FATED
HEARTS
SERIES
4

PERFECT
Fit

INTERNATIONAL BESTSELLING AUTHOR
AIMEE NICOLE WALKER

PERFECT
Fit

CHAPTER
One

JJ

Miller and I didn't meet under ideal circumstances. Honestly, I'm not even sure how I noticed him while I fought with Grayson Wright over a stupid comment I'd made to his boyfriend and my longtime friend, Chase, about why he'd been promoted so fast at Wright Creations. The whole fight had happened fast, but when it was over and the dust had settled, I found myself looking into the lightest blue eyes I had ever seen. Those eyes twinkled with mischief and captivated me right away. I would have introduced myself to him right then, but Jack Murphy forcefully escorted me out of his bar. Damn him and his cock-blocking ways.

My split lip throbbed, and my heart ached painfully in my chest as I walked to my car in the dark. Once again, I had lashed out at the only person in the world who meant anything to me. *Why?* If I was honest with myself, and I always tried to be, I'd have admitted I'd reacted out of fear. My hurtful comment had been a knee-jerk reaction and a self-defense mechanism I had perfected over the years. If I lost Chase, then I'd have no one. *So why not push him away and get it over with?*

"Hey! Your wallet fell out of your suit jacket."

The unfamiliar voice was deep, a little raspy, and very sexy. I turned to see who it belonged to and found myself looking into the twinkling blue eyes I had noticed in the bar. I allowed myself a minute to admire the rest of his physical attributes. He was tall and lean, and he walked toward me with an almost predatory gait. The sexy stranger exuded confidence and sensuality that I wanted to sample for myself. His blond hair shone under the streetlights when he passed beneath them. I just knew the strands would feel silky between my fingers, and I imagined gripping his hair while he sucked me off with his lush mouth.

"It must have flown out when Gray knocked you off your stool." He said this with a bit of snark and familiarity that let me know he was acquainted with Chase's boyfriend. "Although, you got a few good hits in yourself, Jagger." He must have opened my wallet, looked at my license, and saw my name.

I'd hated my name since I was old enough to realize it was odd, which was probably around the time I started school. The other kids mercilessly made fun of it, and I had heard enough snotty remarks about my mom's character and the reason I had the name to last me a lifetime. No kid should hear stuff like "I bet his mom was a groupie, and he knocked her up" or "No way Mick would tap that nasty ass. God only knows where it's been."

Somehow, hearing my name roll off the beautiful blond stranger's tongue made it seem less offensive to me. There was no derision in his tone or in his expression. I only saw the same curiosity I felt about him reflected back at me. Even in the dim light, his eyes sparkled and implored me to be a little bad. I felt the effect of his crooked smile in the pit of my stomach and my groin. "I go by JJ," I told him.

His head tilted to the side as he studied me closely. "That doesn't suit you either."

"It doesn't?" *Who was this guy?*

"No. That's the kind of name you give a boy, and *you* are definitely all man." My body heat rose as his perusal continued. My flesh tingled from head to toe as if he'd touched me everywhere instead of just looking at me. "I think Jag suits you better."

"Jag?" I scoffed a little. I couldn't help myself. No one had ever questioned what I wanted to be called, but this guy was. *Arrogant much?* "And just who might you be? It's obvious you know Clark." I liked to use Clark instead of Grayson because that was what Chase had called Gray until he'd learned his real name. It irritated Gray, which worked out pretty nicely for me.

"Clark? Oh, yeah." The blond shrugged slightly. "I can see the resemblance to Clark Kent." The mysterious man walked closer and held out my wallet to me, which I accepted and slid into my suit coat pocket. "My name is Miller Brexler. I'm Gray's best friend. You must be Chase's best friend whom I've heard so much about." He tilted his head and raked his gaze over me again. "And his former fuck buddy."

"Yeah, that's me."

"What are you going to do now since that avenue is closed?" Miller asked.

"Do you mean *who* am I going to be doing? Are you looking for a dial-a-dick friend, Miller?" I had gotten close enough to feel his body heat, but I couldn't say when exactly that had happened. It was as if my body had moved of its own volition, reacting to the chemistry between us. "Would you like to submit a résumé?" Miller's nostrils flared slightly, which told me I wasn't the only one who felt the connection.

"As tempting as I find the idea, I think I'd better pass." He raised his hand as if to touch me but let it fall back to his side instead. "I think us hooking up might complicate things for our friends and their budding romance."

I released a deep breath, unaware I had been holding it. Had I wanted him to say yes or no? I'd just met the guy, and it wasn't like he had the only available ass in town. Still, I felt a keen disappointment over his answer, even though I knew he was right.

"All right, then," I said." It was nice to meet you, Miller. I'm sure our paths will cross again."

That crooked smile of his reappeared, making me want to kiss it clean off his face. "Definitely. Drive safely, Jag. I'm going to head back inside to make sure Gray doesn't get into any more fights." Miller walked backward a few steps like he wasn't ready to look away from me yet. He offered me one last crooked smile before he turned around and headed back to the bar.

I turned and began walking to my car, even though I wanted to continue to watch him. His subtle reminder about my scuffle with Gray had brought me back to reality and reminded me how much I had hurt Chase. The self-loathing I felt was enough to erase the warm tingly feelings Miller had given me.

I pulled out my phone once I reached my car and tapped out an apology text to Chase. I'd hurt him deeply and regretted the awful thing I'd insinuated. I expected Chase to ignore me for a few days, but he made me suffer for a few weeks before taking pity on me. We hashed things out and I found myself on equal footing once more, except when my mind conjured up images of Miller and his baby blues. It happened more than I liked, and I chalked it up to him being a forbidden fruit I'd never get to sink my teeth into.

Oh, how I wanted to, though.

CHAPTER
Two

Miller

I FOUND MYSELF IN UNCHARTED TERRITORY ONCE GRAY MET AND fell in love with Chase. Even when Gray had been in a long-term relationship with Devon the douche, he'd still made time for us to hang out. After he and Preston had started their own company, our buddy time had been reduced but not nixed completely. But that all changed when he fell in love. Now, his whole world revolved around Chase and the private time he could carve out for them.

At first, I was concerned he was rushing into another relationship too soon. Gray had been miserable during the last several years of his relationship with Devon, so any good friend would worry. Then I'd met Chase and really gotten to know him, and I could easily see why Gray was so enraptured with the guy. He was sweet, funny, and loved Gray so much I knew I could rest easy.

Gray had found his happily ever after; the kind that sorta made me gag because it's almost too sweet, but at the same time, I couldn't help but envy it just a teeny-tiny bit. I never really got caught up in the one-guy-for-ever concept because I didn't think I'd ever find *that* guy—the one I'd want to look at every single day for the rest of my life, forsaking all other tight asses until death do us part. I just didn't see monogamy working for me.

I missed hanging out with Gray, but I understood things had changed, and I needed to adapt or get left behind. That's how I found myself joining a summer basketball league with a bunch of strangers, albeit some super sexy ones. I had a thing for basketball shorts and the way they hung on a man's body. I loved how the silky fabric draped over the round curve of a man's ass then hung loosely over his thighs. It made me want to slide my hands beneath the shorts to feel the hard length of their hamstrings and quadriceps. I was a complete sucker for a set of toned legs. My eyes locked on a particularly scrumptious specimen on the opposite side of the court. I had played against several teams over the summer, but I was positive I hadn't played against him. There was something familiar about the sexy stranger.

I couldn't see his face because he had his back to me, stretching in preparation for the game. The fabric of his navy-blue shorts pulled tight against his ass as he stretched his hamstrings and calves. I found myself so completely distracted by his tall, lean body that I forgot my team had begun passing drills until a basketball hit me in the head.

"Miller, are you all right?" Josh, one of my cute teammates, asked.

The current object of my lust turned around to see what the commotion was, and I found myself looking into gorgeous brown eyes the color of melted dark chocolate. I had looked into the same eyes on one other occasion a few months ago, and the impact had been enough that they often starred in many of my dirty dreams.

Jagger Jackson.

I didn't know why I picked up his dropped wallet and followed him out to the parking lot after the bar fight. There was a sadness about JJ that I couldn't ignore, and I needed to make sure he was okay. But then I couldn't get the jerk off my mind. Never once had I been so fascinated by one guy, and it irritated the hell out of me. Maybe if I just scratched that particular itch…

He smiled at me, and I felt myself smile in return, even though I was certain little cartoon birds were circling over my head from the blunt force of the basketball. I started to take a step in his direction as if some unknown force was pulling me toward him, but Josh called my name, and this time, he sounded more frustrated than concerned. I broke my connection with Jag and looked at Josh. The hateful scowl of disapproval he wore made him downright ugly.

"Pick up dudes on your own time," he added with a sneer. Ahhh, we had ourselves a hater in the mix. As much as I would have loved to knock the derision right off his face, I'd just show him that my basketball skills were probably ten times better than his. I said nothing in return, just threw up my hands in a friendly okay gesture.

Both our teams went through warm-up drills for several more minutes until the referee blew the whistle signaling we needed to get our starters out on the court. I was the best point guard on my team, and I took my position on the court and waited for the ref to throw the jump ball. I also wasn't surprised to see Jag line up against our guy as one of the jumpers. I bet his long legs could really get him off the ground, and they looked strong enough to support my weight up against a wall.

All my lusting stopped the minute the ball went into the air…until Jag's body brushed up against mine. It was innocent at first, subtle brushes of his arm or hand against mine or the rub of our legs together as I went in for a layup that he tried to block. Innocent was soon replaced by a blatant press of his bulge to my ass while I was boxing him out to prevent him from getting an easy rebound. Jag's brazenness threw me off enough that he easily got the offensive rebound and upped the score. The smug look he gave me had me ratcheting up my intensity to a level I hadn't known since the championship game my senior year of high school. For some reason, I felt like I had more to prove that early fall night going up against Jag than I had in high school.

Luckily for me, I was victorious on both occasions. The look in Jag's eyes was indescribable when we lined up and slapped hands. I couldn't remember a time I had been covered in as much sweat, or as turned on, as I was that night.

Topping his team in the game would pale in comparison to topping the man who had unknowingly kept me captivated for months. My body physically shook with the need, and I was certain Jag felt the same way. But instead of claiming my victory fuck, I walked away. I blew out a deep breath of relief as I neared my car and congratulated myself for not letting my dick lead me into trouble. But my celebration was short-lived when I heard Jag call my name. I stopped but didn't turn around.

"You want to grab a beer?" Jag's deep voice, like the man himself, pulled me in and held my body prisoner. I had never found myself in a position of turning away from someone I wanted that badly, but no good would ever come from me taking what he was offering. There was no doubt the beer would lead to sex so hot and primal that we'd scrape and claw each other to the bone. I knew it as surely as I knew my name, but I was just as certain that it would hurt Gray if he found out. Chase might've forgiven JJ but Gray still seethed anytime his name came up in conversation.

Still, my voice was shaky and unconvincing when I turned and said, "It's not a good idea." Jag wasn't used to being told no; I could see it clearly in his expression and body language. I wouldn't say he was hurt, but he was stunned. "Things could get really sticky."

"That was the plan," Jag said, deliberately misunderstanding my comment. He approached me until he was only a few feet away. I was once again caught up in the raw beauty of the man. His chiseled cheekbones, nose, brows, and square jaw reminded me of a comic book superhero. We were both sweaty after the game, and I found his scent intoxicating. My cock twitched beneath my shorts as I imagined having his sweat all over my body. The lascivious look Jag threw my way said he knew how his words had affected me. "It's not like we'd have to tell them. They're not our priests. We don't have to confess our sins."

He was absolutely right, but it still didn't feel like a good idea. I mean, sexually it would feel really, really right, but our best friends were in love, and there would be times when we would be thrown together at events, and things could get really awkward between us. I'd gone through that once with one of Gray's employees, Ben. I made a huge mistake by seducing the guy without thinking things through. We parted amicably and without expectations, but it still felt a little strange when we ran into each other. Gray read the tension for what it was and got really mad at me. I couldn't imagine how he'd feel if I slept with his "enemy."

"As much as I'd love to take you somewhere and fuck you until you couldn't stand"—I adjusted my package for emphasis—"it's not worth the risk to my friendship with Gray."

"Who says you'd be the one doing the fucking?" Jag's answering adjustment to his own growing erection, plus his challenge about who'd be on top, set my blood boiling. His hand lingered on his package, slowly stroking up and down his length over his shorts as his body reacted to mine. I felt my ass clench with a desire to be filled, which hadn't happened for a very long time.

I was about to touch my hardened length too when a loud conversation a few rows over in the parking lot penetrated my thoughts and halted my action. Good God, was I seriously reaching for my cock prepared to stroke myself in front of Jag and anyone else who might be watching? It was the dose of reality I needed to walk away from the delicious temptation in front of me. I could just as easily stroke my dick in the shower. Sure, Jag wouldn't be there, but I wouldn't have to worry that one of my students or colleagues would see me jerking off in public. Jag would just have to appear behind my eyelids instead of in person.

"I always do the fucking," I told him arrogantly. "I just don't want to fuck you." The lie slid easily off my tongue, but he knew I wasn't being honest. There was no disguising my interest in him.

I turned away and pressed the button on my key fob to unlock the door with the intent of walking away from my temptation. I made it as far as opening the door before he spoke again, but this time it was from directly behind me. I felt the heat of his body while his masculine smell permeated my brain. Jag placed his hand firmly on my lower back and pressed his lips to the back of my ear.

"That's too bad because I was going to give you my ass." My knees threatened to buckle, and I opened my mouth to tell him I changed my mind, but his wicked chuckle cut me off. "Maybe next time." Jag licked the outer curve of my ear and chuckled as I shivered.

I mourned the loss of his heat, his touch, when he pulled away from me. I didn't look over my shoulder to watch him walk away, even though I wanted to so badly. I was both dreading and looking forward to seeing him again because I knew right then that sex between us was inevitable. He had something I just couldn't walk away from, and it seemed the feelings were fully reciprocated on his end. My body hummed in anticipation.

CHAPTER
Three

JJ

I DIDN'T SEE MILLER FOR ANOTHER MONTH AFTER OUR PARKING LOT conversation, but that smiling, teasing devil stayed on my mind. I loved the way he challenged me and never backed down during the basketball game or our verbal sparring afterward. He made me want him until the urge became a physical ache. I could have satisfied my needs with someone else, but it wasn't going to work. I instinctively knew that and chose to rub one out myself rather than engage in halfhearted sex.

Yet somehow, Miller's sexy allure and magnetism caught me off guard the next time we ran into one another at a restaurant. I had agreed to go to a celebratory dinner following a big courtroom victory earlier that day. It had been a huge team effort to win our transgender client's workplace discrimination case. It had been an uphill battle with many obstacles and biases to overcome, but we had prevailed, and our client would be awarded a hefty settlement for the horrible way he'd been treated.

All thoughts of work had faded away as soon as I met Miller's gaze over the heads of the dinner crowd. He was also eating with a group of people, most of them men, and I wondered if he was on a date. It didn't seem likely since he was looking at me like he wanted to strip off every piece of clothing I had on my body so he could take what he wanted.

I watched as he slowly raised a bottle of beer to his lips and took a drink. *Was it me or did his cheeks hollow out a bit as if he was sucking on the opening of the bottle instead of pressing it against his lips?* I got his point loud and clear and countered his move, licking my bottom lip afterward to add a little extra something to the tease.

Try as I might, I couldn't get into the work conversations around me. I wanted Miller to think I wasn't that into him, but I wasn't that good an actor. Besides, what the hell was the point of pretending I didn't want him? He already knew, just like I knew he was into me.

The teasing went on throughout our meals, and with every passing minute, I felt my body become more and more alive until I practically vibrated with need. It felt like a thousand bugs were crawling beneath my skin. My knees bounced beneath the table in anticipation until I saw Miller get up and excuse himself from the table.

I rose from my seat without saying a word to my dinner companions and followed Miller to the restroom. I hadn't planned out what I wanted to say to him, but it seemed words weren't needed. Miller took a quick look around to make sure we were alone, then pushed me back against the wall. He placed his hands on the back of my neck and pulled my mouth down to his at the same time he pressed his body against me. Kissing wasn't usually included when I hooked up with another man, but this felt different. I had been craving the feel of his lips against mine.

It wasn't a gentle, get-to-know-you kiss; it was a full-on fucking of mouths. His hands remained firmly on the back of my neck as our teeth scraped and bumped, and tongues dueled for dominance. If Miller's kiss could set me ablaze, what would he do to me once he was inside me? Would his heat sear me and mark me for life?

Miller jerked away from our kiss, ending it as abruptly as it had begun. "I'm going to take what you've been offering me all fucking night." His voice was rough and dark, and it sent shivers up and down my spine. I wanted to hear that voice in my ear as he lived out his promise, but that didn't mean I was going to make it easy for him.

"The offer to tap my ass expired a month ago," I lied. "I'll gladly fuck *you* into next week, though."

"Huh-uh." Miller shook his head. "I'm going to have that ass tonight as long and as hard as I want it."

I screwed up my face into an uncertain expression. "I prefer to top, Miller."

"So do I. Looks like we're at an impasse." He took a slight step backward, just enough to let air flow between our bodies. I wanted to reach for him, but I didn't want to show my hand so easily. I knew a compromise would need to be reached and only one solution came to mind.

"Let's flip for it." My offer was met with a raised, skeptical brow.

"As in a coin to see who gets to top?"

"To see who tops *first*." My words were slow and deliberate, spelling out the dirty images that had just flitted through my brain. Miller's breath hitched and he swallowed hard. I watched the movement of his Adam's apple and longed to sink my teeth into it.

"Jesus, Jag." He sounded breathless as if I'd managed to shock him and turn him inside out all at the same time. "I…Your place is closer," he finally stammered. I was confused for a second—not a surprise since all my blood was flowing toward my dick—then I recalled that he'd looked at my license the night I fought with Gray.

"It's a gated community, so I'll need to leave your name with the attendant if you're not directly behind me."

"Miller Brexler." *As if I'd forgotten his name.* Light blue eyes turned a shade darker and a little turbulent the more excited he got, and I couldn't stop wondering how they'd look when he came. Miller didn't say another word before leaving the bathroom.

I shook my head and followed a few minutes later. My behavior at dinner had been less than professional, and I needed to get my shit together to prevent further embarrassment in front of my colleagues. My thin trousers didn't do much to hide the evidence of my arousal, so I buttoned my suit jacket and hoped for the best as I made my way back to the table.

It turned out that my concern was unnecessary because my table was completely empty when I returned, which made me wonder how long I'd been in the restroom with Miller. My boss, Paul Bergen, had left a note for me. He congratulated me on a job well done that afternoon and said he could tell I had different celebratory plans for the night, and he couldn't blame me. Paul let me know the firm had covered my dinner. Although I appreciated the sentiment, I was still mortified he thought I was hooking up in the bathroom. I felt Miller's eyes on me, and I looked up. The heat I saw in his gaze made all thoughts of work dissipate. I gave Miller a subtle nod and left the restaurant.

Blood hummed in my veins similar to the purr of my BMW's engine. The sensation made me feel alive as I eagerly zipped across town to wait for Miller. I gave his name to the guard on duty and drove home, where I paced the floors, nearly bursting with anticipation. I began removing my tie, jacket, and vest to do something with my hands.

The doorbell rang, signaling the end of my misery. I yanked open the door and found Miller on my doorstep smiling his cocky half smile. I grabbed his shirt and pulled him inside, then slammed the door behind him.

We crashed into each other, hands and mouths all over one another. It was the hottest, most feral joining I had ever experienced, and I knew it was something I wouldn't soon forget. I heard the buttons from my shirt bounce all over the hardwood floor of my foyer when Miller ripped my shirt open. I would have protested, but my breath was stuck in my throat as Miller pressed his kiss-swollen lips to my neck.

"Fuck!" It was the only word I could think in the heat of the moment.

He had reduced my brain to mush, and I acted on natural instinct, prepared to stop at nothing to get what I wanted.

I cupped him through his trousers and teased the hard length straining against the fabric. My ass clenched in eager anticipation of feeling that hard length rasping over my sensitive opening. Sharp teeth pierced the delicate skin over my collarbone, and I cried out in pain and ecstasy. A voice in my brain cautioned that I was in no way prepared for the night I was about to experience, but I refused to give it audience.

"Heads or tails?" Miller's whispered question in my ear sent violent spikes of lust straight to my balls. I could have told him right then that he could have me first, but my devilish side wanted him to earn it.

"Tails," I said naughtily. I reached inside his pocket and made a big show of looking for a coin. In the process, I teased his erection through the thin fabric of his pants. Miller's teeth grabbed hold of my ear and bit hard enough to get my attention. I slowly pulled out a quarter and held it up for him to take.

Miller took a step back so he could flip the coin, and I immediately missed his heat. He flipped the quarter high in the air, and it seemed like slow motion as I watched it arc and spin in the air before it descended to land by our feet.

"Heads." His triumphant voice was paired with a devious smile. "Take me to your bedroom, right. Fucking. Now." Miller made his demand in a raspy growl that had me reaching for his hand and pulling him to my room.

Clothes and shoes went flying between kisses that lit a bonfire in my soul as we crossed the threshold into my bedroom. There was nothing gentle about the way Miller maneuvered us to my bed or the way he pushed me down on top of it, but it wasn't cruel. I wasn't afraid of him—just the relentless neediness he made me feel—because even then I knew there was something entirely different between us.

I spread my legs, and Miller made himself comfortable between them. I had expected him to ask for the lube and condoms and get things started, but he surprised me with more kisses and exploring touches. His hands left a trail of sparks and fire in their wake as he learned the contours of my upper body, all the while rubbing his erection against mine.

I wasn't about to let Miller have all the fun, so I coasted my hands over the tightly formed muscles of his back until I reached the curved swells of his luscious ass. I grabbed hold of his firm cheeks with both hands and pulled his hips tighter against me. I felt our combined precum drip onto my stomach, and it caused me to leak even more.

Miller broke our kiss and raised his head to look at me. His pupils had expanded but not so much that I couldn't still see the pale blue of his irises. Not a word was spoken as he leaned over and opened the bedside table drawer. It seemed like foreplay time was over and Miller was ready to fuck.

I watched as Miller slid a condom onto his long length before he reached for the lube. My ass clenched eagerly as he made a deliberate show of oiling up his fingers. Miller leaned back until he sat on his heels between my legs. I spread my legs wider, exposing my entrance to him.

"So sexy. Miller pressed a blunt fingertip against my puckered hole and traced a circle around the rim, stimulating the nerve endings to make his finger slide inside me easier. He pushed in all the way to the knuckle and my mouth fell open on a silent cry. "So fucking hot."

My ass clenched and tightened around his penetration urging him to give me more. Miller answered my silent plea by sliding a second finger deep inside me before he curled them up to tease the spot that made me shake and quiver in pleasure.

"More." It was all I could muster at that point because my whole focus was aimed on his skillful manipulations. Miller bit his bottom lip as he worked his magical fingers in and out of me. "Fuck me now."

Miller said nothing as he withdrew his fingers and reached for more lube. Blue eyes held mine as he coated the condom. Miller placed one hand beside my head on my pillow as he leaned his perfectly toned body over mine. He aligned his dick to my hole, where he teased me for moments before he pushed the wide head inside my tight clinch.

The burn was intense but very welcome as Miller worked his way slowly inside me until I took him all the way to his root. I expected him to fuck me in earnest, but instead, Miller lowered himself on top of me and ravished my mouth slowly and completely. It was sweet and sexy, but I needed more.

I wrapped my legs around his waist, squeezed him tightly with my inner thighs, and thrust my hips upward to take his dick deeper inside me. Miller chuckled against my lips but took the hint and began to move inside me, slowly at first. I appreciated his consideration, but I wanted it hard and fast. I needed him to drive me to my limit and beyond. I raised my head off the pillow and bit his bottom lip hard enough to make him gasp.

I licked the indentation I left and smiled wickedly as his thrusts picked up in intensity. I was torn between trying to make him lose control and come inside me or making him hold off his orgasm until I could fuck it out of him. Either way, I'd be the reason he lost his load and his mind.

One of my favorite benefits of being tall was having long limbs, which I took advantage of while Miller fucked wildly into me. I kept my eyes locked on his while reaching for the lube. The *snick* of the bottle opening sounded louder than normal, but maybe my senses were just more in tune to everything around me. I lowered my legs to give me room to play and torment him.

I used my free hand to pour some lube down the crack of Miller's sexy-as-sin ass. Miller groaned loudly when the cool liquid dribbled over his heated flesh. I teased his opening just as he'd done to me before I breached his tight passage with one finger. Miller's thrusts lost their rhythm as I slid my finger in as deep as I could.

The groans coming from his throat were animalistic and ferocious. Miller angled his hips to peg my prostate with every sharp thrust forward, and it was my turn to falter. His wicked smile told me he knew exactly what he was doing. The urge to let go and come all over us both was intense, but I refused to give in that easily—not until I was buried deep inside his heat.

I continued to stretch him until he was pliable and ready, and he continued to plunder my depths until sweat beaded all over my body from the exertion of holding back my orgasm. My balls drew up ready to explode, and I knew it was time to flip or lose my load. If I only had one night with Miller, I needed to make it count.

I retracted my fingers from his tight entrance and used my strong legs to roll him over until he was the one on his back, and I was between his legs. I pulled the condom off his cock and tossed it to the floor. I smiled evilly when he practically snarled his outrage from beneath me. It seemed I wasn't the only one about to come.

I grabbed a wrapped condom and held it up. "My turn, sexy." I made quick work of rolling it on and lubing up before I pressed my cock to his ass and pushed inside him.

"Jag." He roared my name as I penetrated him for the first time. I liked my name on his lips more than I should for a casual fuck, but there was no time to contemplate what that meant when his heat threatened to burn me alive. "Show me what you've got, big guy."

I grabbed Miller's hands, pinned them above his head, and fucked him mercilessly in response to the challenge. His pupils were so blown I could hardly see the pretty blue color of his eyes. Still, I was held captive in his gaze, unable to look away even if I'd wanted to.

"Come…G-g-going to come." Miller's voice was jagged and raw as if the words were being torn from him. I pressed on, not letting up on either my intensity or the pace. I needed to see him unravel beneath me, but I couldn't say right then why it mattered so damn much. "Jag. Please."

"Come, Miller." Those two words broke something loose inside him, and his cum jetted from him in creamy ribbons that landed all over his stomach.

I lowered my upper body until I felt his slick heat rub against my skin as I chased my own climax. I kept our hands locked together above his head and picked up my pace when I felt the familiar tingle in my spine and the answering zing in my balls. I did something I rarely did with anyone. I lowered my mouth to his for a searing kiss as my orgasm ripped through me. Miller took my cries into his mouth as I spilled inside the condom.

My mouth didn't leave his until the last ripple of my orgasm faded. I slowly pulled my mouth away from his at the same time I eased out of him. I flopped onto my back beside him and looked up at the ceiling while I tried to catch my breath. I couldn't remember a time I'd felt both so alive yet so exhausted at the same time. I turned my head and found him looking at me. A sexy smile split his face, and I answered with one of my own.

"Why did you wait so long?" Miller's teasing question made me laugh because if it had been left up to me, we would have fucked a month ago.

"I wasn't sure we were compatible," I replied cheekily.

"And now?"

"I don't know, Miller." I scrunched my face up to show uncertainty. "Sex this good has to be an anomaly, maybe a fluke." I shrugged my shoulders casually and bit the inside of my cheek to prevent myself from laughing at the sour expression on his face.

"What you're really saying is that you want to go another round, but you don't want to admit it." He nodded toward the door to my en suite bathroom. "How big is your shower?" That was all it took for blood to start rushing back to my dick again.

"Big enough for us to get clean before we get dirty again."

"Let's go then," Miller said as he rolled off the bed. "Bring the condoms and lube."

I smiled at his sassy remark until my eyes landed on the bounce of his gorgeous ass. I had no clue what the hell was happening between us, but I decided not to question it and enjoy whatever it turned out to be.

CHAPTER
Four

Miller

I SQUIRMED IN MY OFFICE CHAIR FOR THE MILLIONTH TIME IN HOPES of finding a more comfortable position for my tender ass. One would have thought the ache would have made a person regret their reckless actions the previous night, but not me. Each zing of discomfort reminded me of how good it had felt to have Jag buried inside me, how dark his eyes had gotten when he neared his orgasm, and the delicious weight of him pinning my hands to the bed above my head. I had zero regrets, except that my body was eager to experience Jag again, but my brain doubted it would ever happen.

"Exciting night?" I hadn't even realized my teaching assistant, Gavin Anderson, had entered the room. His voice startled me, and I jerked my head up to look at him. He wore a shit-eating grin as he stood there with a Starbucks cup in each hand. His grin told me he knew exactly why I was squirming in my damn chair.

"I'm not discussing my personal life with you, Gavin." My gentle rebuke was a reminder that I was the professor, and he was my TA. It had been obvious to me the first day I met Gavin that he was interested in being more, but I valued my job far more than a quick fuck. I had landed my dream job teaching archeology and anthropology at Georgetown. I didn't spend much time on archeological digs like I had dreamed of doing as a hormonal teenager who'd lusted after Indiana Jones, but I loved my job.

"My apologies, Dr. Brexler." The ornery grin never left his face, which told me he wasn't sorry about anything, but he had brought me my favorite latte, so I could forgive him. "You owe me five dollars for the coffee since it wouldn't be *appropriate* for me to buy it for you."

"Smartass," I mumbled beneath my breath as I fished my wallet from my desk drawer and handed him a five-dollar bill along with a stack of papers that needed to be read and graded by the next day. The grin slid off his face as he accepted the cash and the papers before taking a seat at his desk. It was my turn to smile, but at least I waited until he had his back to me.

I did my best to sit still and ignore the ache and tingle from the hard fucking I'd both given and received. I needed to review my lecture notes for my classes the next day to see if I wanted to change anything up. I loved having a free planning day in the middle of the week to catch my breath and prepare for the rest of the week. The fall semester had just started, and I was still making adjustments to my lesson plans. I could at least celebrate the fact that no one had fallen asleep during my lectures up to that point.

Amazingly, my classes were some of the first to fill up semester after semester, which was a great source of pride for me. I tried to be engaging as I educated my students about lost civilizations and cultures. I tried to relate to them and show how learning about our past prevented us from making the same mistakes in our present and future. Gray said my classes filled up so quickly because guys and gals both wanted to sit and stare at me while I lectured like they did in the *Indiana Jones* movies. I found that hard to believe but was flattered nonetheless that he'd compared me to my childhood hero.

I missed my best friend, but I was really happy for him. Chase would be moving into his house the following weekend. Gray had asked me to help, and I'd happily agreed, even though I'd have to suffer through face-sucking and schmoopy banter for hours upon hours. I had made a solemn vow to myself to never call a lover baby or babe.

My mind chose that exact moment to remind me I'd yelled Jag's name a time or two the previous night. I closed my eyes, and a vision of Jag on his knees in his shower floated behind my lids. I'd said a lot of incoherent things while he'd worked my cock with his wicked lips, tongue, and even his teeth. It was the slight scrape of his teeth over the sensitive head of my cock that had me coming all over his swollen lips and chin. Jag was like every porn fantasy I'd ever had and some I hadn't been creative enough to think up. I'd matched him blow for blow judging by my sore scalp.

My body began to respond to the memories of Jag pulling my hair and a strangled sigh escaped my lips before I could stop it. Gavin looked over his shoulder and gave me a knowing wink, which I answered with a fierce enough scowl to scare almost anyone. Gavin shrugged casually and turned back to his work, which allowed me to return to Jagworld, which was way more fun than Disney World.

My legs had been almost too weak to hold me up by the time we finished our shower, but I wasn't the only one with spaghetti limbs. Jag collapsed unceremoniously onto his bed and lay there in a naked sprawl while I found my clothes that had been scattered about the room. By the time I'd redressed, Jag was sound asleep, soft snores escaping through his parted lips. There was something vulnerable about him at that moment, and it tugged at my heartstrings. Maybe that was why I brushed aside a lock of hair that had fallen across his brow with my fingers or why I covered him up with his comforter, unwilling to leave him naked and exposed. I regretted leaving him at all, which was a feeling I'd never had with anyone else.

Jag scared and thrilled me in equal measures. He threatened my balanced life, and instead of running away, I wanted to return to him. I yearned to uncover the secrets this complicated man hid behind the beautiful façade he showed the world. It didn't take long to recognize the keen intelligence reflected in his eyes, and it was impossible to ignore the sheer sexiness of the man. Both were things he wanted the world to see, but I needed to know the secrets he kept hidden. *Needed?* Oh, hell no. Only danger awaited me on that path. I'm talking booby traps far worse than anything Indiana Jones ever faced. Jag would just have to remain an unsolved puzzle.

My cellphone vibrated on my desk with an incoming text message from my errant best friend.

Pizza, beer, and baseball at your place?

It was the first time he'd reached out to me in weeks unless it was to ask for help moving Chase's stuff the following Saturday. I really wasn't bitter about it, but it was taking me longer to adjust to his absence than I thought it would.

You're on! I wasn't about to question why he was suddenly available. I was just glad to hang out with him. **Time?**

I'll be there at 7:00 with the pizza and beer.

Damn straight you're bringing the pizza and beer. Looking forward to it.

Gray was as punctual as ever when he arrived at my house with a pizza box in one hand and a six-pack of Corona in the other. Luckily for me, Gray would only drink one or two beers at the most since he'd be driving home, which left the others for me.

"Long time no see," I said in greeting as I shut the front door.

"I've missed you too," was Gray's simple but heartfelt response. "Where's Indy?" He was referring to my fearless attack pug who happened to be snoring in his dog bed beside the fireplace, totally unaware we had a visitor.

"He'll come running the minute he smells the pizza." I led the way to my kitchen and pulled some plates out of the cabinet. "I was surprised to get your text, but I'm glad to spend time with you."

"Chase had dinner plans with JJ, and I didn't want to sit at home alone." Gray piled a few slices of pizza onto his plate and grabbed a beer, and the reason for his visit clicked into place. I wasn't sure what upset me the most—the fact that I was now Gray's backup plan when Chase was busy or that Chase was spending time with Jag. My thoughts turned a little bitter, but I refused to let irritation ruin my night.

"Well, let's kick back, catch up, and watch some ball." I tried to keep my voice modulated so as not to give away my inner frustrations. I reached up into another cabinet and pulled down an ice bucket I kept for nights like tonight when we'd be too lazy to want to make a fridge run. I thought I might down my four or five beers in record time.

"That came out wrong, Miller." Gray put his hand on my shoulder and stopped me from walking to the built-in ice maker on my refrigerator. "I didn't mean to make you sound like a substitution or afterthought. I don't feel that way at all, and I'm very glad to relax at your house, knock a few beers back, and devour some greasy pizza. I'm only pissed about *who* Chase is having dinner with, not that I'm not with him."

I accepted his apology with a nod, and he released me. "I think you need to let this thing with JJ go, Gray," I told him after I filled the bucket with ice and submerged the beers in the cubes. "Chase is crazy about you, but if you keep harping on him about a relationship that ended a long time ago, you'll push him away."

Gray puffed out a frustrated breath before he said, "I trust Chase completely, and that will have to be enough because JJ isn't going anywhere. Chase said he's JJ's only family, and he won't turn his back on him just because I'm insecure."

I hated to hear that JJ didn't have any family of his own and not just because he was irritating my best friend. I had a mother, father, brother, sister-in-law, a gorgeous niece, and a precocious nephew I adored with all my heart. I cherished every moment spent in their company and couldn't imagine going day to day without them in my life. Damn if Gray hadn't just handed me another piece of the Jag puzzle, making me want to solve it even more. Was that the reason for the vulnerability I saw in him after he fell asleep?

"That is outta here!" Gray yelled as one of the Nationals players hit a home run. Indy barked happily as if he knew what was going on. I knew better. The little scamp was hoping someone would sneak him a celebration pepperoni.

Gray got too caught up in the game to notice he'd rocked my world by bringing up Jag, and I hoped to keep it that way. I meant what I'd said to Jag. No good would come of Gray and Chase learning about the night I shared with him. It was probably a good thing it wouldn't be happening again. The thought wasn't as comforting as I had hoped, and I found myself reaching for my beer instead of the pizza since I no longer had an appetite.

CHAPTER
Five

JJ

CHASE'S DINNER INVITATION WAS A HUGE SURPRISE, BUT THE news he had shared with me was even more surprising. We had exchanged texts quite a bit, and I'd seen Chase and Gray at Ava's wedding, so I knew things were going really well for them. Still, moving in together was a huge step.

"I never thought I could find this kind of happiness," Chase said, staring off into space. "I knew it happened for other people, hell, I'd even helped set some of them up. I just didn't think it was meant for me."

"I knew." My words captured his attention, and he turned his soulful brown eyes on me. "I always knew you were meant to find this kind of love, just like I knew I could never be the one to give it to you." *Whoa!* I had never really planned on delving into the reasons why Chase and

I hadn't worked out, even though he deserved more of an explanation than I had given him then or was willing to tell him now.

I knew Chase almost better than I knew myself, and I didn't think he could handle the truth of what had happened during Christmas break all those years ago that had ruined our burgeoning relationship. I couldn't take the chance that he'd somehow blame himself when all the responsibility rested on my shoulders. He had forgiven me for breaking his heart, we'd moved on, and I needed that to be enough. "You were meant for Gray, and he knows how to treat you the way you deserve." I smiled as I thought about Gray's sappy West Coast effort to win Chase back, although he had never lost him. Chase had belonged to Gray since the moment their eyes met, regardless of the horrible circumstances of that meeting. "I'm very happy for you."

"You'll always be part of my life. You know that, right, J?" I could tell he was trying not to get too emotional because he paused to choose his words. "You never really explained what happened all those years ago, and I never pushed you. I found a way to accept what you were willing to give me, and I moved on, but I'm not sure you did."

His words were a shock to my system. Did he mean he thought I was still in love with him or hung up on the incident that had changed my outlook on the world forever? I opened my mouth to ask, but he raised his hand to stop me.

"Whatever happened to you during Christmas break our freshmen year of college still has a grip on you, and I fear it's holding you back," Chase said. "I've accepted that you don't want to talk to me about it, but I wish you'd talk to someone. Life is too short not to live it to the fullest, and that means experiencing love—giving and receiving. You give and give, but you never let anyone love you back."

I knew he was right and that I had clung to my past in an unhealthy manner as a reminder to myself of what happened when I dared to grab hold of more than what was meant for me. I took a chance once by daring to dream and love by pretending I hadn't been born under a cursed moon. That dream screeched to a bloody, hateful halt, and I was not willing to try again. The reasonable, mature adult I was trying to become reared its pragmatic head occasionally to protest that I was being ridiculous and using the tragedy from my past as an excuse to keep an emotional distance from everyone. It cautioned me that if I didn't put my heart out there, I could never experience the true happiness Chase had described.

"I'll take your counsel under advisement."

"I just want you to be happy, J."

"I am happy."

Chase narrowed his eyes because he didn't believe me, but I was content for the most part, and there were moments of happiness. I loved my career, and there was Miller's visit, which had really made me happy, even though it was just sex. My heart lurched as I remembered Miller's gentle touch. He'd woken me when he swept my hair off my forehead, but I pretended to stay asleep to avoid any awkwardness. There was something tender about the way Miller had covered me up before he left. I'd almost given up my ruse and asked him to stay, but I remained silent. I didn't do gentle and tender, and I sure as hell never asked anyone to stay. We hooked up and nothing more.

"Okay," Chase said in surrender. "I'll mind my own business."

"Do you need help moving?" I wanted to change the subject but was surprised at the path I took.

"That would be awesome. You can get to know Gray better," Chase replied, beaming from ear to ear. Inwardly, I cringed because getting to know me was probably the last thing Gray wanted to do. Outwardly, I smiled because I'd do just about anything to make Chase happy.

And that was how I found myself standing inside Gray's apartment looking into two sets of hostile eyes the following Saturday. I understood Gray's animosity. He saw me as a threat, and I would do my best to put him at ease unless he proved to be an asshole, then I'd push his buttons. Miller's hostility, though, came as a complete surprise. Those baby blues had once twinkled with mirth or darkened with desire when he looked at me, but now, they were cold and distant. It felt like I was seeing a different man. An evil twin, perhaps.

"Oh, hey, J," Chase said, walking out from the back hallway with two boxes in his arms. "You're just in time to do some heavy lifting."

"Let me help you, babe," Gray said, moving over to take the top box off the stack.

"Thanks, honey." I'd only been there for two minutes, and I was already gagging over their sweetness. I questioned my sanity for subjecting myself to this lovefest. "Oh, you and Miller haven't formally met, have you? Dr. Miller Brexler, meet my good friend, Jagger Jackson, attorney at law."

"They're two manwhoring peas in a clusterfuck pod," I heard Gray mutter as he and Chase exited the apartment. I would have laughed at his accuracy, but I was still thrown over Miller's chilly demeanor.

"Doctor, huh? Well, I have this ache that..."

"Save it." Miller's snarl cut off what I had intended to say. "First, I'm not that kind of doctor, and second, what the fuck are you doing here?"

"I came here to—"

"Fuck things up for my friend. Look, we have plenty of help, so why don't you just make your excuses and leave."

"Wait a goddamn minute," I replied angrily. "Just who the fuck do you think you are?" I didn't realize I had advanced on him until we were nearly chest to chest. "Neither you nor Gray gets to decide who Chase keeps as a friend. He's a grown man who is fully capable of making his own decisions, Doc." I loved that Miller had to tilt his head back to look into my eyes.

"Is he choosing to keep you around as a friend because he wants to or is it because he feels bad that you don't have anyone else?" His words were like a sharp dagger to my heart. I jerked back as if he'd landed a physical blow instead of hurling a verbal barb. My only consolation was the look of horror that spread across his face as soon as he realized what he'd said. He opened his mouth as if to apologize, but he didn't get the chance.

"JJ has me," came a furious female voice from behind me. I couldn't help but smile at Ava, ready to swoop in and save the day. She was Chase's best friend and my friend by proxy, even though there were plenty of times she wanted to strangle me. I often had that effect on people. This time her fury was aimed at Miller, and I felt pretty smug about it.

"Uh…" Miller's stammer only made me smile more.

"J has Xavier too. He is not alone and *never* will be." She came to stand beside me, hands on her hips in full diva mode. "I don't know what's going on here, but I think we need to come to an agreement moving forward." Miller and I just continued to stare at one another, but it was obvious she had our full attention. "We can all get along for Chase and Gray's sake like one big happy family or we can throw down right here, right now. But I will not listen to any petty fighting about where Chase's heart lies or stupid remarks that he needs to choose between his friends and his lover. Gray's insecurity over JJ's existence is Gray's problem, not Chase's and not JJ's. I appreciate that you're in Gray's corner, but as his best friend, you need to assure him that Chase loves him and stop creating a problem where there isn't one. How do you think Chase would feel if he'd overheard what you just said instead of me?" She blew out a frustrated breath and took a step back. "You two fools work this shit out. Now." She turned on her heel and headed back to the hallway, her curls bouncing with every angry step.

"I'd do what the lady says, fellas." I hadn't realized her husband, Brandon, was even in the room until he spoke. He slapped my shoulder as he followed his wife.

"She's kind of scary," Miller muttered softly so only I could hear. I'd always thought she was scary in an awesome way, but I held my opinion to myself. Instead, I stepped around him so I could start boxing up the kitchen. "Wait," Miller said, then grabbed my bicep. I chose to look straight ahead rather than meet his gaze. I didn't want to see pity or derision in them. In fact, if I couldn't look into baby blues and see happiness, humor, or desire, I didn't want to look into them at all. "I was way out of line, Jag."

I tensed when he used the nickname he had given me. Before, I had liked hearing it roll off his tongue, but right then, it just felt wrong. "Don't worry about it," I said, blowing him off with a casualness I didn't feel. "I won't say anything to Chase or Gray, and we can forget it happened. Ava's right, Miller. We don't have to like each other, but we do have to get along. As pitiful as it might sound to you, Chase, Ava, and Xavier are my only family, and I won't do anything to hurt them."

I pulled my arm out of his grip and walked away without letting him respond. As I packed up the kitchen, I contemplated why the shift in Miller's personality bothered me so damn much. Hell, I didn't know a damn thing about the guy, but there was a hollowness in my chest that hadn't been there before, like I'd lost something important. My feelings were still an unsolved mystery by the time I'd packed up the items in the kitchen cabinets, leaving only the refrigerator and freezer to tackle.

I pulled open the refrigerator and was relieved to see that there wasn't much inside, just two bottles of beer. I was pretty thirsty, and I helped myself to one. I opened the bottle and flipped the cap into the trash can before I took a swig and shut the door.

"Is there another one of those? All this *baby* and *sweetie* bullshit, plus all the kissing, is making me nauseous." I nearly choked. I hadn't realized Miller was standing on the other side of the refrigerator door. The ornery twinkle in his eyes had returned, and I found it hard to hold on to my ire with him looking so irresistible. I opened the door and pulled out the last beer for him. "Thank you."

"Less shit I have to pack." My response was less conciliatory than it could have been, and I found myself not wanting to hold a grudge any longer. I could only imagine the horror stories Gray had told him about me, even if they weren't true. I raised my bottle and said, "Confirmed bachelors unite."

"Amen."

Miller clinked his bottle to mine, and the tension from earlier faded until all that was left were two guys sharing a beer while their best friends dreamed of fairy tales, happily ever afters, and probably a unicorn ring bearer at their future wedding. They weren't engaged yet, but we all knew it was just a matter of time. The teasing glint in Miller's eyes changed to something darker and blatantly sexual, but I did my best to ignore it. He had been absolutely right when he'd cautioned that starting anything between us would only make the situation more complicated. I had no regrets about the night we'd spent together, but I was determined it wouldn't happen again.

CHAPTER
Six

Miller

L EAVING MY NIECE'S BIRTHDAY PARTY EARLY TO ATTEND AN ALUMNI
mixer at the university was not my idea of a good time. Holiday break
was supposed to be just that—a holiday. Instead, I found myself surrounded by stuffed suits all trying to convince an important alumnus who
had deep pockets to donate to his beloved alma mater. I much preferred
wearing a party hat and being mauled by my niece and her tiny friends.

Unfortunately, my attendance was required since I was the master-
mind behind the joint Mayan artifact project between the university and
the Smithsonian, even though my department head, Micah Halverston,
had taken all the credit. I wasn't exactly sure why he needed me to be in
attendance. Oh, right, in case someone had questions he couldn't answer
because his interest in the project had been next to nil until articles praising

the exhibit had begun cropping up. Quite honestly, I was tired of saving his lazy ass every time something like this happened, although this was the first time it was happening on a national level.

Micah had to defer to me to answer one too many questions and the wealthiest alumnus in attendance, Senator Baxter Thompson, narrowed his shrewd, gray eyes at Halverston before turning his attention to me. "I think you and your students did an amazing job, Dr. Brexler, and you should be very proud of the positive press the archeology and anthropology departments are receiving."

"Thank you, Senator Thompson, for acknowledging my students' dedication to seeing this exhibit become a reality. They worked tirelessly to make it all happen." I had to admit I was a little bit of a Senator Thompson fanboy. He was openly gay and a champion for LGBTQ rights, not to mention extremely handsome. He was one of the brightest minds to attend Georgetown Law as well as one of the youngest members of Congress, and he'd had people fawning all over him all night long.

"It sounds like your students had some amazing instruction." The senator turned his full charm on me, and I felt myself turn a little pink under his praise. He smiled charmingly, and I returned the gesture. I half expected an invitation to get to know him a little better, but his attention was suddenly diverted. "It has been lovely getting to know you, Dr. Brexler, but I see an old acquaintance, and I need to say hello." He shook my hand in a hurry and made a beeline for someone behind me. I was curious to know who he was talking about and turned to watch his progress but wished I hadn't.

I watched as Jag waved in the senator's direction. A huge smile split his face, and I found an unfamiliar feeling burning in the pit of my stomach. I didn't like Jag smiling at Senator Thompson like that, and I certainly didn't like the hug they exchanged. I knew right then what kind of acquaintances they had been and understood the senator's burning desire to reacquaint himself with Jag. I sure as hell had spent several nights tossing and turning, burning with desire I had started to suspect only Jag could satisfy. Damn it, *I* wanted to reacquaint myself with his body.

The fiery sensation intensified, burning a path up my esophagus until I could taste the jealousy on my tongue. There was part of me that wanted to stomp over there and break up their little reunion before anything could even get started, but I held myself back. I'd made a big enough asshole of myself the last time I'd seen Jag, and I refused to do so again.

Dr. Halverston yammered on about this alum and that alum, but I tuned him out and focused on the two gorgeous men engaged in a conversation full of smiles and laughter. It was during this intense scrutiny that I noticed Jag's smile didn't quite reach his eyes. My jealousy faded somewhat as I remembered the times I'd seen the smile in his eyes when he'd looked into mine. Okay, so we'd either been playing basketball, fucking, or sucking each other off, but still...I had been on the receiving end of his genuine smile. The urge to see it again struck me hard enough to make me dizzy, causing me to blink several times while I gathered myself.

"Are you okay, Miller?" I heard the forced concern in Dr. Halverston's voice. "You're not intoxicated, are you? That would make the department look bad in front of our esteemed alumni."

"Too much birthday cake at my niece's party this afternoon, sir. I think my blood sugar dropped suddenly and left me a little lightheaded. I'll grab a bite to eat from the buffet and be just fine." I kept my voice modulated so as not to show my disdain for the man who thought I'd get tanked at a university event.

"Dr. Brexler," Gavin said, walking up beside me, "there are a few benefactors here who'd like to talk to you about future projects." Thank God for Gavin who knew how much I disliked the clueless department head.

"Perhaps I should come along as well," Micah said. I would have hung my head in embarrassment for him, but Jag chose that exact moment to look at me.

Time had not diminished the impact of his penetrating gaze. Jag tilted his head slightly in acknowledgment before turning his focus back on the senator. It felt more like a dismissal than a greeting, and the burning sensation returned in full force.

"There are so many people for you to talk with, Dr. Halverston," Gavin answered. "If Dr. Brexler needs your assistance, I will come find you." Gavin's ass kissing was met by a harrumph and hearty slap on his back before the penguin-shaped man waddled off into the crowd. "Is that him?" Gavin asked as soon as Halverston was out of earshot.

"I don't know what you're talking about, Gavin." I pivoted on my heel and made my way to the buffet table to get a bite to eat. The excuse I'd given Halverston wasn't far from the truth. I had eaten too much birthday cake and not enough of anything else.

"Don't play coy with me, Dr. Brexler," Gavin said as he followed behind me. I had hoped if I ignored him, he'd walk away and find someone else to annoy, but no such luck. "I saw the way you were looking at the tall, dark, and sexy man talking to the senator."

"You saw no such thing, Gavin." *Deny. Deny. Deny.*

"He's the one that had you wiggling in your chair a few months ago, right? The one you were sighing over as you looked through your planner like you couldn't get the memory of how he made you feel out of your mind."

"Perhaps you should switch your major to romantic literature since you seem to have the knack for it."

"I know what I saw on your face in the office that day. I haven't seen that expression again until tonight, so who are you trying to fool? Me or yourself?"

"Look—"

"Yeah, Doc, who are you trying to fool?" Jag's dark, sexy voice came out of nowhere and caught me by surprise. "Let me help you with that," he said as he eased an arm around me and plucked the plate out of my hand. "I'm going to borrow him for a bit," Jag said to Gavin. "I hope you don't mind."

Gavin looked Jag up and down like he was a life-sized hot fudge sundae. "Take all the time you need." He gave me a jaunty little salute and an impish smile. I was ready to give him a scalding retort, but Jag took my upper arm in his free hand and began guiding me to a table.

"You're a doctor who studies bones, yes?" That was a unique way of referring to my job, but I knew which *bone* he was referring to, and it had nothing to do with archeological digs or lost civilizations.

"In a manner of speaking," I replied as I sat down at a vacant table. "You've just met my teaching assistant, Gavin Anderson."

"He's a scrumptious little cupcake with sprinkles on top," Jag replied. I did not want to hear about his past or future conquests, so the question that popped out of my mouth shocked me.

"You've fucked Senator Thompson, huh?" Luckily, I didn't blurt it out as loudly as I could have, but it was still loud enough that Jag looked around to make sure I hadn't been heard.

"Oh, good. People in Southeast Asia didn't hear you," he said sarcastically once he looked back at me. I tried to play it off like I didn't care by stabbing a meatball with my fork and bringing it to my mouth. I caught Jag staring at my lips, so I played up the situation to make eating the saucy balls as sexy as I could. In spite of knowing better, I wanted to remind him of our joint shower when I had sucked his balls into my mouth one at a time. It seemed to be something he liked a hell of a lot. Jag leaned closer until his lips nearly brushed against my ear. "Yes, I did fuck the good senator, and yes, he wants me to fuck him again, but do you know what?"

"What?" My voice sounded strangled and a little raspier than I had been aiming for, but it was hard to put on a front when I had an erection trying to bust out of my trousers. It only took his deep, dirty voice in my ear to get me primed and ready.

"Senator Thompson doesn't have the ass I've been dying to ride again." *Gulp.* I knew where he was heading, and I couldn't resist following. I set my fork down and slid my plate away as food became the last thing I wanted right then. No, there was definitely something else I wanted in my mouth.

"He doesn't?" I asked.

"No." Jag placed his hand on my thigh beneath the table and slid it upward until he cupped my straining hard-on through the thin fabric of my dress pants. "Why don't you show me your office, Bones? I'd like to see the chair you wiggled in the day after I claimed that sweet ass." Jag's breath ghosted over my ear. "I felt you for days too." My skin and clothes suddenly felt too tight as memories of our night together flashed behind my closed eyes. Jag gave my cock a firm squeeze, then rose to his feet, giving me a chance to go with him or watch him walk away—probably right to the good senator.

I stood up without a word and led the way to my office, which included a walk across campus in the frigid December air. The chilly wind that swept between the buildings did nothing to diminish the heat that boiled in my veins because I knew I would soon be filled with Jag's burning heat and all else would fade away as he mastered my body.

There was no need to use my keys to get into the building because guests were encouraged to meander through the university that night. My office, however, was locked, so I pulled my keys out of my coat pocket and attempted to unlock the door. It took several tries because my hands were shaking as Jag rubbed his erection against my ass in the empty hallway and bit my ear.

"I haven't come in my underwear since I was a teenager, Bones, but you're making it really hard to hold back. God, I love your ass." Jag gripped my cheeks in his large hands and massaged them. "I need to be inside you."

Finally, I fit the key into the lock and opened the door. Jag shoved me inside my office before he slammed the door hard enough to rattle the frame. The only sound besides our pounding hearts and labored breathing was the click of the lock engaging beneath his masterful hands.

"I don't have any protection here. Please tell me you have something with you."

Jag smiled wickedly before he said, "I've got us covered, Bones. I wasn't a Boy Scout, but I'm always prepared."

"I was a Boy Scout, and that wasn't what they meant about being prepared." I took off my jacket and tossed it onto the small couch where I liked to read with a cup of hot coffee in the late afternoon. I reached for my tie and began to loosen it, but Jag's words stopped me.

"Leave the tie and shirt on." He pulled me into his arms and took my mouth in a ravaging, almost bruising kiss for several long, sexy minutes. "I'm going to bend you over your desk and fuck you the way your body is begging me to." Jag whipped my chair out from behind the desk and positioned me the way he wanted me. He reached around to my tie and loosened the knot so it hung free a few inches. He lifted the knot in front of my mouth and said, "Bite this to keep from crying out, Bones, unless you want someone to hear you cry out as I give you the hard fucking you want."

Jag's dominant side drove me wild, and I eagerly obeyed him by chomping down on my tie. He made quick work of unbuckling my belt and unfastening my pants. The slide of the fabric down my legs caused me to shiver in expectation. I knew no matter how hard he'd ridden me the first time, it would pale in comparison to the pounding he was about to deliver.

Jag tossed his wallet onto the desk with a soft *thud*, then came the rustling as he pushed down his own pants. I nearly groaned with anticipation when his belt buckle hit the hardwood floor with a *clank*.

I turned my head and watched Jag pull out two lube packets and a condom from his wallet. The sound of the packets tearing was the sexiest thing I had heard since the last time we were together. I missed watching him roll the latex down his steely length, but I didn't have time to pout because his long, confident fingers began to work the lube inside my tight hole. It didn't take me long to be grateful he'd recommended I bite my tie because it dulled the sound of the heavy groans he ripped from me.

"Just imagine how much you'll want to shout once I've worked my dick inside you." Jag pressed his cock to my opening to tease me. I thrust backward to take him inside me, but he pulled back. "You're still so tight, Bones, and you threaten my control. I want to fuck you good and hard, but I don't want to hurt you." He continued stretching me until he thought I was ready to receive him. "Press your chest flat against your desk and grab onto the edge on the other side. The only thing I want in the air is your gorgeous ass." I did as he asked and was rewarded with his hot, teasing hands on my ball sac and a wicked thumb massaging my taint.

As excited as I was to be giving my ass up to him again, I found myself holding my breath as he started to enter me. "Jag," his name was a mumbled curse against knotted silk as he drew out my torture, entering me one tiny fraction of an inch at a time.

Jag pressed his chest against my back and placed his mouth against my ear. "Such a greedy ass you've got, Bones." He laid his hands on top of mine just like he had the first time he'd claimed me, then he drove in deep, bottoming out in one hard thrust.

I screamed his name behind my impromptu gag as black dots danced in my vision and intense pleasure rocked me. Jag kept his thrusts slow and steady at first and allowed me to adjust to his girth, then he increased the intensity until I heard and felt the slap of his pelvis against my ass. I wished I could see how his hips looked as he powered in and out of me. I found myself longing for a mirror or some way to watch us because I knew Jag taking his pleasure from me and giving it to me in return would be the sexiest thing I ever saw.

"Don't move," he whispered hungrily in my ear. He lifted his weight off me until he stood behind me with his hands on my hips. "I need to watch your ass take me deep, Bones." It felt like he was trying to memorize every sensation just like I was.

I resented the gag, wishing I could tell him how I wanted him to fuck me. I wanted to beg him, but I wasn't sure what I would plead for. I yearned to shout his name and let him know he turned me inside out.

Jag held my hips in his strong hands, hard enough to bruise, and pounded into me. The sound of flesh smacking together echoed around my office, and I was certain I'd hear the echoes long afterward. Jag moved one hand and pressed down between my shoulder blades as if he feared I might try to escape.

Sweat dripped from my forehead and splashed onto my desk as Jag dialed up his pounding to a level I hadn't known existed. It was beyond feral or animalistic. It was almost as if he was using my body to exorcise some sort of demon. The pleasure was too intense for me to complain.

Suddenly, Jag stilled with his dick buried inside me. "I want you to ride me while I sit in your chair, Bones. It'll give you more memories to make you wiggle in your seat." Jag pulled me up so I stood in front of him with his dick still lodged in my body and took a few steps back until he fell into my office chair, pulling me down on top of him.

Jag's hands left my hips and slid up my torso, pulling my shirt along with them. I began fucking myself on his hard rod while he pinched my nipples. My cock bounced and slapped against my stomach and the sound spurred me on even more. I was so close to coming, but I didn't want it to end. Jag's fingernails rasped over my hard nipples and sent me flying over the edge. He grabbed my hips and began slamming me onto his shaft when my rhythm faltered and my orgasm flooded my system. I came in a wide arc that landed on my desk and the floor in front of me.

"Jesus, you get so tight when you come that it almost hurts," Jag growled between his teeth.

I was so exhausted I could do nothing but lie back against his chest while he fucked into me, chasing his own orgasm. Jag was that damn good. Even better was the way he bit into my shoulder to keep from roaring as he flooded the condom inside me.

He thrust up into me twice more before he wrapped his arms around me and held me tight against him. He leaned his head so that his temple was pressed against the side of my sweaty neck. He pulled the tie out of my mouth and turned my head for a hot kiss. I hadn't realized how much I missed his lips during sex until then. We kissed until our breathing and heart rates returned to normal.

"Next time, I want to hear all the sexy things you say during sex," he whispered hotly in my ear. *Next time?* I should've put up a token argument, but we both knew this wouldn't be the last time I surrendered my body to him.

"Next time, you'll be the one making all the hungry sounds while I fuck you."

Silence and then finally, "Okay."

We didn't say anything else while we cleaned up in the tiny bathroom attached to my office then wiped down my desk, the floor, and my chair. After, Jag handed me his phone, and I knew what he was asking without words. I programmed my contact info into his phone, saved under the name Bones, and handed it back to him. I handed him my phone and watched as he saved his info in my phone too.

One last soft, lingering kiss, then he left me alone in my office to think about what had just happened. It wasn't the sex part that had me floundering but the kiss he'd given me before he left. All the other kisses we'd shared had been hungry preludes to hard fucking. That goodbye kiss was sweet and remained on my lips long after he left.

I sat down in my chair and could still feel the heat of his body on the leather and smell his scent and the fragrance of our combined releases in the air. I wondered, not for the first time, what I was doing with Jag and why it seemed like I couldn't let go? Sure, he was a mystery I wanted to solve, but there was more to it than that. This was more than dial-a-dick, and I guessed only time would tell exactly what was happening between us.

CHAPTER
Seven

JJ

A MONTH HAD PASSED, AND I HADN'T HEARD FROM BONES, WHICH left me feeling irritated and conflicted. My confliction came from the hurt and disappointment I felt growing stronger each day that went by without a word from him. I didn't want our interactions to be important enough to hurt me, but I still ended up feeling rejected. I was irritated I had set myself up for disappointment by handing him my phone in the first place. I'd asked myself a hundred times in thirty days what I had been thinking that night. The answer came easily each time as I sat alone inside my house.

Miller made me forget. He took away the pain and numbness and made me feel. I wanted to hold on to that, but at the same time, I was too afraid to try.

That night at the university alumni event had been the anniversary of the worst day of my life. It was a night when I usually got smashed to hide from the pain, but I would wake up the next morning and remember that my selfishness nine years ago had cost the life of someone I loved so much, someone who'd trusted me to keep him safe, and I'd failed. I wanted to feel miserable and alone for the rest of my life because I didn't deserve any better.

Somewhere along the way, I'd stopped wanting to be miserable and alone, but I didn't know how to move forward. I had built so many barriers and blockades to keep everyone away that I wasn't quite sure how to take them down. Did I slowly remove them one at a time or just kick them all down one right after another? Handing my phone to Miller was my attempt to slowly remove the barriers, to dip my toes into dark, murky water to see what lurked beneath the surface. His lack of response wasn't inspiring, even though our goodbye kiss had held so much promise. I'd made the first move, and I needed him to make the next one.

In the meantime, I decided to get a cat to combat the loneliness. I had gotten acquainted with Chase and Gray's cat, Oliver, the few times I had been over and found his purring to be comforting. I also loved his smartass personality if you could say that about a cat. I'd even extended an olive branch to Gray by way of asking him where he'd adopted Oliver. I thought by complimenting his choice in cats it would somehow work in my favor. I figured he'd be less hostile since he and Chase had gotten engaged, but it seemed he still hadn't warmed up to me yet. In fact, Oliver taking a liking to me seemed to make things worse. Gray was probably thinking I was after his man *and* his cat.

I felt some of my sadness ease over thoughts of tormenting Gray a little later that afternoon. I had been invited to their house for pizza and beer while we watched the first round of the NFL playoffs. I wasn't sure who else was invited, but my heartbeat picked up at the thought of seeing Miller again. Would it be awkward? Would I be able to avoid making a fool of myself over him again? Would I be petulant and demand to know why he hadn't called? I hoped to hell I wouldn't give him the satisfaction of seeing how much he'd gotten under my skin.

I took my time grooming myself just in case he made an appearance. Just in case he wanted to apologize for his absence by dropping to his knees to blow me later when we could be alone. *A guy could dream, right?* I believed in being prepared for any occasion, which was why I also stopped at the drug store on my way to buy more lube packets. *Just in case.*

I turned down the family planning and personal hygiene aisle and came to a screeching halt when I saw Ava standing in the aisle studying the boxes in front of her. I couldn't help but smile at the long trench coat and Hollywood-style sunglasses she wore. I wasn't sure if she was trying to disguise herself or if she was about to start flashing people. She leaned over to get a closer look at the boxes instead of picking one up as if she were afraid it might bite her.

"You could read it better if you took off those sunglasses, Ms. Monroe," I said, comparing her to the famous blonde bombshell. Ava clutched her chest and gasped before she spun around to face me. Then she promptly burst into tears. "Ava, what's the matter?" I asked. I walked to her and wrapped my arms around her. I couldn't recall a time I had seen her cry in all the years I had known her. "Surely, it can't be that bad." I looked over at the display she had been studying and saw they were early pregnancy tests.

"I-I-I'm not ready for this, J." She began to cry a little harder, so I hugged her tighter. "I had hoped it would be just the two of us for a little while longer." Two women had entered the aisle and were giving me the evil eye as if I was the one who'd knocked her up and made her cry. "I want to have kids, I really do, but I…"

"It's okay, Ava." My words were met with more sobs. "Does Brandon know yet?"

"No." Her voice sounded small and broken. "He's waiting for me to come home so we can go to his brother's house to watch football." Ava pulled back from my chest and tilted her head back so she could look at me. "What if he's mad at me for being careless, J? I take my birth control really seriously, and I don't know what happened. Maybe I'm just late. I don't want to say anything to him until I know for sure." I couldn't take her seriously with those damn glasses on, so I slid them up onto the top of her head. Her blue eyes were so full of worry I nearly slid the glasses back down.

"This is Brandon we're talking about, Ava. He's not going to be mad at you. The man worships the ground you walk on. He's almost as sappy as Grayson Wright." Ava gave me a wobbly smile at the comparison because she knew it was true. I used the sleeve of my coat to wipe the tears from her face. "Besides, it takes two to make a baby, and if he was hell bent on preventing pregnancy, he should've worn a condom in addition to the birth control you're taking. Buy your test, take it home, and tell him what you're going through. Brandon wouldn't want you to worry about this all alone. Hell, he'd probably hold the stick for you to pee on." Ava laughed loudly at my ridiculousness.

Ava stood on her tiptoes, but I still had to lean down so she could land a kiss on my cheek. "I love you, J." It had been a very long time since someone had told me they loved me, and I didn't quite know how to respond. I did know that those three words were a balm to my desolate, dry soul. She pulled back quickly and gave me a genuine, megawatt smile before she pivoted and grabbed the first test she saw on the shelf. "You're right. I'm going to go home and tell Brandon what I suspect is going on. I'll pee on the stick by myself, but I'll let him hold my hand while we wait for the results. Thank you. I'll text you later and let you know if you're going to be an uncle."

"Thank you, Ava." It meant a lot to me that she wanted to include me in her new family. A year ago, I might have scoffed at the sentiment, but something was gradually shifting inside me, and I wanted something bigger than my shallow existence. I knew exactly who was responsible for the shift which made me even more pissy that he hadn't called.

I was still smiling when I arrived at Chase and Gray's. Gray met my happiness with narrowed eyes behind his black-rimmed glasses. I planted my ass on the couch while he headed into the kitchen. I heard him muttering every step of the way. Oliver jumped onto the couch and began rubbing his head on my arm to get my attention as if the fifteen pounds of fur and fluff wasn't enough to gain my notice.

"You sure are a pretty kitty," I said to Oliver as I scratched his head between his ears. He closed his eyes and purred even louder. I felt Gray's hostility growing when he returned to the room, and I couldn't help but play it up a bit. He was such an easy target after all. You'd have thought I was stroking Chase by the way he glared at me. "Smart too, aren't you?"

Gray sat on the loveseat and did his best to ignore me while I cooed to his cat just so I could watch his jaw muscles twitch from clamping down so hard. As much as the guy irritated me, I had to give him credit. I didn't think I would have been nearly as accepting if the situation were reversed, so I decided to cut him some slack. He was really trying to make an effort. The least I could do was meet him halfway.

"Seriously, Gray, where did you adopt Oliver?" He turned and studied me to see if I was being serious or just yanking his chain again.

He must have seen something he liked, or at least found acceptable, because he said, "River's Crossing Pet Shelter. My stepfather works with them a lot, and he recommended them to me. They have a lot of animals that need homes, and it was hard to walk out of there with just one cat."

"Thank you."

Gray responded with a simple nod, but it was enough. It seemed we had taken a slight step forward, and I was grateful for the ease in tension.

Chase came in with snacks a few minutes later. He laid them down on the coffee table and curled into Gray's side on the loveseat. I had to admit they were as cute as fluffy kitties together, but I wasn't going to confess that out loud to either of them. As they snuggled, I found myself wondering where Miller was and what, or who, he might be doing. *Why did snuggling remind me of Miller?* It was a Saturday afternoon. Maybe he just had other things to do. I didn't have to ponder for much longer because he showed up a little bit later. He wasn't alone.

"I found this cutie lingering outside," Miller said. "What's your name again?"

"Kit," the blond guy said. *Kit? Short for Kit Kat? Would Miller be his*

Knight Rider? "I work at Wright Creations. Gray invited me because he wanted to introduce me to his friend."

Just fucking great. Was I supposed to just sit back and watch Miller seduce this guy? Since Gray and Chase were in the kitchen refilling drinks, Miller went around the room and introduced everyone to the newcomer.

"Oh," Kit said when Miller got to me. "Hi." He gave me a little finger wave, which I returned in kind. "Has anyone ever told you that you look like Bruce Wayne?"

"Nope."

Kit smiled and I had to admit he was pretty. "Do you happen to be the friend Gray invited me to meet?" he asked.

Miller threw back his head and laughed. "Oh, sweetie. This is the kind of guy your mama has warned you about. Pretty sure you're here to meet me."

I quirked a brow at Miller because he was no better than I was.

Kit laughed and raked his eyes over Miller. "My boss has excellent taste."

What the hell had Gray been thinking with this setup? If I didn't know better, I'd think he did it on purpose to... What? Make me jealous? That was preposterous, yet an unfamiliar emotion stirred in my gut and grew stronger each time the kid laughed at one of Miller's stupid jokes.

My phone beeped in my pocket midway through the first quarter, and I knew it was probably a text from Ava. They didn't need to know that, and I needed an excuse to get out of there. "There's the bat signal now. I'm needed elsewhere."

"I hope you're able to stop whatever villain is wreaking havoc all over our fair city," Kit said playfully.

I rose from the couch and turned to face the two men who remained seated. My eyes remained on Miller's when I replied to Kit's remark. "It's not that kind of emergency, kid." I took immense pleasure in watching the smug smile slip from Miller's face. "Night all."

"Night, J." Chase was the only one to reply as I made a hasty retreat.

It was ten degrees outside, but I didn't bother putting on my coat. I needed the frigid air to cool the fury I had building inside me. I started my car and retrieved the message I had received in the house. As I suspected, it was from Ava.

Thank you for your support today! You're going to be an uncle later this year. <3

I was excited for her and Brandon, and I was glad she'd spoken to him.

You're going to be an amazing mom! <3

I pulled up the internet on my phone and did a search for River's Crossing Pet Shelter. I could've gone out and hooked up with a random stranger to fuck Miller out of my system, but my house would still be lonely afterward. According to their website, the shelter was open for another two hours, so I aimed my car that direction. It felt like I was knocking over another barrier in my attempt to find a bit of happiness for myself. Hopefully, this would turn out better than the barrier I'd knocked down for Miller.

CHAPTER
Eight

Miller

"**B**RUCE WAYNE?" THE IRRITATION I HEARD IN GRAY'S VOICE through the phone made me smile. I had to bite my lip to keep from laughing as I pictured the look of disgust on his face as I repeated the parts of the conversation he missed while they were filling drinks. "He's the villain, not the hero."

His outrage made me laugh harder than I had in ages. "Only Chase could date both Batman and Superman," I teased.

"Oh, shut the fuck up, dickhead. I don't even know why I love you."

"Oh my God, Gray, you need help."

But he wasn't the only one. I waited a month for Jag to call or text me. I had stupidly read more into us exchanging numbers or the tender kiss we'd shared before he left me alone in my office. He was the one who'd wanted to exchange numbers, so he should've been the one to initiate our next arrangement. My dick perked up at the thought of a convenient arrangement with Jag, one where we both got what we needed without any entanglements or complications.

My best friend sighed heavily. "JJ's happiness means a lot to Chase, and I have to accept the guy in my life whether I like it or not. You need to be my ally, not the person who stirs shit up because you think it's funny. Okay?"

"No problem." Truthfully, I found nothing funny about JJ and Chase being former lovers. It gnawed on my nerves and irritated me in a way I didn't understand. It felt a lot like the jealousy I experienced when I realized Jag and Senator Thompson had been lovers. It was something that didn't make any sense to me at all. In my mind, you had to be in love with someone to feel jealous. I wasn't in love with Jag, but my body craved the things he did to me. I was smart enough to know the difference, so why did I care about his past so much?

I chatted with Gray for several more minutes, and we made tentative plans to play racquetball sometime the following week. My mind was stuck on the situation with Jag long after I disconnected the call. It was as if I couldn't move on once I'd thought about what a casual arrangement with Jag might look like. My heart sped up as I rolled the possibilities through my brain—a lot of sex that didn't require disastrous dates or explanations about my position on love and romance. I wanted to see how far I could push Jag and how far he could push me in return. It would be simple and uncomplicated.

I sat staring at my phone for a long time before I worked up the nerve to send him a simple text with three innocuous words. **Are you busy?** There, I'd taken the first step and sat back, trying to relax as I waited to see how long it would take him to respond if he did at all.

No.

His one-word answer came two hours later. Two hours! He must've been busy if he couldn't answer me for two fucking hours. Maybe he'd been busy with someone else for those two hours and only answered me when he was finally free. I groaned out loud when I realized I sounded like an angry, jilted lover. I had a nice set of balls, and it was time I used them and took a chance.

Can I come over? Go big or stay home. This time his response was immediate.

I'll leave your name at the security gate.

I showered, shaved, and brushed and flossed my teeth. My grooming had more to do with ridding myself of nervous energy than any real expectation of what would happen at his house. Okay, wishful thinking might have played a big part in the way I'd manscaped before I put on a pair of ass-hugging jeans and a sweatshirt.

I showed my ID to the guard on duty, and he opened the gate for me. My heartbeat accelerated as I drove through Jag's neighborhood. I hadn't really worked through what I wanted to say in the hours that I'd waited for him to respond, and I was no closer to a plan when he opened the door after I rang the bell.

I didn't know what I expected to see in his dark eyes, but the wariness in his expression took me by complete surprise. My excitement faded at the thought that I might be to blame for his hesitation. Well, fuck. Instead of him grabbing me by my shirt and hauling me over the threshold, he quietly stepped aside so I could enter.

"Where do you want to do this?" Gone was the hot, hungry voice I had come to associate with him, and in its place was sad resignation that doused any lusty feelings I had. I turned in his foyer to face him.

"What?"

"You came here for sex, right? I would have thought you wore yourself out with the twink last night, but apparently, he wasn't enough to get it done. So where do you want to do this?"

"I didn't come here for sex." *Lie.* Jag's expression said he didn't believe a word I'd just said. "And nothing happened between Kit and me." I thought I saw a spark of happiness in his eyes, which both thrilled and irritated me. "You're one to talk, *Bruce*. You ran off to attend to someone's 'emergency' needs last night, so why are you giving me shit? Afraid you can't get it up so soon?"

"Are doubting my virility now, Bones?" Jag's nostrils flared as he advanced on me. "Just to set the record straight, that was a text from a friend who'd had a tumultuous day. I think you're just picking a fight so we can tussle before we fuck it out of our systems? There's no need to pretend. You're here to get fucked, and I'm *up* for the task." I backed up, countering every step he took forward, until his large frame pressed me against a wall. He was *up* all right and making it very hard for me to concentrate.

"I didn't come here to fight or get fucked." I licked my lips that had suddenly gone dry from all my labored breathing. He made me so crazy with lust that I feared he'd have me panting like a begging dog. "Besides, it's my turn to do the fucking."

Jag pulled back from me slowly, his hooded eyes locked on mine. "Come and get it, then."

He turned and walked into his living room. I followed him after I picked my jaw up off the floor. I had almost caught up to him when a streak of gray fluff followed by a black one ran in front of me and knocked me off-balance. I tripped forward and crashed into his back, which knocked him to his hands and knees. I landed draped all over him in just about the perfect mounting position. My dick twitched happily in my briefs at the thought of filling him again.

"So you want to scrap after all," Jag said as he dropped and rolled to his side. I collapsed once his supporting weight was no longer beneath me. Jag took advantage and rolled us until I was pinned beneath him. "I love your aggressiveness and eagerness to fuck me, Bones, but you could've broken my dick just now."

He lowered his head at the same time I raised mine and our mouths met in the middle for a savage kiss. There was no other way to describe the almost painful passion that erupted between us every time we came together. He bit my lip hard enough to draw blood, and I hissed angrily between parted lips. Just as quickly, soothing swipes of his tongue over the offended flesh dulled the anger to a lust so intense I completely lost sight of myself. My only thought was pinning him down and taking his ass again because no one else made me feel what he did.

"That's right, Bones," he whispered wickedly in between nips and bites to my neck. "Show me what you want from me." He was taller and probably had more than thirty pounds on me, but I liked the challenge he presented.

I should've been appalled Jag had a stash of condoms and lube handy in his coffee table drawer, but right then, I was just thankful as I began stretching him open to receive me. Gratitude turned into elation as his tight rim strangled the head of my dick.

"Fuck me already," he snarled as I took my sweet time letting him adjust to my penetration. He kept bucking his hips back onto my cock, and it was enough to snap what little control I had. "Miller!" He roared my name as I slammed deep inside him and rode his ass like it was my last rodeo. Jag played the role of a bucking bronco very well, but he wasn't trying to unseat me. His ass eagerly met every thrust until we were reduced to a spunky, sweaty pile of tangled limbs on his living room floor.

"I actually only came over here to talk to you," I told him once some of my blood had returned to my brain. "Sex was just wishful thinking."

"Talk?" His incredulous snort told me he didn't believe me. "Give me a few minutes and we can 'talk' some more."

"Seriously, Jag." I eased my dick out of him and rolled over onto my back. I turned my head and looked into his suspicious dark eyes. "I hadn't even planned on taking you up on your offer until your critters tripped me and knocked me into you." I wasn't even sure what type of animals had run in front of me.

"You're going to blame my kittens for you knocking me to the floor and fucking me senseless?"

"Yes, I'm blaming your kittens because it's the truth." I was thrilled to hear him say I'd fucked him senseless, but my mind kept going back to him owning kittens. He didn't strike me as the fuzzy kitty type, which made me wonder what else he might be hiding beneath his sexy veneer.

I sensed there were even more layers to him than I'd first thought, and damn if I didn't want to peel back every single layer to discover the real Jagger Jackson.

"Riiiiight. I'll play along, Bones, because I'm curious what you're going to say next. If you didn't come here for sex, then what did you come here to talk about?" His smug tone challenged me, but I wasn't backing down.

"Sex." His right eyebrow shot up.

"Like you need some pointers or advice?"

I rolled my eyes, reached over, and twisted one of his nipples until he cried out. "Does it look like I need pointers on how to fuck? Do I need to remind you of the pleading and begging you did just now?" He narrowed his eyes at me and rubbed his hand over his aching nipple. "I wanted to talk to you about us having sex more often than once every few months." He looked skeptical about my proposal but didn't say anything. "We're really good together, Jag, and I trust you. I love having sex, but I hate the complications of trying to find someone who also doesn't want a relationship."

"Miller, I don't think people can hook up and have a lot of sex without someone developing feelings or getting attached to the other person. I really like having sex with you too, but I won't be able to give you anything more. It's just not in the cards for someone like me." Was he saying he didn't think he deserved to be loved? That was a far cry from just not believing in love. I wanted to ask more, but he spoke first. "If sex is all you expect or want from me, then I'm in."

I should've said more or even asked some questions, but Jag pressed his lips to mine and pulled me tight against his body. My brain short-circuited as his hands roamed all over my body as if they had missed the feel of my skin. My only thought was experiencing the pleasure that only he could give me. Had I been more cognizant, I would've worried about becoming addicted to him and the way he made me feel.

CHAPTER
Nine

JJ

MILLER'S SUGGESTION FOR US TO HOOK UP ON A MORE REGULAR basis shocked and delighted me. To say I was sexually attracted to him was putting it mildly. Bones turned me on and drove me wild like no other man had before, but his intelligence, humor, and personality made him even more appealing. I found myself in the uncomfortable position of fearing I would be the one to fall in love and get hurt.

Our hookups started out once or twice a week, but gradually, over a few months, became three or four times a week. I didn't know how else to describe the way he made me feel except to say he was like an addiction. I got twitchy and became withdrawn until I got my Miller fix. He brought so much more into my life than just sex.

He became the person I talked to about my work, and I was his sounding board too when he wanted to talk about the idiot who ran his department. I loved how passionate Miller was about his work and his students. He told me he admired the way I fought for our community, even though the things I battled for were things I didn't want for myself. Miller called me selfless when most would describe me as selfish. It seemed he saw more in me than others did, including myself.

Miller was so much more than just the affable playboy I had first thought. One of the things I admired most about him was his dedication to his family. I didn't know too many single men who gave up their weekends to babysit their niece and nephew so their parents could take a weekend getaway here and there, but he did. I loved how he had a spare bedroom just for them at his house and how he hung up the pictures they colored for him on his refrigerator. I loved to listen to him talk about his family, and I wondered what it must have been like to grow up surrounded by so much love. The beautiful man he'd become was a testament to the kind of parents he had. Every child deserved to be loved the way Miller was, regardless of the number of parents a child had or their sexual orientation. Love and acceptance could eclipse a lot of shitty circumstances.

He was wonderful to my purr babies, Ursula and Maleficent, when he came to my house. There was a lot of teasing on his part when he recognized I'd named my cats after two Disney villains. He often brought them treats or toys and spent time playing with them. It seemed the way to my heart was to be good to my kitties, and I definitely showed him my appreciation each and every time.

I did the same for his adorable dog, Indy, who was probably the smartest dog I had ever met. I'd never pictured Miller with a dog, but if I had, I would have guessed a Labrador or some other large breed. Once I'd met Indy, I couldn't imagine him with any other dog. They were cute as hell together, especially when Miller talked to him and Indy cocked his head to the side as if he was listening very closely. I'd had to pay Miller back by giving him a hard time for naming his dog after Indiana Jones.

Casual lunches and dinners got added into the mix about four months after our arrangement began in January. I didn't refer to them as dates because they were impromptu meetups that were totally random and didn't involve sex afterward. I thought we kept it that way on purpose so we didn't veer into territory that we'd promised to stay away from.

Yet for Miller's birthday, I planned an *Indiana Jones* movie marathon and takeout from his favorite Chinese restaurant. It was my turn to go to his house and spunk up his sheets, so I took the DVDs and food over to his place around five. I was nervous he would reject my birthday gesture because it was too much like a date, but he seemed genuinely pleased at my thoughtfulness.

We dug into the food and settled on the couch to begin our movie marathon. I found myself eagerly anticipating the time in his company and the birthday sex I'd planned for later that night. The doorbell rang about halfway through the first movie, jolting me out of my sensual thoughts. Miller paused the movie and left the room to answer the door. I started to worry it might be Gray stopping by to wish him a happy birthday. Miller was still adamant Chase and Gray not find out about our arrangement because he didn't think either would understand or approve.

Two rowdy kids ran into the room looking for Indy followed by two adults. A silly part of me wondered if I should hide in Miller's bedroom until his company left. But he didn't act like he wanted me to make myself scarce, so I stayed on the couch and waited to follow Miller's lead.

The kids came to a screeching halt when they spotted me. They stood there looking at me with blue eyes that were identical to Miller's. The adults were so busy apologizing for missing Miller's birthday brunch that it took them a few minutes to realize the room had gone completely silent. They turned and saw me sitting on the couch and smiled politely.

"Oh, I didn't know you had company. We're so sorry for intruding," the woman said as she looked back and forth between Miller and me. "I'm Destiny Brexler." She crossed the room and held out her hand. I rose to my feet and shook her hand in greeting. "I'm married to Miller's brother, Darryl, and I'm mother to Lucas and Lily." She gestured at her blond-haired, blue-eyed children who were still sizing me up. "You must be Jag."

I was stunned she knew my name because the only way she could possibly know it was if Miller had talked about me to her. Why would he do that, though? I looked over at him, but he didn't meet my eyes. Instead, he looked down at his feet. I decided to play it cool so I wouldn't make the moment more awkward.

"Yes, I'm Jag. It's very nice to meet you, Destiny, and you too, Darryl." I turned and offered my hand to Miller's brother, who shook it with a wry smile on his face.

"It's nice to meet you, Jag." He turned back to Miller. "Sorry we burst in on your date, bro. Lucas and Lily wanted to give their favorite uncle a birthday hug and kiss." Darryl knelt down beside his children. "Why don't you say hello to Uncle Miller's friend Jag, then give Uncle Miller his birthday kisses and hugs so we can let them get on with their evening."

"Hello, Jag," Lily said in the sweetest little voice. She gave me a tentative smile. "I'm Lily, and I'm four years old."

"Hi, Lily. It's nice to meet you." I was completely out of my league with this impromptu meet and greet and was flying by the seat of my pants. Lucas walked up to me and offered his hand like a little man. I smiled down into his twinkling blue eyes and shook his hand. "It's nice to meet you too, Lucas. Your uncle Miller talks about you guys all the time."

"He does?" Lily asked.

"What does he say?" Lucas looked suspiciously at his uncle.

"He just tells me funny stories," I told him. "Like how you dress Indy in Lily's dress-up costumes or how you sometimes hide Lily's favorite book because you're sick of hearing the same book over and over."

"Uncle Miller," Lucas whined as if Miller had somehow given away his biggest secrets. He looked back at me with an earnest expression as if he was pleading for me to understand him. "Do you know how many times I've heard *Green Eggs and Ham*? A trillion!"

Hearing the title of that book shifted me back in time to when I'd sat with another little boy with big blue eyes who'd pleaded with me to read it to him just one more time. That book drove me crazy, but it was his favorite. If only I had the chance to read the book to him one more time.

"I understand, buddy." I dug deep for composure and tried not to let my devastation show in front of everyone. "You'll look back someday, and that book will be a fond memory instead of an annoyance. I promise."

"If you say so." Lucas added a dramatic eye roll to his droll reply, which made the adults in the room laugh.

"Munchkins, give Uncle Miller his hugs and kisses so we can get going," their mother said.

They ran to Miller, and he acted like they knocked him down. They pounced on him with delighted squeals and kissed his face repeatedly while they clung to his neck. It was a beautiful moment that helped pull me away from the ghosts of my past. Darryl and Destiny laughingly pulled their children off Miller and bid him farewell before leaving.

Miller returned to the living room and plopped down on the couch beside me after he walked them out to their car. He picked up the remote and turned the movie back on without another word. I recognized the move as one of avoidance, and I let it go. He didn't want to discuss that he'd talked about me to his family, and that was fine with me because I was suddenly plagued with memories I had suppressed for nine long years.

I kept my eyes on the movie and recognized that Indiana Jones had found himself in a bit of a jam, but I wasn't giving him any thought. Instead, my brain chose that moment to display every minute of my little brother's short life that I could remember. Damn, I had forgotten how much he'd looked like Tweety Bird, which had earned him the nickname Tweety. So many memories flooded through me, one right after the next, like a home movie that was cut way too short by my selfishness. I hadn't realized I had started crying until Miller spoke from beside me.

"It's okay, Jag. Indy always finds a way to survive, get the girl, and his treasure." Miller was going for flippant, but he couldn't hide the concern in his voice. I was unable to do anything but shake my head. "Hey, what's wrong?" Miller's soft voice and the feel of his hand gently wiping tears from my cheeks broke through the dam I had built to keep the misery away. It was the final blockade left, and I found myself wrapped tightly in his arms once it came down. "I got you, Jag. I got you."

He rocked me back and forth as he sifted his fingers through my hair to soothe and comfort me. I didn't know how long we stayed like that before I stopped crying and just lay in the circle of his arms with my head against his chest.

"Here I thought the *Indiana Jones* movies were comedies, not tragedies." I knew Miller was attempting to lighten up the moment and I appreciated it more than he could ever know, but I was humiliated that I was unable to keep in control of my emotions.

"I'm sorry I ruined your birthday." I lifted my head from Miller's chest and tried to move away from him, but he pulled me back.

"You didn't ruin anything, Jag." He dropped a soft kiss on the top of my head. "I wanted to spend it with you, and that hasn't changed." Miller rubbed his hand up and down my back until I relaxed into him. "I've always known you were hiding a lot of sadness inside, and I'm always willing to listen if you want to talk. I promise what you tell me will stay between us, just like Vegas."

I couldn't help but chuckle over his Vegas joke, but I knew that I could trust Miller without his promise. At first, I didn't want to take him up on his offer. I wanted to pretend my breakdown hadn't happened and continue on with our night. Then I realized I was so damn tired of pretending.

"My brother's name was Will." It hurt so bad to say his name out loud. It felt like Mola Ram had punched through my chest and ripped out my heart with his bare hand. "He was only five years old when he died in a fire."

"Oh, Jag." Miller's arms tightened around me, anchoring me against his chest. "I'm so sorry." I heard his sorrowful condolence, but I didn't stop to acknowledge it. I knew that if I stopped telling the story, I might not start again. I wanted to heal and stop hurting, and telling Will's story was the first step toward healing.

"My mom wasn't June Cleaver by any stretch of the imagination. She brought one abusive bastard into our home after another. I spent my entire childhood living in fear of being beaten by her latest lover or starving to death when they got tired of pounding on her and moved on. It was a vicious cycle she just couldn't break until one of her boyfriends turned his anger on me one night when I stepped in to stop him from hitting her." I shuddered at the memory of being hit repeatedly with a belt while white hot rage built inside me. "I was thirteen or fourteen and really big for my age. I don't know where the strength came from, but I dug deep and came up swinging. I gave that asshole a taste of his own medicine, and he was the one that left our house bloody and limping." I remembered feeling pride pierce through my fear as I watched that asshole speed off down the road as I yelled at him to never come back.

"Something changed my mom for the good that night, Miller. She stopped drinking and started working two jobs instead of relying on loser men to help us get by. I started doing lawn care and odd jobs for our neighbors to help. My mom was really trying to turn her life around, and my resentment toward her slowly started to turn into respect. A month later, she discovered she was pregnant." I shook my head and smiled sadly when I remembered how upset I was that I was going to have a little baby brother or sister to look after when she was working. "I wasn't too thrilled," I confessed.

"I can imagine," he said softly. His hand was still rubbing my back, and it helped me unwind enough to tell the rest of the story.

"It was really hard, but we were making it. Will was the best baby you could imagine." My voice broke and new tears threatened, so I cleared my throat to gather my composure. "He hardly cried or fussed and was ready with a smile every time I looked at him. I adored him from the moment I held him the first time. He was so tiny, and I felt this strong feeling of pro- tectiveness come over me." I couldn't stop the tears that time, and Miller just waited patiently while I worked my way through them.

"He was my little shadow, following me everywhere I went. People asked me if I resented him, but I never did. I wanted to be his protector forever, but I let him down. I was selfish, and Will paid the price."

"What do you mean you were selfish? Wasn't the fire an accident?" Miller asked me.

"My mom promised me she would stay sober and be a great mom to Will when I left for college. She was so proud of me for getting scholarships to a prestigious school and promised me I had nothing to worry about. I learned after the fire that her promise had only lasted for one month after I left. She went right back to drinking and dating bad men again. One of those losers passed out drunk with a lit cigarette in his hand. The fire burned down our house and killed everyone inside." I started imagining a terrified Will screaming for me to save him, but I never came.

"You're blaming yourself for going to college and wanting a better life, Jag?"

"I should've been home that night, but I was on a Greyhound bus instead. I wanted to spend a few more days with Chase before I went home for holiday break. If I hadn't been selfish about spending time away from Chase, then I would've been home the night of the fire, and I could've gotten my brother out alive."

"Or you could've died too," Miller interjected. "Jag, you may look a little like Bruce Wayne, but you're not a superhero. You have no way of knowing what would've happened if you had been home when the fire started."

"I would've run that fucker off before the fire even started," I snarled. "I could've transferred schools and lived closer to home and helped my mom out again. I knew how hard she struggled to stay sober, but I wanted to believe she could do it because it made it easier for me to leave. I hadn't thought of her or Will, not when I went to college and not when I stayed extra days to spend time with Chase."

"So that's why you broke up with him so abruptly? Did you blame him for what happened?"

"No. Never." It was the truth. "I never blamed Chase for any of it, just myself. I knew better than to think I deserved a good life. People like me don't get fairy-tale endings, Miller. I was mad at the only people responsible—my mom, her boyfriend, and myself."

"People like you? I don't understand."

"People from the wrong side of the tracks, Bones. You've heard all the phrases and probably used a few of them. Have you ever referred to someone as white trash or trailer trash? If so, you were describing me."

"I've never said those horrible things, and I'm calling bullshit right now." Miller's voice had taken on a firm note, and he pushed at me until

I sat up and looked at him. "You are none of those things." I was about to tell him he had no idea where I came from, but he stopped me with a press of his lips to mine. I closed my eyes and let Miller's touch soothe my battered heart. "I don't care where you were born or to whom. You"—he held my chin in his hand—"are a brilliant, beautiful man who tries to hide how deeply he cares about people. You're the kind of guy who can't just adopt one fluffy kitty and leave her sister behind. What happened to your little brother is tragic and horrible, Jag, but it's not your fault. You could've died too, and the thought of you not being here really hurts."

The intellectual side of me knew Miller was right, but the broken-hearted teenager still had a lot of control over me, and his self-esteem and feelings of self-worth were very low. The lonely adult I had become wanted to cling to Miller's words, to take them into my heart and hold them dear. I wanted to be worthy and deserving of love.

"Have you ever told Chase about what happened?"

"I've only told you, Bones."

"I think you should tell him. I think Chase deserves to hear the truth and not keep thinking you just suddenly didn't want to be with him." Miller's voice was still compassionate, but a hint of something else was there too. I just couldn't name the other emotion.

I cocked my head to the side and studied him, but he gave nothing away. I only saw caring in his baby blues, not pity or disgust. "Do you think it still matters after so long? Have you seen how deliriously happy he is with Gray and the life they're making with each other? I don't want to bring a second of sorrow to his life."

"Jag, can I ask you a really personal question?"

"You're asking me permission after everything I just unloaded on you?" I gave Miller a disbelieving look and gestured for him to bring it on.

"Are you still in love with Chase?" He grimaced once the question left his mouth, and I wondered how long he'd been thinking about that.

"No." That was my short answer, but I saw in his eyes that he needed more from me. "I thought I was in love with him for a very long time. I realized that what I had been feeling was love but not the passionate kind.

I was in love with the memories I had of a happier time in my life. I love Chase with all my heart, but I am not *in* love with him anymore." I had maintained eye contact with Miller while I answered his question. I wanted him to hear my words and see the truth of them in my gaze.

"Okay," he finally said. "I still think you should tell him just so you can have a truly clean slate. It's obvious he's not carrying any grudges against you, but it's very possible he's hurt you won't confide in him as a friend would. If Gray refused to confide something in me, it would really bother me."

"I'm afraid he might blame himself because he asked me to hang back a few extra days. I wanted to stay, and his asking made it easy for me to say yes. Chase is a very sensitive person, and I don't want to do anything that will hurt him. Besides, if I make him cry, your BFF will kill me, and you'll be forced to settle for second-rate sex again." I was tired of being sad and talking about morose things.

"It's your decision, and I support you, Jag." Miller leaned in and kissed me softly.

We eventually settled in to resume his *Indiana Jones* birthday marathon. His couch was big enough that we could both lie down. I lay behind Miller and held him tight in my arms while I watched Indy's adventures play out on the screen and listened to Indy the pug snore by our feet. It was just what I needed after I'd cut myself open and bled out all my pain for Miller to see.

It wasn't long before my eyes got heavy, and I had a hard time staying awake. I knew I should get up and go home because sleepovers weren't part of our agreement. It was the first time I held Miller in my arms out of comfort rather than passion, and it felt like pure heaven. I didn't want to walk away. I turned my brain off and let myself drift off feeling content and at peace for the first time in a very long time.

CHAPTER
Ten

Miller

I HADN'T MEANT TO FALL ASLEEP ON THE COUCH WITH JAG BECAUSE it blurred the lines we'd established. I was surprised when I woke up in the middle of the night and discovered I had turned into his arms. My nose was pressed to his throat, and his arms held me tightly against his sleeping body so I wouldn't fall off the couch. Jag was a natural-born protector, and it spilled over into his sleep.

I lay there in the dark for several minutes before I realized the room shouldn't be dark. The TV should've been on with the screen showing the DVD menu for the movie. At some point, Jag must've turned off the TV and decided to stay with me on the couch instead of going home. I wasn't foolish enough to think the gesture meant anything more than Jag needing comfort from me.

Tears burned the back of my eyes, and my nose began to sting as I replayed what he had divulged. It broke my heart to hear all the pain Jag had been carrying inside himself for so long. I hated that he felt so alone with no one to share his burdens. I hated even more that Jag didn't think he deserved to be loved and somehow felt the universe had punished him by taking away Will because he had dared to love and dream. I was truly grateful he'd trusted me with his hurts and turned to me for comfort.

I had held my shit together when Jag was telling his story because I knew he needed me to be strong for him, but I allowed myself to release my tears and cry for the broken boy he used to be. That wasn't the man who held me in his arms, though. He had moved so far beyond that kid. Jag just needed to see it for himself. Maybe then he would realize he was meant to have so much more than a lonely, loveless life.

I debated waking him up and taking him upstairs to sleep once I gathered my composure and dried my tears. I worried Jag would think I was upset that he'd stayed over, and that wasn't the case at all. He needed me, and I was glad I could be there for him. I decided to take a chance and kissed him awake.

"I'm sorry I fell asleep." Jag unwrapped his arms from around me to stretch his body. "Just give me a few minutes to wake up, and I'll take off."

"I didn't wake you up to leave. I woke you up so we could go to my bed where there's more room." Silence met my statement, but I swore I heard a hamster in his brain running triple time in its wheel as he struggled to think through my offer. "You're thinking way too hard, Jag." I gave him a quick kiss, then climbed off the couch. "You know your way to my bedroom. My offer of a large comfortable bed and warm body stands. No hurt feelings if you want to stay down here, okay?" I patted my leg a few times, and Indy jumped down off the couch and followed me upstairs to my bedroom.

I stripped down to my underwear and put Indy on the bed before climbing between the sheets. I lay there in complete silence as I listened to see what Jag decided to do. After several minutes, he was still on the couch, and I squashed my feelings of disappointment before they could take root. I was just about to fall asleep when I heard his feet on the stairs.

I remained silent as he undressed in the darkness of my bedroom. I tried not to giggle when I heard him give Indy a good night scratch and a kiss on the top of his head. I attempted to keep my breathing even as if I was asleep, but the brush of his bare legs against mine ruined my efforts. I kept my eyes shut and lay still, even though I wanted to curl into his heat. Luckily for me, I wasn't the only one who wanted to cuddle because Jag rolled over onto his side and curled around my body.

"Thank you for being there for me, Bones. I think I needed to talk about my past more than I realized." Jag pressed a kiss to the back of my neck and let out a pent-up breath.

"Anytime, Jag, and I mean that."

I fell asleep wrapped up in his heat but woke up alone. I always woke up alone, so it shouldn't have bothered me. I should've been glad we'd avoided any awkwardness and could just go back to screwing the next time we hooked up. Instead, I missed Jag's heat and the smell of his skin. I pouted like a petulant child because I hadn't gotten the birthday sex I had been looking forward to the previous day. Okay, I was more upset about Jag leaving without a goodbye than I was about the lack of sex. For some stupid reason, I'd woken up wanting things to be different between us.

I still didn't believe I could ever settle down with one guy. So what if Jag had been the only one I'd had sex with since we first got together several months ago. That didn't mean I was falling in love or wanted to settle down with him. I'd just gotten comfortable, and I liked it. Ha! There wasn't anything comfortable about the passion I shared with Jag. I rolled over and punched my pillow in frustration, and that was when I discovered the note on the vacant pillow beside me.

Went to the bakery for pastries and coffee. Be back in a few.

Maybe I should've been embarrassed Jag had discovered the dinosaur stationery my mother had given me for Christmas, but all I could concentrate on was that he was coming back. My dick perked up, and my body came alive at the thought of a birthday orgasm. Jag had told me earlier in the week that I could have any kind of birthday orgasm I wanted. My mind nearly overloaded with images of all the dirty things we could do. *Maybe I could talk him into staying all day and giving me multiple orgasms.*

It didn't take much convincing. Jag came back with two cups of coffee and a variety of pastries, but the only thing I wanted in my mouth was his tongue or dick. He read the desire in my eyes and set the items on the bedside table to be forgotten for a very long time. What started out as playful birthday spankings turned into the most erotic sex I had ever had. There wasn't a part of me Jag didn't worship with his entire body. He brought me to the brink of orgasm only to hold me back from falling over the edge. When he finally let me come, it was the most explosive experience of my life. Once I caught my breath, I wanted to do it all over again, but I wanted to be the one driving him insane with burning need that shook him to his core. He gladly gave his pleasure over to me, and it was the best birthday gift I had ever received. I didn't think we left my room until late in the afternoon, and that was only because we needed something more sustainable than sugary baked goods.

We grilled steaks and finished our movie marathon curled up like lovers on my couch. Neither of us put a name to what we were feeling or discussed it out loud. It seemed we had both made a conscious effort to silently acknowledge that our feelings had moved beyond sexual gratification. I had never experienced anything like my current emotions, and it felt like I was adrift in the middle of the ocean without any sort of life preserver. I was awed by the sheer beauty and power of the ocean surrounding me but terrified of what I couldn't see beneath the water's surface. I was floating and drowning at the same time.

I wished I could talk to Gray, but that was out of the question. He couldn't be objective when it came to Jag. He was convinced Jag was still in love with Chase, and nothing anyone said would change his mind. I knew only time would fix the problem, but that didn't help me when I needed advice immediately. I didn't want to wait months or years for Gray to come around. So I decided to keep my thoughts to myself and see where things took us one day at a time.

CHAPTER
Eleven

JJ

THE MORE TIME I SPENT AROUND MILLER, THE HARDER I FELL FOR him. It was impossible not to be charmed by his every word, touch, and kiss. Talking to him about my past had eased so much of the weight I had been carrying on my shoulders for so long. Before I'd unburdened myself to Miller, it felt like I had a dark cloud of doom floating over my head that prevented the sunlight from reaching me. After telling him about my past, I finally felt the warmth of the sun on my skin.

Our sexual relationship had changed as well. Our connection felt more intense. We spent more time drawing out each other's pleasure instead of fucking furiously while we chased our orgasms. The touches and kisses lingered, and more time was spent on foreplay. Every inch of Miller's beautiful body was burned into my mind. I knew there was something very different about having sex with Miller from our very first encounter. We had maintained eye contact the whole time, and that wasn't how random hookups usually went. I would bend someone over and pound them six ways to Sunday, but I never once looked them in the eyes. That was too personal. With Miller, it had been personal from the onset, and I'd been fooling myself when I'd chosen to believe differently.

What I didn't know was how Miller felt about our arrangement. We had spent several more nights together since our first sleepover, taking turns so our animals didn't feel lonely. In fact, Miller brought Indy to my house with him when he slept over. It almost felt as if we were forming a little family of our own, but I didn't let myself dwell on those thoughts or get my hopes up too high. It was a good thing I'd kept my feet planted firmly on the ground because if not, Miller would have surely knocked me back to earth.

He'd made it abundantly clear he still didn't want anyone to know about our *arrangement*. Fuck, I hated that goddamned word. Miller said it would only confuse people and fire up their matchmaking. I told him we were grown-ass adults, and it wasn't anyone's business. I didn't like being his dirty little secret, but I kept that thought to myself. I figured a sure-fire way to kill our *arrangement* would be to start acting needy. It hurt, though. It was hard enough to hide the feelings I was developing for Miller from him, but I wasn't sure I could pull it off in front of Chase.

It took me a long time to re-erect the arrogant, bored mask that everyone expected me to wear at Chase's bachelor bowling party. I didn't want to go, but I didn't want to disappoint Chase who wanted me there. I knew he battled Gray over our friendship, and I didn't want it to be for nothing. I pulled on my big boy briefs and went to his party, but unfortunately, all my hesitating had made me a little late.

The first thing I saw when I walked into the bowling alley was Miller sizing up Xavier. It was the first time I had seen Miller interact in a group since the alumni event in December. I hadn't liked seeing him flirt with Senator Thompson, and because of that, I might have led the good senator to believe I wanted to reacquaint myself with his body when all I really wanted to do was get him away from Miller. The possessiveness I felt that night had driven me to take Miller like a crazed animal in his office. But those feelings of jealousy and possessiveness paled in comparison to how I felt when I saw Miller chatting up Xavier.

Luckily for me, Gray recognized what was going on and intervened. I wouldn't admit it out loud to anyone, but I was quickly becoming one of Grayson Wright's biggest fans. Not only did he treat Chase like a prince and make him deliriously happy, but he saved me from making an ass of myself that night. If Xavier had given the green light, would Miller have taken him for a ride? The thought made me physically ill. Miller walked away from the group and headed to the bar, and I almost left the bowling alley. I could text Chase the next morning and apologize for missing his party and blame it on work, but Gray's eyes locked on mine. He said something and nodded in my direction causing those around him to look at me. *So much for a quick escape.*

I wanted to believe the regret I saw in Miller's eyes when he rejoined the group was a plea for me to understand he was just flirting, but in actuality it was probably regret his plans for the night had been foiled. My gaze landed on Chase, and I forgot all about my disappointment and anger. My friend radiated so much happiness it nearly hurt my eyes to look at him. I couldn't help but smile as he practically levitated with joy and bliss. The party was about him, to honor his bright future with the man he loved, so I forced myself to focus on him and not Miller.

"Hey, cutie." I pulled Xavier into a one-armed hug and ruffled his hair. I looked into Xavier's dark eyes and noticed the lack of sparkle that was usually present. Whatever had kept him away from home for so long had really done a number on him. I recognized the look in Xavier's eyes because I'd worn the same one for many years growing up in an unstable and often violent home. I hated whoever had hurt this sweet, sensitive soul so badly.

"You're still so freaking annoying," Xavier said as he jabbed me in the ribs with his elbow until I turned him loose. Xavier's crooked grin as he straightened his hair told me he wasn't as annoyed as he let on.

I looked up and my gaze locked on hostile gray eyes that were assessing me as a threat. I had been around Ben a few times at the gatherings I'd attended at Chase and Gray's. He seemed like a nice enough guy, but he sure as hell didn't like me touching Xavier in any way. Xavier hadn't been home yesterday when I'd talked to Chase, so the little shit had been home for less than twenty-four hours and already had two sexy guys chasing his tail.

"Let's get to bowling," Gram said, coming up behind us. "Lennie wants to go home soon so I can tuck him in." Chase and Xavier nearly threw up while the rest of us hooted with laughter. I loved that crazy lady, even though she'd wanted to throttle me more often than not. There was no pretentiousness about Agnes Simmons. She put herself out there and dared the world to say something to her. She was a woman who'd taken in a broken and beaten Xavier when he was just a little boy and raised him like her own. As much as I admired her confidence and boldness, I adored her huge capacity to love even more.

The beers started to flow, but I kept myself to just one since I'd be driving. It was obvious Miller wasn't too concerned about driving as he knocked them back pretty damn fast. Because it was expected of us, Miller and I started making jokes about monogamy and marriage.

"I mean, don't you get sick of having sex with him?" Miller slurred his words as he pointed to Gray. "I'm not saying you suck in the bedroom," he explained to Gray, "well, I'm sure you suck there and other places too, but what I meant was don't you get worried about just having sex with each other? Forever!"

We listened as Chase and Gray cooed over how lucky they were to have one another. As happy as I was for them, I was fucking miserable. Miller and I had been seeing each other exclusively for several months, or so I'd thought. That was what we'd agreed to, and I never questioned him. Then I recalled the lusty way he'd appraised Xavier and had to wonder if I was the only one staying true to our exclusive arrangement. The uncertainty I felt created turbulence I had a hard time handling, so I used those feelings of irritation and projected them toward my distaste for commitment and monogamy. Besides, I wasn't about to be the weak one in this thing I had going on with Miller, so I had to put my two cents in.

"I might puke," I said to Chase and Gray as they smooched and fawned all over each other, only I knew my words were actually addressed to Miller, who still flirted with Xavier every chance he got.

Miller mistook my statement as an agreement with his assessment of committed relationships and held up his fist for a bump. I obliged him rather than leaving him hanging and tried to ignore the zip and zing of electricity that jolted up my arm after I bumped my fist to his. I could tell he felt it too from the widening of his gorgeous blue eyes and the parting of his lips. That was all it took to remind him of all the nights we'd spent pleasuring each other. It should've been enough to ease the irritation I felt, but it didn't.

I spent the rest of the evening ignoring Miller as I tried my best to kick his team's ass. There were many times I caught him staring at me when I turned around after releasing my ball down the lane. Miller had confessed how much he loved my long legs, and I would've gladly wrapped them around him, but I was anything but turned on by his behavior. I had never seen him drunk before, and I had to say, it wasn't appealing in the least.

It looked like Ben was trying to give Miller a run for his money. I wasn't sure how they were still able to bowl so competitively considering the amount of beer they'd consumed, but they didn't seem to be affected. In fact, the more beer they drank, the better they bowled. Under normal circumstances, I would've been impressed, but the anger and jealousy that burned through my blood diminished any positive thoughts I felt toward Miller.

"Come sit by me for a minute, J," Ava called out from where she had been sitting with Xavier's sister, Ellie. "Keep me company for a few minutes, will you? Ellie went home because she wasn't feeling very well, and I'm all alone." I sat down next to Ava as she rubbed her rounded baby bump.

"How are you feeling, sweetheart?" She was beauty personified and good to her core. She would be a wonderful mother to the bundle of baby joy she had on board.

"Pretty good for the most part. I'm in the final stretch now with only a few months left to go. We have the nursery all set up, and that makes me happy." Ava cocked her head to the side and studied me through narrowed eyes. "I didn't invite you to sit down so we could discuss baby stuff, though." She leaned closer and lowered her voice. "How long have you and Miller been sexing each other up?"

"Huh?" My mind began to spin as I thought back to all the times Miller, Ava, and I had been at the same gathering. There had only been a few occasions since Miller and I had started having sex, and I couldn't recall a single incident that could have given us away.

"It's the body language you two have when you're near each other," Ava replied. "There's a spark between you when you look into each other's eyes. I thought maybe it was because of the way Miller was hitting on Xavier, but I realized he's only doing that to hide how he feels about you. I take it you guys don't want Chase or Gray to know?"

"*He* doesn't want them to know. I don't care who knows." I'd confessed a lot to her with just a few words.

"Ah," Ava said, then smiled tenderly at me. "So it's finally happened, then? You've fallen in love." Heat washed over me, and my skin suddenly felt tight. "If it makes you feel any better, I think he feels the same way too. I think he's flirting so hard and drinking so much to fight what he's feeling." I turned and looked at Miller where he stood talking to Gray. As if he felt my eyes on him, he turned and looked at me. I thought I saw desire in his eyes, but it was hard to see beyond the glazed drunkenness.

"I don't think so, Ava." I turned my attention back to her. "It's just sex between us, and I think it's run its course." I took hold of her hand and raised it to my lips for a kiss. "Not everyone finds the perfect person for them like you and Chase did. Some of us aren't meant for that kind of happiness."

"Bullshit," Ava said with a roll of her eyes. "That's just an excuse people use when they're scared. You're going to find your own happiness someday.

If not with Miller, then with someone else. He's going to be a really lucky guy too." I leaned forward and gave her a tender kiss on her forehead. It was nice to know that she was still my champion after all these years.

"You're one of a kind, Ava."

"Right back atcha."

I felt bad leaving her when it was my next turn to bowl. I felt Miller's eyes on me once again when I walked up the steps and got into position. It was my last frame, and I was torn between rolling strikes to help my team win or just throwing it down the lane so I could close the door on the night and go home to my cats and bed. I was starting to sound like the crazy cat gay.

Our team won, much to Chase's delight. Gray had already told Miller he'd drop him off, so I knew he had a ride home. Like a coward, I waited until Miller had gone to the restroom to say my goodbyes and leave. It wasn't like we could've had a conversation anyway with everyone around. It felt wrong to drive away without saying goodbye to him, but I didn't trust myself to keep it together. I was angry and hurt. I could have tried to deny I felt those things, but it would've been pointless.

The night ended completely different than what I had expected. I thought we'd go to the party, then end up at one of our houses for a night of passion. Instead, I climbed into my empty bed and lay awake for a long time pondering the future for Miller and me while Mal and Urs curled into each other and purred as they slept on the pillow next to mine. I was grateful for the comfort my gals gave me, but I would have much preferred for them to be sleeping at my feet so my extra pillow could be taken up by Miller instead.

It was obvious that I was going to get hurt when this thing ended between us, and I wondered if maybe I should terminate it on my terms instead of waiting for him to do it for me. My heart squeezed painfully in my chest just thinking about telling Miller that I wanted to end things. I couldn't imagine the pain if I actually uttered the words out loud to him. Would he care? Would he miss me and my touch? Would Miller remember all the laughs we shared and the memories we made outside the bedroom, or was I just another faceless fuck to him?

I guessed I would find out when things came to a screeching halt, but it wouldn't be because I walked away from him. I wanted to take control of the situation to prevent more heartache, but I wasn't ready to stop making memories with him. I would cling to them once he had moved on and I was alone again. I could take them out and remember a time when I'd felt carefree and unburdened by life. I would remember how the warm sun felt against my skin instead of the constant chill of an overhead cloud. I would reminisce a passion so consuming it made me forget about the tragedies of my past. The memories of us would have to be enough because I knew I wouldn't have Miller for much longer.

CHAPTER
Twelve

Miller

I HAD BOXED MYSELF INTO A CORNER, AND I WASN'T SURE HOW TO fight my way out of it. I had told Jag I didn't want Gray and Chase to know about our arrangement, and because of that, I found myself flirting with Xavier like an idiot right in front of Jag. Tension had radiated off him in waves, and I was worried he misunderstood my flirting as real interest in Xavier. If I hadn't found myself hooked on Jag, I would've been flirting with Xavier for real because the man was stunning.

But Jag had caught me—hook, line, and sinker. I tried to convince myself it was just lust, and it would fade, but I couldn't fool myself. I somehow must have kept my true feelings hidden from Jag, though, because I'd seen the hurt in his eyes the night of the bachelor party.

I resented the ruse I'd insisted on playing in front of our mutual friends and had no one to blame but myself. I hated that I was falling so deeply in love with Jag that I didn't want to spend a night away from him, and he didn't return those feelings. He tried to warn me that prolonged sex would lead to one of us developing feelings for the other, but I didn't listen. I was so arrogant to believe that I would never fall in love with another man and want to commit myself to him. Ha! Of all the men I could fall in love with, it had to be the one who couldn't love me in return.

I chose to drink away my frustrations and misery, but all I'd accomplished was pushing Jag further and further away. I had planned on spending the night at his house after the party, but that was completely out of the question after I got wasted and had to be taken home by Chase and Gray.

Gray lectured me about my behavior like he was my father, not my best friend, while Chase just gave me sympathetic looks. I knew worry was the reason for Gray's gruff demeanor during the ride home. I hadn't gotten drunk since our early college years, and I knew I was going to regret it in the morning.

I drank a ton of water and took some ibuprofen and a long shower once I got home. While I was definitely intoxicated, I wasn't falling-down drunk. I stood beneath the spray and thought about how I wanted to go forward with Jag. If I even still had that chance. Jag was right. It was no one's business what we did together. We were consenting adults, and if we wanted to hook up and have sex, then that was what we would do. We weren't hurting anyone by being together, so why did I want to keep us a secret?

I was afraid. I had insisted on secrecy so no one would know just how badly I was hurt when we were over. I didn't want pitying glances because of my broken heart. I didn't want sympathetic pats on the arm to go with trite advice on how I'd move on in time.

I let the hot water ease the tension in my body as I dropped all my defenses and blinders so I could really evaluate my relationship with Jag. Yes, it had become a relationship, and there was no other way to describe it. I wasn't *falling* in love with him; I was *in* love with him. A goofy smile spread across my face as I let that truth sink in. I was in love for the first time in my life, and I was screwing it up royally. The latter part of my thought caused the smile to slip from my face.

The way I saw it, I had two options. One, I could keep pretending things with Jag were just a sexual arrangement and let the fling run its course, then walk away with a broken heart when it was over. Or two, I could tell Jag just how I felt about him and see what happened. The worst-case scenario would be that he didn't return my feelings, and he would end our relationship. Either way had the potential to lead to heartbreak, unless he returned my feelings, which I wouldn't know unless I talked to him. I knew in my heart his feelings for me went beyond sex, but I wasn't sure how far. I went to bed with a clear plan in mind to call Jag and apologize to him for the way I'd behaved at the party. I wanted to tell him how I really felt about him and promise I was done playing games.

Unfortunately, I woke up with a hangover so bad it hurt just to breathe. There was no way I could give him some great speech about being willing to take a chance on us. Luckily for me, I didn't vomit. I was the world's biggest baby when that happened. I'd suffer anything over vomiting any day of the week.

I gingerly brushed my teeth to avoid gagging and went downstairs to make a cup of strong coffee. I had just entered the kitchen when my doorbell rang. My body knew who was on the other side of the door before I even opened it. My hangover had no impact on my body's ability to crave the man who played it like a finely tuned instrument.

The smile slid off my face when I saw his posture and expression. Even though he held two coffees and a pastry bag from Adam and Steve's Bakery, it looked like he had come over prepared to battle or maybe to say goodbye. My nausea increased tenfold at the thought of us being over. It was so bad I nearly clutched my stomach and moaned out loud. He must have seen how badly I was hurting because the tension in his face softened, and he offered a small smile.

"I thought you could use some strong caffeine and some sugar this morning."

"Or a time machine so I could go back and do last night over." I stepped aside to let him in. Instead of walking by me, he stopped and gave me the gentlest, sweetest kiss I had ever received. "I feel better already," I said honestly, not caring how cheesy I sounded. He wouldn't kiss me like that if he was telling me goodbye. His simple kiss alleviated a large portion of my suffering.

I doctored my coffee with creamer and sugar while Jag placed the assorted donuts and pastries on a plate. I was so grateful for his presence that I decided not to confess my feelings out of fear that he'd leave. I just couldn't deal with that devastation on top of my hangover, so I kept my mouth shut. However, I did owe him an apology for my behavior at the bachelor party.

"Jag, I am sorry for flirting with Xavier so obnoxiously and for getting drunk last night." I turned on the couch to face him because I needed him to see the sincerity in my eyes. Jag looked up from feeding a tiny bite of a strawberry-and-cream-flavored cake donut to Indy. "My behavior was atrocious, and I regret it."

"It's okay." Jag's casual voice didn't match his stiff posture, and I knew he was either trying to avoid a conversation or taking pity on me in my wretched state.

"It's not okay. I need you to know two things, then I'll shut up." Jag nodded for me to continue, but he couldn't hide the skepticism in his eyes. "I flirted with Xavier because it was expected of me. He's a hot, single guy who I would flirt with under normal circumstances. If I didn't, Gray would've pounced, and the whole night would've been him interrogating me about who I was seeing and whether it was serious."

"Okay." The sad resignation I heard in his voice was like a stab to the heart. I had hurt him by insisting we keep our relationship a secret and through my callous behavior the previous night.

"I'm not done yet." I took a deep breath before I continued. "Flirting with Xavier felt wrong to me, Jag, so I tried to bury my discontent in alcohol. I promise it won't happen again."

"Come here," Jag said as he turned and reclined against the arm of the couch. I lay on my side between his legs and rested my head on his chest. He ran his long fingers through my hair and massaged gentle circles into my scalp and temple.

I fell asleep against his strong chest and stayed that way for a few hours. When I woke, my headache was gone, and the guy I had fallen in love with was looking at me with forgiveness in his eyes. I should've told him right then what I was feeling, but I chickened out. *One more day,* I told myself because I was convinced Jag would walk once I told him the truth.

I gave my body and heart to him and hoped he could feel the difference in my touch and the way my lips lingered on his flesh. I made love to Jag instead of fucking him. We had been moving closer and closer to lovemaking every time we were together. My toes curled tightly when he finally slid inside me. The expression in Jag's eyes gave me hope that we could have more, but I still wasn't willing to risk it. Afterward, I returned to my spot against his chest and pushed the world and my worries away so I could bask in him—in us.

It felt like a turning point, and the weeks that led up to Gray and Chase's wedding were wonderful. We spent most of our free time together, and I convinced myself that Jag returned my feelings but was just as nervous as I was when it came to divulging them. I decided I would tell Gray the truth after they returned from their honeymoon. Once I could be honest with my best friend, I would tell Jag I had fallen for him.

The day of the wedding was gorgeous with just the right amount of sunshine and low humidity. I arrived at the church and went in search of Gray so I could have a private word with him before the ceremony.

"Your bow tie is a little crooked," I said as I gave it a slight adjustment. "I might tease you mercilessly, Gray, but I'm so happy for you today." His smile was so radiant it was almost blinding. "Chase is the best thing to ever happen to you, and I am so proud of you for taking the chance and putting your heart out there. The two of you are really inspiring to the rest of us jokers stumbling around through life." I pulled Gray into a tight hug and slapped his back several times. "I love you, Gray."

"I love you too, Miller." Gray returned the backslapping and pulled back to look at me. "I can't wait until you stop running and let some amazing guy catch you." I gave him the half-disgusted, half-skeptical look that he was expecting because it was easier to fall back into my normal routine than to tell him I had already been caught. "Loving someone the way I love Chase makes it all worth it, buddy."

Preston entered the room just then, preventing me from saying anything else. "Gray, Pastor Simms wants the best men to take their places at the altar. I'm going to go get Xavier and get into position." Preston hugged his brother and bumped my fist before he left the room.

Chase and Gray decided to only have their brothers stand up beside them during the ceremony. Gray wanted me with him, but if he included his best friend then Chase would've wanted to include his best friend too. There was no way in hell Gray would allow Jag to be included in the wedding party.

"This is it," I said to Gray. Happy tears welled up in his eyes because the day meant so much to him. It was truly a touching moment I was grateful to witness.

"I'm ready."

One final hug and I left his room to take my seat on the side of the church designated for Gray's friends and family. I tried to stop myself from looking, but I couldn't resist seeking Jag's face in the crowd. He smiled tentatively when our eyes met. I regretted that he hesitated because I knew my stupid rule was the reason. It was something I could easily fix when he came over after the wedding.

The ceremony was beautiful and poignant. I heard so much genuine adoration in their voices and saw such raw emotion on their faces when they exchanged their vows. Tears flowed throughout the church, and I found myself tearing up too. It was hard not to respond in the presence of the genuine love the two men shared.

I stood in line to congratulate the newlyweds and watched as they were hugged by one person after the next. I saw Jag approach the couple and held my breath as he gave Chase a hug and offered his hand to Gray. The air expelled from my lungs in relief when Gray smiled crookedly and shook Jag's hand.

I watched Jag walk away from the church and wished we were riding to the reception together. I also wished we were sitting at the same table and were free to dance together. I had really messed things up, and my only consolation was that there would be other events where we could dance together in the future. *If* we had a future.

Jag was seated on the opposite side of the reception from me, with Ava and her husband, while I shared a table with some of the grooms' work friends, including Ben. I didn't have to worry about it being awkward with him because he couldn't take his eyes off Xavier. Toasts were given, and we all watched while Xavier sang and the newlyweds had their first dance.

I made the mistake of looking over at Jag and wished I hadn't. He watched the couple with an expression that could only be described as longing. The food I had just consumed turned sour in my stomach as I realized Jag hadn't been honest with me. He *was* still in love with Chase and would never return my feelings. As unhappy as I felt, I refused to let it show or give in to the urge to drink away my misery. I wouldn't let him or anyone else see how unhappy I was. Instead, I tried to figure out a way to end things with Jag before I got hurt worse if that was even possible.

I sat alone at my table and watched people celebrate all around me. I thought the only other person not dancing the night away was Jag, but I couldn't bring myself to look at him again. I didn't want to see him pining away for another man. I wanted all his focus and emotion aimed at me and was ill-prepared for anything else.

My skin began to itch with irritation over the situation, so I decided to step away for a breath of fresh air. I hadn't made it very far down the hallway before I heard the echo of shoes on the marble floor, and I knew without turning around that Jag had followed me. A small part of me wanted to speed up and run away from him because I knew I couldn't resist him once his hands were on my body. The part of me that needed his touch stomped out the sane part, though. My need for Jag won the battle, and I slowed down so he could catch me.

Instead of pushing me through the door to go outside, Jag pushed me into some sort of large cleaning closet. "I need you, Bones." My heart pinched painfully because it knew he only wanted a physical release.

"Jag, this isn't the right place. We could get caught." I threw that out as an excuse not to make a complete fool of myself. Would he take my body and make me beg for him while he pretended I was someone else? *Was I truly that desperate to have him at any cost?*

"Bones, I've gone along with your idiotic decision to hide our relationship. We've sat on the sidelines and watched everyone else dance and be happy while we pretended we didn't want to be in each other's arms." Jag walked me backward until I was pushed up against a metal shelving unit that held cleaning supplies.

"That's not how it looked to me and everyone else out there." Jag scowled at me in confusion. My heart lurched painfully in my chest, and it felt like it stopped completely before stuttering to a start again. I knew my next words might be the nail in our coffin, but I couldn't just give in and have sex with him without saying how I felt. "It looked like you couldn't take your eyes off Chase while they danced. You looked at him with so much longing that it..."

"Don't." His reply was practically snarled as he cut me off. "Do not tell me how I feel. I'm so sick and fucking tired of everyone thinking I can't get over Chase. I already told you I'm not in love with him. What more do you want from me?" As mad as he was, he couldn't pry his body away from mine, and I couldn't stop mine from responding to his nearness. "Did you ever think maybe I wished it could be us dancing in front of everyone?"

"No. Why would I think that?" Jag jerked back like I'd hit him, but I refused to back down. "What indication have you given me that you wanted anything more than what we have right now? I thought you were happy with the way things were between us. You don't believe in love, dating, and sappily ever after." I threw his words and beliefs back at him.

"Bones." His voice was pleading, but what did he need me to grasp? "I'm sorry if that's the impression I gave you and everyone else in that room. If you want me to, I'll go in there and take the microphone away from the DJ and announce to everyone that I wasn't pining after Chase but wishing I could dance with you. I don't want to put a stupid label on what we have because I hate them. I think what we have is amazing and I don't want to ruin it. I want you, Bones. Just you. I think about you all the time, and I wish we were together when we're apart. I..."

I didn't let him say another word because what he'd said was enough. We came together, our mouths meeting halfway. My worries and jealousy dissipated beneath the spark of desire that zipped through my body. My fear of getting caught also vanished, and I found myself lowering his zipper and fondling his erection through the cotton fabric of his briefs. No one had ever made me feel so alive, and I clung to the emotion as if my very life depended on it.

I spun us until Jag's back was pressed against the shelving and lowered myself to my knees in front of him. I knew how much he loved getting head, and I loved giving it to him. I kept my eyes locked on his so there could be no doubt who was worshipping Jag's cock with hands, lips, and tongue.

"Bones, I'm not going to last long with you sucking my cock like that...Jesus...so damn good." I felt him shaking as his body primed to unload into my mouth. I reached between his legs and rolled his firm balls in my hand before I tugged them firmly just how he liked. "Miller." My name barely passed through his gritted teeth before he released inside my eager mouth. I cleaned him thoroughly before I tucked his softening cock back inside his underwear and zipped him back up. Jag grabbed me under my armpits and pulled me to my feet. "Your turn," he said before he kissed me.

It didn't take him long to work me into a frenzy with his mouth and hands once he dropped to his knees to return the favor. I looked down into his brown eyes, and the intimacy of the moment combined with the threat of getting caught had me revved up and unloading on his tongue in record time. I would've been embarrassed by how fast I'd come, but the wicked, smug smile on Jag's lips told me how glad he was that I'd lost control for him.

By the time we righted our clothes and hair, the grooms had already left the reception. I was disappointed I didn't get a chance to see them off, but I wasn't sorry for the reason I'd missed them. I said my goodbyes to the others as if I hadn't just been in a closet getting off with Jag and went home to wait for him to show up.

He didn't make me wait long, and the sexy gleam in his eyes promised me he was worth it. Jag poured us a glass of champagne from a bottle he'd pilfered from the reception, and we drank while eating cake he'd also helped himself to. *How long had we been in that closet? We'd missed the cake cutting and the final send-off.*

I hit a button on my remote to start some music, and Frank Sinatra's "Fly Me to the Moon" began to play. I held out my hand to Jag and said, "Dance with me."

It was the first time I'd danced with another man. I hadn't come out to my family until I was in college, so my senior prom date had been a girl who'd also been a very good friend. I never attended any dances in college and hadn't really had an occasion to dance with another man, not that I would have anyway. Dancing was personal and intimate, which were the exact opposite of the types of encounters I'd wanted until I met Jag. It only seemed fitting that my first dance was with the first guy I'd loved.

It was a moment I knew I'd never forget for as long as I lived. It was obvious Jag cared for me on some level and enjoyed what we had built together, but did he love me? There was only one way to find out. I needed to dig up the courage to ask him. I decided not to bring it up that night because I didn't want anything to ruin the most perfect evening I'd ever had. I wanted to wait for the right moment when I wasn't feeling so emotional.

CHAPTER
Thirteen

JJ

I DIDN'T WANT TO GO TO CHASE AND GRAY'S FOURTH OF JULY PARTY. I was tired of pretending Miller wasn't someone very special to me. The disappointed pout I couldn't seem to wipe off my face was going to be mistaken for pining after Chase. Again. The only way people, especially Gray, would get over that notion was for them to realize I had moved on and had feelings for someone else. Chase insisted I come to the party, and everyone knew I was prone to give in to him.

The only things that finally got me motivated to attend was the idea of being around Miller while he wore swim trunks and the possibility of a secret touch or a stolen kiss. The image of our bodies brushing up against each other in the pool sent licks of fire straight to my balls. Hell, we'd had each other in every conceivable way, so I was surprised I was reacting so intensely to the thought of relatively innocent foreplay.

I arrived before most of the guests and greeted the newlyweds affectionately. Gray was still giving me narrow-eyed looks, but we were making progress. It helped that I always brought Oliver a little treat or toy when I showed up. I was turning out to be his favorite uncle.

"How are your kitties doing?" Gray asked to make small talk.

"They've brought a lot of happiness to my life. Their playfulness takes the stress right out of my day." I felt myself turning a little pink over my kitty love confession.

Gray raised both eyebrows in surprise at the same time a smile split his face; the first genuine smile he had ever given me. "Damn, Bruce, you might actually be a nice guy beneath that hard-ass exterior."

I leaned closer because my words were for him only. "Don't go telling people I'm nice, Clark, or I'll bring kryptonite to your next party." Gray laughed at my empty threat and slapped me on the shoulder.

"Are you any good at volleyball? I'm not going to go easy on Chase just because he's my husband now," Gray asked just as quietly. "I'm trying to build a kick-ass team while he's busy playing host."

"I'm almost six and a half feet tall, so I make a good blocker up front." I thought their competitiveness was cute, and I suspected, like everyone else did, that it was a source of foreplay for them. I was torn about wanting to be on Miller's team to sneak in a few touches or playing against him and using the competition as a build-up to fabulous sex.

"I'm putting you on my team," Gray said before he moved on to greet his next guest.

Miller came straight to me when he arrived, shocking the hell out of me. I was lounging in a chaise by the pool, and he stood right beside me. "You look good enough to eat," he said low enough for my ears only. I had already stripped down to just my trunks so I could soak up some sunshine. "Make them go away so I can climb onto your lap and grind against you."

His words heated me in places the sun wasn't reaching, and I found myself responding to his nearness. If he kept it up much longer, I'd need to jump into the pool to cool off and hide my erection. The smug smile he wore told me he knew exactly what he was doing to me and liked every second of it. Yeah, well, two could play that game.

I looked around to make sure no one could overhear my words because there would be no doubt in their mind about the kind of relationship I had with Miller. "Mmmm, I can almost feel your skin all slick with tanning lotion as you slide against me, riding my dick while yours grinds against my stomach and leaves behind a slick trail of its own."

"Jag."

I couldn't see Miller's beautiful blue eyes because they were hidden behind his sunglasses, but I had no doubt his pupils were enlarged with excitement. Gray had his form of foreplay, and I had mine. I let my eyes travel down the length of Miller's body, but his T-shirt came down far enough to hide any physical reaction he might've had to my words. That was when I noticed the dinosaurs on his trunks.

"Bones, I'm digging your shorts." My intended pun earned me a sweet smile, which eased the sexual tension between us. "I can't wait to see them around your ankles later." Miller's mouth opened and closed silently a few times as if he wanted to say something, but his mouth was too dry to speak.

"Hey, you two, we're picking teams," Gray hollered from the other side of the pool. He didn't let on if he suspected something was going on between us.

"Come on, Bones. If we end up on separate teams, the winner gets to top tonight." In all honesty, I loved to bottom for Miller, but it was fun to tease him about who got to top.

"You're on." Miller's face lit up over the challenge I had thrown down.

Miller and I stood together and waited for everyone else to gather around. That was when I noticed Liam, the cute bartender from Bottoms Up, had come to the party too. I recalled the time I tried to pick him up but had been warned off verbally by Chase followed by a death glare from the bar owner, Jack. I had no doubt Jack would rearrange my face if I took one step in Liam's direction.

Liam stood sort of off to the side as if he didn't feel one hundred percent comfortable or welcome, and it was a feeling I understood. There was something else about him that grabbed my attention, but I couldn't place what. It wasn't his looks, although he was a hottie. There was something familiar about him as if I should recognize him from somewhere but didn't.

"Try not to strain yourself, darling," Miller sneered quietly in my ear. He mistook my interest for something other than what it was.

"I don't want him, Bones. There's something familiar about him. I know him from somewhere, and I can't figure it out."

"Mmm hmmm. He was probably a bathroom hookup at the bar." Although I didn't like the implication that I was slutty, I loved the jealous tone of his voice. I could almost imagine him turning green like the Grinch.

"I've never had sex with that guy, and I gave up bathroom hookups years ago. That's just unsanitary and gross." I told him the truth, and that would have to be enough for him. I wasn't going to apologize for my past, and I didn't expect him to either. "I'm telling you. I know him from somewhere, and it's making me nuts."

Ben looked over at us as we studied Liam and gave us a look that would've made Jack very proud. Miller and I both threw our hands up in surrender and turned our focus back to one another before everyone got the wrong idea about our interest in Liam.

"I love your nuts," Miller said, effectively diverting my attention. The guy was cruising for a hard fucking. He gave me a playful wink that let me know driving me insane with lust was part of his strategy to beat me at water volleyball.

Picking teams turned out to be a hilarious battle with both grooms protesting the other's choices, so someone wisely recommended we all draw straws—red straws on one team and blue on the other. Gray and Chase picked first, and we all collectively groaned when Gray chose a red straw and Chase drew a blue straw. I smiled when I chose a blue straw and Miller chose red. I'm sure people thought I was smiling because I was on Chase's team, but that wasn't it at all.

"You two idiots will fall the hardest," Gram said from her lounge chair beneath an oversized rainbow umbrella.

"Every rake has his day," Ava added.

The remarks went on and on and on with Miller and me reacting as expected. I couldn't imagine what they would think if they knew Miller and I had been together for nearly ten months. We had been seeing each other exclusively for six months, but it had been only Miller for me since the first time we had sex more than three months prior to establishing our arrangement. Miller still hadn't told Chase and Gray about us, and I tried not to think about why he hadn't told them as soon as the happy grooms returned from their vacation. The most obvious reason was that Miller didn't feel as strongly about me as I did him. I knew he had genuine affection for me, but was that love?

I shoved those thoughts aside to focus on the volleyball game. Truthfully, that line of questioning led me to feelings of self-doubt and sadness. I had worked too hard to get away from despondency, and I didn't want to go back. What I needed to do was come to terms with the fact that happiness could still exist for me if Miller and I were to end our relationship. I wasn't to that place yet and chose to live in denial for a little while longer, focusing on something positive like kicking some volleyball ass.

Our team won the best of three matches in volleyball but got our asses kicked in water polo. Miller gave me a private look that said my ass was his for the taking. My pucker twitched in excitement, and I wondered how much longer we had to stick around before we could go home and fuck like wild animals. I knew I'd be wearing his teeth marks on my skin for days after he got a hold of me.

The food was almost finished, but I was hungry for something different. I saw Miller pick up his bag so he could change, and a wicked part of me decided I couldn't wait any longer to feel him inside me. The smile he wore when he saw me get up with my bag to follow told me that he felt the same way.

I crowded him into the small half bath on the main floor and closed the door behind us. His mouth was on mine the second he heard the lock engage. Our hands went into immediate action and began stripping our wet shorts off each other.

"Please tell me you have condoms in your bag." I growled the words against his throat as I stroked his hard length. I didn't wait for him to answer before I dropped to my knees and took him into my mouth. Miller made no attempt to hold back the excited noises he made, and I wanted to pull more sounds out of him.

I worked Miller's cock until his legs began to shake and his balls retracted. I released his dick from my mouth and began digging in his bag for supplies. "Side pocket," Miller said breathlessly. I found the supplies and slid the condom down until it was snug around the base of his erection. "It's so much sexier when you do that," Miller said once I rose to my feet with a little bottle of lube in my hand.

I turned around, leaned over, and placed my palms on the vanity so I could present my ass to him. My eyes met Miller's in the mirror and stayed locked on him while he prepared my ass with lubed fingers. It felt so good that I wanted to close my eyes, but I didn't want to miss a second of the way he looked as he took me. My breath whooshed out of me as he pressed inside me with one stroke. The slight burn of his claiming excited me almost as much as the feral look on his face when he bottomed out. He loved the feel of my tight channel around him as he worked himself in and out—slowly at first, then hard and fast once the need to come overtook him.

I had watched Miller take me many times, but there was something different about watching in a mirror. I was attached and engaged with my body, but my brain treated the coupling like it was watching from afar. I could only take my eyes off his face when I wanted to see his hands on my body. I loved the way he gripped my hips while he pulled me back onto him again and again. Miller moved his hands up to my chest so he could pinch and tease my nipples, which tugged some invisible string that must have been connected to my balls.

My senses were threatening to short-circuit my brain, but Bones wasn't done with me yet. He slid his arms beneath my pits and bent his arms so they hooked under and around my shoulders. He placed both of his hands around my neck similar to some wrestling move I saw once on TV. He laid his chest against my back until I was completely surrounded by his heat. His hot breath puffed against the back of my ear as he fucked me with a vigor he hadn't shown me before.

Our eyes met once again in the mirror, and I thought I saw an answer to the question about how he felt about me. Yes, there was raw lust and an animalistic drive to come, but there was more. There was a depth of feeling he hadn't shown me until then, and I had hope he might love me too. Miller stood on his tiptoes and changed the angle of his penetration so he pegged my prostate in just the way I needed to explode all over the vanity after a few more strokes. My forceful orgasm caused my ass to squeeze his dick hard enough to tip him over the edge right after me.

Miller rested his forehead between my shoulder blades as our hard breathing echoed around the small space. He dropped a kiss on my shoulder before he eased his softening cock from my body. I slowly stood up and turned to face him. I expected him to remove the condom and begin to clean up, but instead, he pulled me to him for a kiss. He seemed completely unconcerned that quite a few people could be making their way into the house in search of a bathroom to change in. The hope I had soared to levels I hadn't experienced in years, making it hard for me to breathe.

I knew in that moment that things would work out for us. The touching and kissing continued while I cleaned up my spunk and he disposed of the condom before we got dressed. I opened the door and was about to suggest we blow off the party and start one of our own as I walked out, but I saw Ben and Xavier turn into the hallway leading to the bathroom. There was no mistaking what Miller and I had just done because we were still sorting out our hair and straightening our clothes when we stepped into the hallway.

"I'll be damned," Ben said with a smirk on his face.

I felt Miller tense beside me, and the happiness and hope I'd experienced a few minutes before faded away. "Shut up." I aimed my frustration at Ben rather than Miller because I wasn't sure what else to do. I watched with regret as Miller walked away without a backward glance. Ben looked at me with sympathy in his eyes, letting me know he was onto the way I felt about Miller. I wasn't prepared to discuss it with anyone, so I followed after Miller without another word.

I found him sitting beneath an umbrella drinking a bottle of water. I figured he could use something stronger, so I snatched two beers out of the cooler and sat down beside him. His eyes met mine briefly when I slid the bottle to him. I longed to kiss away the worry that was evident in his creased brow and the frown of his firm lips. I started to worry it might be the end of us. I opened my mouth to speak, but Gram stood up and announced she was getting married. Her statement was followed by a lot of cheering and chatting, and I used the distraction to turn Miller's attention back on me.

I found I was unwilling to walk this tightrope with him anymore. I wanted to be with him, and I was tired of hiding it. It made me feel like Gray's feelings were more important than mine or that he was ashamed of being with me. Either one made me feel irrelevant when I'd finally believed I deserved more, and I was no longer willing to play his games.

"You did know getting caught was a risk we faced when we decided to fuck in our friends' bathroom, right?" Miller nodded slightly but avoided looking into my eyes. "Was that a deal breaker for you, Miller? Are we over?" I was direct and to the point, placing the ball solidly in his court. He was the one with all the rules from the very beginning, so I was letting him decide our fate. He jerked his head up as if I had shocked him. If anything, his worried expression intensified at my questions.

"Is that"—his voice cracked, and he cleared his throat—"what you want, Jag?"

"No, but you're deflecting by answering my question with a question." I looked him square in the eyes and didn't so much as blink. "Is the possibility of Ben or Xavier telling Chase or Gray about us a deal breaker? Is your friendship with Gray more important than what we've built together?" I wanted to take back the words as soon as they left my mouth. I found myself holding my breath as I waited for a response.

"Are you asking me to choose?"

"That isn't what I asked you. Again, you're deflecting." There was no disguising my irritation. I figured his unwillingness to answer *was* his answer. "Look, why don't I just make this really easy for you, Bones." I started to stand up, but his hand on my leg stopped me.

"Don't go." The plea I heard in his voice stopped me. "I just didn't want him to find out this way." I eased back down into my chair and covered his hand where it remained on my leg. "I l-l-like what we have together, and Gray finding out isn't a deal breaker for me. Just let me tell him in my own way, okay?" My heart stuttered in my chest when I thought Miller was going to use a different L-word instead of *like*. Miller *liked* what we had while I was in *love* with him. There was a world of difference between the two.

I nodded and looked over to where Ben and Xavier were snuggling on a chaise together as the sky darkened. I wanted to be able to hold Miller that way but settled for linking my fingers through his beneath the table. It was a tiny step in the right direction for us. I found myself staring at his lips and wishing I could kiss him under the stars.

The first explosion of fireworks lit up the sky, and everyone turned to look upward. I chose to watch their reflection in Miller's brilliant eyes instead. It was on the tip of my tongue to tell him just how much he meant to me, but I wouldn't risk pushing him any further than I already had that night. Miller felt my attention on him and looked away from the fireworks display to meet my eyes. I knew he could feel and see my intensity. A beautiful smile lit up his face, brighter than any pyrotechnic explosion in the sky. The hope I had felt earlier returned and intensified. I needed to be alone with him, to wrap myself around him so tightly that just maybe I could hold on to him with more than just my body. I wanted to wrap myself around his heart until his every heartbeat became mine. The level of sappiness I felt was making me feel a little nauseous, but I pushed on.

"Come home with me, Bones," I said, leaning into him.

"As if there was ever a doubt, Jag."

CHAPTER
Fourteen

Miller

I LOVED THE MONTH OF JULY. IT WAS THE ONLY TIME I TOOK OFF FROM the university, and it was normally spent on a beach chasing sexy, tight, and scantily clad asses. Once I met Jag, I still noticed the other guys on the beach, but he was the only sexy, tight, and scantily clad ass I wanted.

I had talked him into taking off a week and going on vacation with me. It was seven days filled with sun, sand, and sex that was hot enough to singe the hair on my arms and legs. We kept our phones turned off and focused solely on one another, and dear God in heaven, I loved being his sole focus. I was going to turn into a sappy, lovesick fool if I wasn't careful, and that would surely push him away from me. We had a beautiful thing going, and I didn't want anything to ruin it.

My promise to tell Gray about us lingered in the back of my mind and was the only dark spot in an otherwise perfect vacation. I wasn't stupid enough to think that Jag and I were still engaging in a casual hookup, but I wasn't brave enough to discuss it with him. It seemed we were both completely happy with how things were going, and there was no need to hash out feelings and slap a label on it. It wasn't the way we operated.

I was undeniably in love with him, and I was pretty sure he felt the same way about me. It could've been wishful thinking on my part, but the look in his eyes when he held me or the way he reached for my hand as we strolled down the beach told me I was right. I convinced myself Jag knew how I felt about him too and that we didn't need to say the words. Things would change once those words were spoken, and I didn't want or need anything to change. I had Jag, and that was all I wanted—or so I thought.

Our vacation went by too quickly, and we were forced to return to real life. Jag spent long hours catching up on his cases in the weeks that followed, and the next thing I knew, it was mid-August. He had made as much time for us as he could, and I did my best to properly express my appreciation to him. But it was time for me to get serious about the new school year with the fall semester closing in, so I started spending longer days in my office with Gavin.

Jag didn't care for all the time I spent with my TA, and I tried to hide how much I adored his jealousy and possessiveness, but he made it so hard when I loved to be reminded who owned my ass. Jag's possessive feelings didn't make me feel like my life was in danger, but I couldn't say the same about my heart. I had arrived at the point where I wanted the words. I needed to know if Jag saw a future with me. I also knew in my heart that I was the person holding us back because I still hadn't told Gray about us.

If I wanted Jag to see a future with me, I needed to give him something to believe in. I wasn't foolish enough to believe he suddenly understood he was worthy of a life of love. Almost a year had passed since we'd had sex for the first time. This was the longest I'd been exclusive with anyone and Jag had confessed the same to me while we soaked in the bathtub one evening.

"You ruined me for all other men," I told Jag as I lounged against him. "I guess you're stuck with me now."

"I'll gladly serve my penance, Bones." Jag kissed my temple sweetly and ran his hands up and down my chest. "You've been the best thing to ever happen to me." It was the closest to a confession of love I'd gotten from him, and I gladly took it. He slid his hands between my spread thighs and cupped my balls firmly in his hands. "But if you ever refer to me as your bae, I will twist these clean off." Jag squeezed my sac a little harder to emphasize his threat.

I burst into laughter over the thought. I promised I'd never say such a thing, then I turned my attention to the endearing comment he'd made prior to his threat. I was so overwhelmed by the emotions his words stirred inside me that I said the first thing that came to my mind. Unfortunately, it was a famous line from the movie *Jerry Maguire*. "You complete me." I wanted to take the words back and say something sincere from my heart, but his arms wrapped around me, holding me tight, and laughter rumbled in his chest before it spilled out. I had never heard him laugh so hard, and I would've been offended, but his next words assured me he wasn't laughing at me—just near me.

"You had me at hello, Bones."

From that moment on, we frequently used movie lines to communicate. My favorite was when he left my house one morning to go to work and said, "Bye, Felicia." That line from the movie *Friday* had become part of pop culture and was hard to follow up, but I did my best.

"It's Britney, bitch." Okay, so I'd quoted Britney Spears's music and not a movie, but Jag's laughter and his smiling kiss afterward told me it was still hilarious.

"You got me this time, Bones." Jag's lips lingered on mine, and I began to wonder if he would end up late for work again.

I was happy, ridiculously so, and it came as no surprise that Gray noticed the smile I couldn't wipe off my face when we met for lunch in early September. "The unthinkable has happened," he said smugly. "Miller Brexler has fallen in love."

"You're an idiot."

Gray threw up his hands and shook his head while wearing a smug grin. I loved the guy as much as I loved my brother, but I was ready to punch him in the mouth. "I know you usually go to the cabin with your family for Labor Day weekend, but I still wanted to invite you to our party." I was grateful for the change of subject, but once again I was angry at myself for not telling him the whole truth.

"I am going to the cabin with the fam, but I appreciate the invite." I conveniently left out the part where I was taking Jag with me or that I had already introduced him to my family.

They were instantly smitten with Jag once they saw how much Luke and Lily, who had hung out with us on several occasions, loved him. My mom greatly admired his pursuits for equal rights, and my dad liked the way he made me smile and laugh. My mom even cut out an article that had been written about him and framed it for Jag to hang in his office.

Labor Day weekend with Jag and my family was absolutely perfect. He was comfortable around them and unafraid to show me affection. Sure, we couldn't go at each other as hard as we wanted to at night with a cabin full of people, but that was okay because the tender way he took me was even better. I missed being able to shout out his name when he made me come, but he made it worth it when he captured my sounds with his mouth.

The following weekend was the final barbecue of the year at the Wrights'. In fact, it was the last barbecue they'd be having at that house period. They were in the process of buying a new home together that they wanted to one day fill with kids. I hoped every one of their dreams came true because they deserved it.

I woke up the morning of the party and decided there would be no more hiding and no more games. I would've told Jag my thoughts right away, but it was hard to think coherently with my morning wood in his mouth nor could I properly verbalize my intentions when I had a mouthful of his cock when I returned the favor. It was my favorite way to start the day, so I waited until we were in the shower before I brought up the party.

"Let's ride together." Jag had been rinsing the shampoo out of his hair while I swirled my finger through the suds that were sliding down his body. I looked up and found he had stopped midmotion with his hands still in his hair. "No more hiding, okay? I promised you months ago that I would tell Gray about us, and today is the day." My voice sounded firm and confident, and after a few minutes of self-evaluation, I realized I truly meant what I'd said.

"Bones, I know it's an awkward position to be in, but I think you'll find Gray is okay with us. He and I have formed a truce since the wedding, and it's going to be okay."

"I don't think it's so much Gray knowing that gives me pause. I introduced you to my family, and believe it or not, their opinions count more than Gray's." I took a deep breath while I searched for the right words to say to him. "My problem is that I don't want outside influences putting pressure on what we have, Jag."

"What do you mean putting pressure on us?" he asked after he finished rinsing his hair. "Like for a commitment or something?" He didn't look or sound squirrelly over the C-word, but he was good at hiding his feelings.

"Jag, we've been committed to each other for a long time." He nodded in agreement but waited for me to say more. "I really love what we share. We understand one another. I can't help but feel that we'll start acting differently once everyone knows about us and starts expecting certain things from us."

"It's that phobia of slapping a label on us and watching it crumble. I understand how you feel, but aren't you and I in charge of us? If someone asks when you're going to make an honest man out of me, you can simply tell them to mind their own business or tell them I'm already an honest man. Right?"

"True," I replied, but I suspected it wouldn't be that simple.

"We can tell Chase and Gray together if you want. Chase is going to be pretty upset that I didn't trust him enough to share this part of my life with him. Gray won't be the only one who hesitates or has hurt feelings."

He had a valid point, and it was one I hadn't stopped to think about while I worried about covering my own ass.

"Let's do it after the party. We'll tell them once everyone else has gone home. It's obvious Ben and Xavier didn't say anything to them, or we would've known by now. Why do you think they kept it quiet?"

"They probably figured it wasn't their story to tell." Jag shrugged, then added, "Or they didn't want everyone to know they were heading to the bathroom for the exact same reason."

We arrived at the party together, but it didn't seem like anyone noticed or cared. The weather was gorgeous, so most of us stayed outside and socialized. I went inside to use the bathroom, and Jag followed me to grab some more lemonade. We found Xavier and Chase standing together and gossiping while they prepared some food. It was obvious they hadn't heard us come through the back door.

"I'm serious. There was no mistaking what JJ and Miller had just done in your bathroom." Jag and I froze in place, hearing Xavier drop the bomb on Chase. Jag recovered first and pointed to the hallway, where we could listen without being seen. "Ben and I got the impression it wasn't the first time either. JJ made a comment to Ben at the charity event about Miller wanting me and always getting everything he wanted. It was said as though JJ had personal knowledge of just how convincing Miller could be."

"Ben ought to know," Chase said snarkily, then gasped at what he'd just told Xavier. I listened as Xavier explained that he had known about Ben and me, and it didn't bother him. I had never told Jag about the one night I'd shared with Ben, and fear of his reaction twisted my guts. I missed the rest of what they said because Jag whipped me around and silently pushed me up against the wall.

"It doesn't matter," he whispered as if he could read my mind. "Our pasts are just that—the past." He lowered his lips and kissed me softly until all my tension melted.

"Miller and JJ, huh?" Chase asked, pulling our attention back to the other men. "Well, they have gotten closer since Gray and I met. They're kind of thrown together at these things since they're the only two swinging dicks left. Do you get the impression they've been screwing each other for a long time?" It bothered me to hear our relationship described in that way because it had grown into so much more.

"Where'd they go?" Xavier asked, and we realized they had looked outside and noticed we were missing. "Oh man. I bet they're in here screwing."

"Let's have some fun," Jag whispered in my ear. He tugged me behind him until we had closed ourselves in the bathroom. Jag pushed me against the vanity, and I slammed my hands on the counter to make a thumping noise.

"Ohhh. God that feels so good," I moaned and groaned like he was really putting it to me. I looked at his reflection in the mirror and saw the wicked gleam in his eyes. He started banging his body against mine for effect.

"You like that? Right there?"

"Fuck yes," I cried, doing my best porn voice, "but harder, J. I need it harder." Jag continued to pound away. I tried so hard to remind my body we were only playing around, but my dick started to swell anyway. "J. Oh, fuck! More, baby."

Jag let out a long groan as if he was coming hard and filling me. Then he put his finger to his lips as he stealthily reached for the door. He turned the knob suddenly and jerked the door open so fast it was amazing Chase and Xavier didn't fall into the bathroom with us.

"Caught you didn't we, you little assholes," I said playfully as I jabbed at Chase's stomach with my fists.

"You little gossip gays were so busy yapping you didn't hear us walk in. We stood there listening to you talking about us having sex." Jag looked at me, then back to the guilty-looking busybodies. "What we are or aren't doing is our business."

Jag hooked his arm around Xavier's neck and pulled him into a headlock then began to give him noogies. Xavier struggled against Jag, and it didn't dawn on me that he was in distress until he started making panicked noises in the back of his throat.

"What's going on in here?" Gray said, appearing in the hallway. His voice was full of mischief rather than suspicion, which was a good sign.

"JJ and Miller are trying to talk us into a foursome," Chase joked. "See? J is trying to pull X into the bathroom."

"Let go of him, JJ." Ben had entered the hallway and didn't like what he saw. Jag immediately let go of Xavier, and I was shocked to see Xavier struggling to pull air into his lungs because Jag hadn't been holding him that tightly. Ben took Xavier into a loving embrace and asked, "Can we have a private moment please?" He didn't wait for an answer before he shut the door.

We all stood staring at each other wondering what had just happened. Jag looked mortified that he'd upset Xavier so badly. Xavier's reaction wasn't typical, and I could tell by the look in Jag's eyes he was sympathizing with whatever X was going through. I reached out for his hand and leaned into him for a kiss.

"He'll be okay. Ben will calm him down, then you can talk to him." Jag was too upset to reply, but he nodded in acknowledgment. It was then I felt Chase's and Gray's eyes on us. Gray looked shocked while Chase stood there smiling at me. "Gray, can we go somewhere and talk privately?"

"Yeah, I think that's a good idea." He turned on his heel and left me standing there with Chase and Jag. I kissed Jag once more and patted Chase on the shoulder as I followed my best friend upstairs to their guest bedroom. "How long has this been going on?" he asked as soon as I walked into the room.

"A year." I factored in the time we'd been having sex before our agreement. I'd been his from the word go.

"*A year?*" He ran his hands through his hair and looked at me with accusing eyes, but what was he accusing me of exactly? "You've been dating for a year, and you didn't tell me? Why would you keep something like that from me?"

"We're not *dating*," I said, correcting him.

"Fucking then," Gray countered with a sneer.

"Stop!" I didn't like Gray's tone. I took a deep breath to keep my composure. "Jag and I don't want to label what we have, and we really don't feel like we owe anyone an explanation. We're both consenting adults, Gray."

"*Jag*?" Gray asked. I gave him a look that let him know I wasn't going to take any crap from him. "Why the secrecy if neither of you care what others think?"

"I didn't think you could handle it." He looked taken aback by my honest answer. "You were convinced Jag was a horrible person who was trying to steal Chase away from you. I didn't know how long Jag and I would last, and I didn't think it was worth upsetting you if it turned out to be a brief fling."

"And now?" Gray had lost his skeptical, judgmental look and tone.

"I care very deeply about him." I swallowed hard to dislodge the emotional lump that was stuck in my throat. "He's very important to me and I would appreciate it if you could just accept that I'm happy with the way things are with Jag and support me."

Gray studied me for a very long time, which had me squirming. I loved Gray with all my heart, but it was nothing close to what I felt for Jag. "I knew you'd fallen in love," was his response.

"Gray, I…"

"I know love when I see it, Miller. You can run and hide from it, but sooner or later you'll have to acknowledge it or risk losing it. Say what you will about your no-labels lifestyle, but eventually one or both of you will want some sort of definition on how you feel about one another. You know what?" Gray asked as he hooked his arm around my neck. "It's all worth it."

"I refuse to turn into a lovesick sap." My protest sounded weak even to my own ears, and Gray's laughter confirmed he wasn't buying it either.

Gray's expression sobered, and I knew I wasn't going to like what he said next. "I just don't want to see you get hurt. I'm not sure he's capable of a healthy relationship, and I want better for you."

"I'm a big boy, Gray. I know what I'm doing." The look I gave him let him know my relationship with Jag wasn't up for debate. There was nothing Gray could say to dissuade me from seeing him.

"Point taken. Let's get downstairs so we can rescue our food from Preston. I had to put him in charge of the grill, and we'll be lucky if anything is edible."

"We can always order pizza," I offered as I followed my best friend down the stairs.

"Always thinking, Doc. I love that about you." Jag was waiting for me at the bottom of the steps, and he looked hesitantly between me and Gray. "He's all yours, buddy," Gray said to Jag, punching him playfully in the shoulder. Jag and I both breathed a sigh of relief that Gray wasn't making this hard on either one of us.

"Bones, if it's okay with you, I'd still like to stay late so I can talk to Chase. I think you were right about me needing to be completely honest so I can really move forward with my life."

"Of course," I replied. "I'm proud of you, Jag. I'll be wherever you need me to be and do whatever I can to help you through it."

Jag pulled me into his arms and held me tight as if he didn't want to let go. "I know I can always count on you, Bones." His faith in me never failed to make me smile.

CHAPTER
Fifteen

JJ

CHASE WAS SILENT FOR SEVERAL LONG MOMENTS AFTER I TOLD HIM the truth about why I had abruptly ended our relationship. He just sat there with his eyes closed as if he was trying to absorb and process the horrific story. I somehow kept my shit together a lot better than when I'd told Miller, but then again, my confession to Miller had been the first time I had ever spoken about what happened.

I just stared at the way the pool lights threw reflections all around and allowed him the time he needed. I had lived with the truth for more than nine years while he had known for closer to nine minutes. I looked into the house, and my eyes connected with Miller's. The affection in his steady gaze calmed me like nothing else could. Miller's patient and complete affection healed a broken part of me I never thought could be mended. I felt like telling Chase the unvarnished truth was the final step to becoming the man I always wanted to be. I kept my eyes locked on Miller's and looked forward to when I could be alone with him, and our menagerie of pets, again.

"Did you—do you—blame me because I asked you to stay?" Chase's broken voice pulled my attention from Miller and had me focusing on him. Chase was chewing his bottom lip as he waited for me to answer. I saw the hurt I had always wanted to avoid in his soulful eyes. I knew he'd blame himself, and I couldn't leave his house until I made him believe I had never blamed him.

I reached across the distance between our loungers and took both his hands in mine. It was a risky move that could ruin the burgeoning trust I had been building with Gray, but I needed the connection. I just had to trust that Miller could reason with Gray and prevent him from coming outside.

"I never blamed you for one second, Chase. Not one. If you believe nothing else that ever comes from my lips again, I need you to hear me and believe me right now." I paused to rein in my emotions. "I wanted to stay with you and celebrate the holiday, and you asking me to stay a few extra days was the best present you could've given me that year." I squeezed his hands and offered him a smile I hoped was convincing. His brow was still deeply creased, and I knew I needed to explain more.

"I blamed myself because I dared to dream of a better life than I thought I deserved." I told him about my mom's addictions to alcohol and abusive men followed by her attempt at a better life once she found out she was pregnant with Will. I explained that I had started to believe, for once in my life, that I wasn't the white trash people claimed. "I thought it was fate's way of reminding me who I was and where I came from and that I wasn't good enough to clean your shoes, let alone deserve your love. I might've been able to save them both had I been there."

"Or you could've died, J. I'm so very sorry about what happened to Will and your mom, but I can't be sorry that you didn't die too." His voice broke, and I could tell tears threatened.

"That's what Miller said too."

"We'll get to you and Miller in a bit," he said wryly. "We've been through a lot together, and yes, you broke my heart when I was eighteen." His words caused me to tense, which he must have felt because he gave my hands another reassuring squeeze. "You've also been the best friend a guy could ever ask for, J. It might have taken us a while to get over our broken romance, but what came out of it was a friendship I'll cherish for the rest of my life. It's one I fought my husband to keep, and I'll keep fighting him if that's what it takes. I wish you had trusted me enough all those years ago so I could've helped you through it."

"You would've blamed yourself, and I couldn't stand the thought of you being guilt-ridden over something I felt was my responsibility. I handled it the best way I knew how at the time. Looking back at the incident through adult eyes I see how wrong I was for not telling you. Thank you, Chase, for being my friend, even when I didn't deserve it." I cleared my throat to buy myself time so I could choose the right words. "You've grown a lot since you've met Gray. You're much more confident and assertive than you used to be. You're an example of what being in love with the right person does. It makes us grow and become the best versions of ourselves. I'm truly glad you found that with Gray."

"You've found that with Miller." It was a statement, not a question. Chase cocked his head to the side and studied my face while he waited for my response. If I even tried to lie to him, he'd know. I confided in Miller about something huge, which told Chase that my relationship with him went way beyond physical.

"I have." It was true. Miller made me a better man. I could've said more, but it wasn't right for me to tell Chase how I felt about Miller before I told the man himself. I was on the receiving end of one of Chase Wright's radiant smiles because I had reached a pinnacle he feared I'd never reach. It wasn't from lack of trying on his part, though. "We better get back in there because I'm not sure how much longer Miller can hold your husband back. I mean, we've been out here holding hands for quite some time."

Chase dropped my hands and looked through the patio door where his husband stood beside Miller. I felt the heat of Gray's glare from across the pool and could only hope he'd calm down once he had a chance to talk to Chase.

"It's okay for you to tell Gray what we discussed. I don't want you to feel like you need to keep this a secret from your husband. I'd explain it myself, but I'm suddenly tired of talking." I needed Miller's quiet comfort.

"Ready?" Miller asked me once I walked inside the house, and I answered him with a kiss.

Miller said goodbye for both of us then steered me toward the door. I was too wiped out to drive, so I decided to ride shotgun. I leaned my head back against the headrest and closed my eyes. I only had to wait a minute before Miller climbed behind the steering wheel and adjusted the seat.

"A couple of inches makes a difference in some instances," he teased. I opened my eyes and turned to look at him. Miller's voice was playful and light but his baby blues were heavy with worry.

"Take me home, Bones, and make me forget."

We stopped to pick up Indy on the way to my house. Miller getting his ass chewed by his dog for being gone so long brought a smile to my face. "I tried to get him to come home hours ago, little buddy," I said. The dog cocked his head to the side as he often did. It was as if he understood exactly what I said because the look he gave Miller afterward was priceless.

"He lies, Indy!" Miller slugged me painfully in the arm. There we were, two grown-ass men, standing in Miller's living room talking to a dog like he was a human and understood us. I wouldn't have had it any other way.

Maleficent and Ursula puffed up like attack cats the minute I set Indy down on the foyer floor. They stared each other down for half a minute before the cats scrambled, knowing full well that Indy would pursue them. It was the game they played every time they were together. I never took the cats to Miller's house on the nights I stayed over. Miller offered to put litter boxes in the utility room for them, but I explained that the cats didn't like to travel. I'd learned that the hard way when I took them to the vet for their shots. I laughed at Indy's playful bark as he chased Mal and Urs through every room in the house.

"Do you want to talk about it?" I knew he was referring to my conversation with Chase. I would gladly tell him every detail but not right then.

"Can we talk tomorrow? Right now, I just want to curl up on the couch and watch a movie or something."

Miller smiled with understanding and reached for my hand, tugging on it so I'd follow. I expected him to head into the living room, but instead, he headed toward the stairs. "Let's take a long, hot soak in your tub, then we'll climb into bed and watch a movie."

"Mmmm. That sounds perfect, Bones." Hot water and a naked Miller in my arms was just what I needed.

"The doctor knows best," Miller said playfully.

"I thought you weren't that kind of doctor." I used his own words against him.

Miller whipped around on the step and cupped my dick through my pants again. "I specialize in bones and boners, but they don't give doctorates for the latter."

My cock was already at half-mast, and he had barely begun to touch me. It was on the tip of my tongue to tell him I was in love with him. He had brought so much light and happiness to my life, and I wanted him to know how much he meant to me. I opened my mouth to speak the words, but they were cut off by a passionate kiss.

It was how we communicated. Some couples, like the Wrights, spoke freely and openly about their feelings. That worked really well for Gray and Chase, but Miller and I weren't like that. We used our mouths in a completely different way to express our feelings for one another, yet it was just as poignant. I didn't need Miller to yell out how much he loved me because I felt it in his touch, saw it in his eyes, and tasted it in his kisses. It might not work for some, but it worked for us.

That night, I showed Miller how he made me feel. I lovingly touched every wet, slick part of his body while he straddled my hips in the generous tub. I pressed worshipful kisses to his naked chest as he raised and lowered himself on my dick. Miller tangled his fingers in my hair and tilted my head back so he could ravish my mouth as he rode me. His kiss told me so much more than simple words ever could, and if given the choice, I'd choose his physical demonstrations over verbal ones every time.

Miller was so sexy when he came undone in the circle of my arms with his head thrown back and incoherent words tumbling from his lips. His orgasm triggered mine, and I refused to close my eyes so he could see how he made me feel. No words were needed.

I stayed awake for quite some time after Miller fell asleep. I held him in my arms and let the comfort he gave me be the catalyst I needed to forgive and heal. I forgave my mother for her weaknesses and remembered the good times I'd shared with her. I let myself remember Will and the joy he brought into my life. I hoped I was a man he could be proud of. I finally forgave myself for wanting to be loved, and I accepted that the circumstances I was born into didn't have to dictate the rest of my life.

I was free from burden and guilt, and I owed it all to the beautiful man who lay beside me. The man who had accepted my flaws and loved me anyway. I placed a kiss on the back of his neck and snuggled tighter against him. I fought off sleep so I could enjoy my newfound feelings for just a little longer.

"Go to sleep, already," Miller muttered. "Indy can't sleep with you thinking so loudly." The pug let out a loud snore at the foot of the bed. "He's just faking so you won't feel bad."

"Well, he does need his rest so he can chase his mortal enemies tomorrow." I glanced down at the foot of the bed and could just make out the silhouettes of my cats where they curled together beside Indy.

"You need your sleep so you can put up with my family at brunch."

I groaned like I was miserable, but in reality, I loved being included in the Brexlers' brunches and outings. "Yes, dear." They were the last words I spoke before I gave in to my exhaustion.

CHAPTER
Sixteen

Miller

HALLOWEEN ROLLED AROUND, AND INSTEAD OF JAG BEING WITH
me at Bottoms Up to watch our friends perform in the costume karaoke competition, he was at a business dinner with Senator Baxter
Thompson. Our various individual professional projects had kept us apart
the past few weeks and it was wearing me down. Jag was working with
Baxter on a national workplace equality campaign, and I was heading up
another joint project with the Smithsonian. Jag was every bit as jealous
of the time I spent closed up with Gavin in my office as I was over the
time he was spending with the senator, and I took his chest thumping as
a good sign he still cared. It was hard to know how he felt because neither
one of us talked about feelings and emotions. We just took it one day at

a time and got together whenever we could, which lately had been only a few times a week. God, I missed him.

"Where's your boyfriend again?" Gray asked me, already knowing the answer to his question.

"For the hundredth time, we're not dating. He's not my boyfriend. We don't do labels, Gray. I wish you could respect how I feel and let things go." My outburst earned me a smug smile from my asshole of a best friend. Going to the Halloween party was probably a mistake, but I was already there, and I planned to make the best of it. Gray threw up his hands in surrender about the same time the bar owner, Jack, stopped by our table for a brief visit.

"I'm sorry, Miller," Gray said once Jack moved on. I looked at my friend and saw the sincerity in his expression. "I don't understand what you two have going on, but then again, it's not my life. You've been so happy lately, but tonight you look miserable. If he's hurt you…"

"He hasn't," I said, not allowing Gray to finish. "Look, Gray, I appreciate your concern. I really do. Let's just keep in mind that you didn't listen to a word I said during the disastrous relationship you had with Devon. Jag and I are still figuring this relationship stuff out as we go, and what we really need is support from our friends."

"Ha! You just admitted you're in a relationship. I'll take that as a step in the right direction." Gray's smile was the goofiest damn thing I had ever seen, and I couldn't help but respond in kind. "It's only a matter of time before you're swapping keys to each other's houses and planning weekend getaways." The grin on my face stretched until it was nearly painful. "You've already done those things, haven't you?"

"You're a few months behind, buddy."

"Fine then," Gray said in an exaggerated huff, which earned him another smile. "Soon you'll be picking out rings and china patterns." I wasn't sure those things would ever happen with Jag, but it was fun to mislead Gray with another goofy grin. "Now I know you're playing with me." Gray narrowed his eyes and pointed his finger at me. "I can't wait for my 'I told you so' moment."

The karaoke competition started, and we watched the performers take turns on the stage. I found myself enjoying the show so much I forgot about my jealousy and insecurity over the time Jag had been spending with Bax. Gray cheered loudly when his husband and brother-in-law, Liam, took the stage. It was no wonder Jag had thought Liam was familiar. Chase had only just learned the truth of why Liam had moved to town a year and a half ago. Gray told me Chase had been shocked and hurt that Liam hadn't told him sooner, but it didn't take him long to forgive Liam and work on building a relationship together.

They performed Katy Perry's "Dark Horse" with Liam dressed as Katy and Chase dressed as the rapper Juicy J. They did a great job and were the frontrunners to win until Xavier and Ben took the stage. They performed "You're the One That I Want" from *Grease* with Ben dressed up like Sandy and Xavier as Danny.

"I didn't know your husband had those kinds of moves," I said to Gray, referring to Chase's dirty dancing.

"I did." Gray leered in his husband's direction.

Xavier and Ben were called to the stage to accept their trophy, then Xavier did something that surprised everyone. He dropped to one knee and asked Ben to marry him. We collectively held our breaths, but Ben didn't make us wait long before he accepted. I clapped and cheered with everyone else, but a part of me was the tiniest bit envious.

I congratulated the newly engaged couple then waited for Gray to search out his husband in the crowd before I snuck away. I checked my phone on my way to my car and saw that I had missed a few texts from Jag while I was in the bar.

Home from dinner.

I really want to see you tonight. Do you want me to come to the party?

An hour had passed between his two texts, and I felt terrible that I missed them. I sent Jag a quick reply that I was leaving, grabbing Indy, and heading over. I had a little surprise planned for Jag, but the closer I got to my house the more I doubted myself. In the end, I went through with the plan and put on my Halloween costume. Indy gave me a disbelieving look when he saw what I was wearing. The noise he made almost sounded like an indignant snort.

"You coming or not?" Indy gave a short bark and headed to the front door. I buckled him into his doggy car seat and headed over to Jag's.

"Hi, Dr. Brexler," the gate attendant said to me. She took in my costume and couldn't keep the smile off her face. Indy barked from the back seat as if in complete agreement with her assessment. The smile broke into full-out laughter as she handed me a dog biscuit for my back-stabbing dog.

"Hello, Molly." I was on a first-name basis with all the gate attendants.

"Enjoy your night," she replied once she stopped laughing.

I almost turned my car around and went home, but the need to see Jag won out over my self-doubt. Indy led the way to the house like he always did, but instead of unlocking the door like usual, I rang the doorbell and waited.

"Trick or…" The words died on my tongue as I feasted my eyes on Jag.

"Treat," Jag finished for me. He grabbed me by my billowy, black pirate shirt and pulled me into his home. His eyes raked over the leather boots and pants I wore and worked their way up my body until they looked into my eyes. "Oh, my dear Captain Hook, I have waited so long for you to plunder my depths." He smiled broadly and gave me another once-over. "Nice guyliner."

"Thanks." Jag stood in his foyer looking better than any fantasy or wet dream I'd ever had as a teenager. He wore the Indiana Jones look better than anyone I knew. He'd completed his look with a fake whip on his hip and a sexy hat on his head. "Doctor Jones, I've got just the right tool for the job." I gestured to the bulge beneath my leather pants.

We burst into insane laughter over our cheesiness, and I realized just how much I'd missed the easy banter between us. The sex had still been incredible, but we'd let jealousies and stupidity ruin the amazing comfort we'd found in one another. I didn't want our relationship to regress to just the physical, which is what had happened over the last few weeks.

We'd gone at it like two frenzied lovers who didn't know when they'd get their next fix.

Jag pulled me into his arms and kissed me softly and slowly, which told me I wasn't the only person who'd missed the way things used to be. Of course, my dick was ready to spring into action, but I ignored him. I needed so much more from Jag than an orgasm in that moment. I needed to feel connected to him. I rolled my eyes at how needy my internal thoughts sounded.

Jag pulled back from our kiss and looked into my eyes. "Did you eat dinner?" He didn't wait for me to answer. He grabbed my hand and began walking to his kitchen. "I stopped and picked up some Mexican in hopes that you hadn't eaten yet. I went ahead and ate when you didn't respond to my text, but I saved you some. My blood sugar tanked from going so long without food, and I was starting to get a nasty headache." He released my hand so he could pull leftovers out of the refrigerator.

"I thought you had dinner plans with Senator Thompson?" I purposely chose to use Baxter's title rather than his name to keep their relationship professional in my mind. "What happened?"

Jag froze momentarily as he opened the cabinet where he kept his plates. He took a deep breath and pulled out a plate before he shut the cabinet and turned to face me. "Let's just say the senator had ulterior motives for asking for my assistance on the campaign."

"You mean he just wanted to fuck you?"

Jag nodded as he loaded up my plate and put it in the microwave to reheat. "Which he made abundantly clear tonight."

Tension seized my body and I stood there frozen. "What happened?"

Jag turned to look at me, and I saw the dark emotion in his eyes. The hunger that had been gnawing at my guts turned to dread. In my heart, I knew Jag wasn't unfaithful. Remorse or guilt wasn't the look I saw in his eyes. Instead, I saw humiliation and hurt. No matter how much I didn't want to hear what he had to say, I needed to let him talk it out with me. I reached for his hand and tugged him closer.

"Talk to me, Jag."

"I showed up at the hotel where I thought we were having a meeting with a group of supporters. It turned out to be just the two of us in a private dining room. I should've left right then, but my ego wouldn't let me. I wanted to work on the national campaign, so I pushed aside the warnings and stayed." He cupped my face in his hands. "I didn't do anything, Bones. I need you to believe me."

"I do." I turned my face and kissed his palm. I reminded myself that beneath Jag's confident exterior was a man who constantly searched for acceptance—personally and professionally. He had thought he could only achieve it professionally. The urge to tell him how much I loved him was so strong, but I held back. I didn't want my confession to look like some knee-jerk reaction from jealousy.

"We sat down for drinks, and I saw the look in his eyes. He was a man on a mission to get laid." Jag swallowed hard before continuing. "I didn't even take the first sip of wine. I looked him in the eyes and told him I was in a committed relationship and very happy." His words were a balm to my franticly beating heart.

"To which he said?" I prompted.

"He said he didn't care, and no one had to know. He had booked a room at the hotel under an assumed name, and we could spend hours getting reacquainted with one another again. He told me he'd never had anyone fuck him the way I had, and he wanted to experience it again."

I would've truly been okay if he'd left the last part out, but I appreciated the fact that he wanted to tell me everything that had transpired. I didn't have the right to be upset about his past. He never pretended he had been a saint, and I had been no different. We both went into our relationship with eyes wide open.

"I told him I wasn't interested, and he got really angry."

"Angry? How angry?" That wasn't a normal reaction when someone said they weren't interested in hooking up. I was sure the arrogant ass wasn't used to being told no, but that didn't give him the right to get angry. I felt my own fury rising and my indignation growing.

"He told me it was a bad move for my career. He basically told me working on the campaign would have cemented my future both in law and politics. He said he could've molded me to reach my full potential and that we could become the most powerful gay couple in the country." Jag shook his head at the memory. "Molded me to reach my full potential?" He gave a short bark of derisive laughter. "Since I'm not interested in fucking him, he doesn't want my help with his campaign. What a putz."

The microwave dinged, and Jag turned to get my food, but I stopped him. "I don't know what to say, Jag. I'm sorry about the campaign. I know how excited you were to be working on something at the national level, and it sucks that he..." Jag silenced me with a finger over my mouth.

"He's an idiot if he thought I'd sell out on what I have with you to work with him. There will be other campaigns, but I'll never find another you." *Oh, dear lord.* His words lit me up on the inside and emboldened me to be brave.

"I love you, Jag." It was the moment I had been waiting for. I held my breath as I waited for his reaction. His eyes widened in shock, then a smile slowly spread across his face.

"Bones," his deep voice sounded raw as if it was painful for him to speak. "I love you too. It feels so fucking good to finally say it out loud."

We stood there grinning at each other for a few moments before we were all over each other like trick-or-treaters on candy. I forgot about being hungry, angry, or any other feeling except the desire to take and be taken.

"It's my turn to top," I said teasingly. "You rode my ass like a champion bull rider the last time."

"You begged me to fuck you, so it doesn't count," Jag growled against my throat. His hands were fondling my ass through my leather pants. "I was prepared to give it up to you, but you were all 'Fuck me hard, Jag,' so what else could I do?"

I pulled back from his embrace and looked into his eyes. "Let's flip for it."

"That sounds very familiar," Jag said, his eyes glittering with adoration.

We reenacted the scene from my maiden visit to his house, but that would be where the similarities ended. It would be the first time we made love with our feelings out in the open, and I knew it would be stronger and more meaningful than anything we'd previously experienced.

I was right. Jag's heat nearly burned me alive when I slid inside him, and he imprinted himself everywhere on my body when it was his turn to top. Neither of us was willing to close our eyes or look away while we truly made love for the first time. The whispered words of love between tender kisses fueled our passion for one another. I had never loved or been loved so thoroughly. My orgasm had never been as strong as when we came together. That night changed everything between us.

I was never eager to disengage from Jag's embrace, and that night, I held on even longer than usual. It was the moment I had been waiting for, and I clung to it as long as I could while we lay in a tangled knot, sharing every breath. I finally understood all the sappy crap Gray had been saying ever since he'd met Chase. Jag breathed life into me and I into him. I wasn't the same person I'd been before he'd come into my life, and I knew the same was true for Jag. Together, we were better.

"Don't you dare let me turn into a fucking sap," I said after we showered and got back into his bed. "I mean it, Jag. I'm on the verge of drawing hearts, writing poems, or sending you flowers."

"I won't let the sickening saps get you, Bones. I'll keep you grounded." His chuckle was the last thing I heard before I fell asleep.

As usual, Jag was gone before I woke up. I went about my normal routine and got ready for work, but it was obvious there was an extra gleam in my eyes and more pep in my step, which was commented on as I made my way to my office. I opened my door and was shocked to find an enormous bouquet of red roses sitting in the middle of my desk. My heart beat erratically in my chest as I pulled the card from the middle of the bouquet. Inside was a roughly drawn heart and the words:

I must have read the card four or five times before I finally stopped laughing. I leaned forward and breathed in the fragrance of the roses. The sickening saps had caught me too and damn if it didn't feel good. I sat in my chair and began to plot my counter move—work was the last thing on my mind. A fun idea occurred to me, but I'd need some help to pull it off. Gavin came through the door and grinned like an idiot when he saw my flowers and the goofy smile on my face.

"Shut up," I said before he could even get a word out of his mouth. "I need you to do something else for me instead of grading papers. It's personal, and I shouldn't ask you to help me, but—"

"I'm in," Gavin replied without hesitation. He listened intently as I laid out the materials I needed him to buy for me while I gave my lecture. I handed him my credit card and shooed him out the door.

I only had a few minutes before my first class, but I couldn't teach without taking the time to thank Jag for his gift. I shot him a quick text that ended with **I love you.**

I whistled through my morning and spent my lunchtime putting together the surprise package for Jag. I barred Gavin from my office and locked the door so no one could witness my humiliating display of sappiness. I would've loved to deliver it in person, but my schedule just wouldn't permit it, so I hired a courier service to deliver the gift to his office.

CHAPTER
Seventeen

JJ

I SAT AT MY DESK A FEW DAYS BEFORE THANKSGIVING AND PONDERED what kind of sappy-ass gift I could give Miller next. Ever since I'd sent him flowers, we had been exchanging gifts that had gotten more and more elaborate over time. I'd started the game with simple flowers and a lame-ass poem that was supposed to make him smile and let him know how serious I had become about our relationship. He'd fired back that same day with an elaborate gift that made me laugh and touched my heart.

I had grinned when my receptionist called me out to the lobby to sign for a package. There had been strict instructions that only I could sign for it. It could've been from any number of people, but I knew in my heart it was from Bones. My pulse sped up when I cut through the tape on the outer box to see what was inside. I lifted a shiny red box out of the larger one and placed it on my desk, then I just stared at it like it was a ticking bomb or something.

I finally lifted the lid off the box and peered inside. At first, I was confused about what I was looking at because it looked like a box of scrap construction paper. I pulled one scrap out, flipped it over, and noticed it had a few words printed on it, but they didn't make sense. They appeared to be random words printed on pieces of paper. Then I noticed the odd shape of the pieces and realized it was a puzzle. I began to pull each piece out one at a time, placing them all on my desk so I could put the puzzle together. Once assembled, I sat in my chair and laughed until my stomach hurt as I read the poem he'd written and cut apart.

I give you my heart and that's a fact
It's yours to keep, I don't want it back
I'm sticking to you like fleas on a dog
If you're a good boy
I'll let you ride my log

I returned my attention to the box because there were still more items inside. I pulled out a box of assorted Belgian chocolates, a small plastic ball and chain, and a red plastic heart that pulled apart like the eggs that went in Easter baskets. Inside were little slivers of paper where Miller had written mushy movie lines.

I didn't think anyone could top my tacky-ass poem, but Miller had definitely taken the prize with his. From then on, we tried to one-up each other at least once a week, but privately instead of involving our workplaces. I bet Miller would be surprised if he knew I'd kept every one of those puzzle pieces and the plastic heart with the movie lines inside my desk. They were meant to be funny and cute, but it was the first romantic gift I had ever received, and it meant the world to me.

The receptionist called me and let me know I had someone there to see me, but they didn't have an appointment. That was something that never happened, and I figured Miller was up to something. So, I was surprised when I entered the lobby and saw Grayson Wright.

"Is something wrong with Chase?" I asked as I led him back to my office.

"Nothing is wrong," he assured me quickly with a warm smile. *Grayson was smiling at me?* "I know I'm the last person you'd expect to see at your office, but it turns out Chase and I need your legal advice." I was sure my surprise showed on my face because Gray chuckled. "We haven't even told our families about this yet." His excitement built with each word until it became a palpable presence in the room. "Pastor Simms recommended Chase and I as adoptive parents to a young lady in her congregation. We met with her and her parents recently and…" Gray paused to swallow hard. "She chose us, JJ. Our daughter will be born in January."

"Gray, that's fantastic news. She's going to be the luckiest little girl in the world, and I sincerely mean that." I was shocked to hear the news from Gray instead of Chase.

Sensing my surprise, Gray smiled and said, "I needed to be the one who asked for your help after the animosity between us. I didn't always treat you very kindly, and I'm sorry for the way I've behaved."

"Gray"—I blew out a relieved breath—"I didn't make it very easy on you most of the time. To be honest, not many guys would have accepted the situation like you did. I appreciate you not making Chase choose between us because I would've lost my best friend."

"He wasn't going to give you up, buddy. Believe me, I tried." Gray offered a wry smile, and for once, I found myself completely comfortable in his presence. "Anyway, we would like to hire you as our legal counsel to make sure the adoption goes through without a hitch. We're a bit overwhelmed right now. Chase and I would love to focus solely on getting our new house ready for the baby and not worry about the legal aspects. To do that, we need someone who will have our backs. And that would be you, J."

"I'll gladly take your case, but I'm not taking your money." Gray opened his mouth to argue, but I cut him off. "It's not up for negotiation. Take the money you would've paid me and put it toward creating the coolest nursery on the planet." There was no give in my voice, and Gray wisely knew to pick his battles because this was not one he would win.

"I appreciate that very much. We'll be making the announcement to our friends on Sunday when we have you all over for dinner. You and Miller are coming, right?"

"Absolutely." For the first time in nearly a decade, I was looking forward to the holidays. In the past, the memories of everyone I'd lost made them unbearable, but things were completely different now that I had Miller. He brought so much happiness and love into my life that I'd never be able to properly express my feelings for him. Just telling him I loved him wasn't enough. I would miss my brother and mother for the rest of my life, but Miller gave me a reason to smile and look for happiness instead of clinging to sadness.

"You know," Gray began, "I don't want to ruin the good thing we have going here"—he gestured between us—"by making comments about your not-a-relationship with Miller, but I just want to say that I've never seen him so happy. I, um, scoffed at the 'no labels' thing, but you know what? It works great for you guys, and it's no one's business but your own."

"Thank you, Gray."

"You're welcome. Enjoy Thanksgiving with the Brexlers. They're a fun bunch of people."

"That they are." Miller had included me in every family function over the last several months, and I had fallen in love with them. It was no surprise Miller had turned out the way he had after growing up in that household. They were boisterous, fun loving, and very accepting of my intrusion into their lives.

"I need to head back to the office to work on some last-minute details before I take the next few days off for the holiday." Gray rose to his feet and offered his hand. "It's okay with me if you share this news with Miller, but tell him to keep his mouth shut. I don't want my parents finding out from his parents."

"Deal." I shook his hand and told him I'd see him later.

I had details of my own to wrap up because it was my last workday before the long holiday weekend. I ended up working later than I wanted, and it was seven before I knew it. I sent a text to Miller asking if he had already eaten and offered to pick something up if not, but he never responded. I called him and left a few voicemails, but he didn't respond to either my texts or phone messages.

I was too worried to stop and get anything to eat. Instead, I drove straight to his house. All the lights were off, and he wasn't home. I drove to my house in a haze of worry, wondering what the hell I should do next if he wasn't there. Call his parents to see if they'd heard from him? That sounded over the top, but I found myself frantic with worry. Then I saw his car in my driveway and breathed a sigh of relief.

"Miller?" I called his name as I walked through my front door. "Bones, where are you?" I found him and Indy sound asleep on the couch. I knelt beside the couch and touched his face. "Bones." My touch startled him, and he jerked into a sitting position. "Are you okay?" His face looked pale, and his skin felt clammy when I touched it.

"Yeah, I guess I was more tired than I thought. I can't remember the last time I slept this hard." He shook his head to clear the sleep fog, then his face scrunched up in irritation. "I had an unexpected visitor at the university this afternoon." I could tell by the sour expression on his face that it wasn't a happy visit like the one I'd had with Gray. "Your buddy, Bax, stopped by to see me."

"What? Why?" I had a really bad feeling in the pit of my stomach. "He's not my buddy."

"Apparently, he's the benefactor behind an archeological and anthropological dig that will occur on a Civil War battlefield. They believe there could be a cache of old Confederate money that was captured and hidden along with munitions and other pieces of history. A Maryland farmer discovered old uniform pins for both the Union and Confederate armies while tilling his ground. He also found some spent ammunition and a little metal tag that one of our history professors believes was used to seal a bag of Confederate money."

"How does any of this involve you?"

"The farmer took the items to a museum, and the curator reached out to our history department because the site of discovery was not on a known battlefield. The history department chalked it up to a minor skirmish that might have occurred between battles. The farmer didn't believe it, so he bought a metal detector and did a little digging on his own. It was obvious from all the hits he got that his land was probably more significant than a small skirmish site. So now, the history, anthropology, and archeology departments will work together to dig up and preserve what we find."

"Ahhh. Bax wants you involved in the dig, is that it?"

"Yep. I guess they've gone through several months of government red tape, although this is the first I've heard about it. Our buddy, Baxter, used his influence to move things along. The dig is set to begin the Saturday after Thanksgiving. They want to get started before the weather gets too cold and the ground freezes. I would normally be excited for this, but I'm suspicious about his involvement. I'm the youngest member of the archeology and anthropolgy departments, yet I was chosen to oversee the dig? He's either figured out we're dating and wants to cause problems for us, or he now thinks I could be the other half of the most powerful gay couple in the country. Either way, I'm not happy with his involvement."

"But you don't have a choice, do you?" I heard the tension and dread in his voice. I told myself Baxter wouldn't dirty himself by hanging out at a dig sight, but I was starting to believe I didn't really know anything about the man he had become. There was hardly anything about him that resembled the good guy I remembered, but then again, power corrupted people.

"No, I don't," Miller agreed. "And honestly, I don't want to walk away from a potential major discovery."

"This is too important to pass up." I leaned forward and kissed his mouth. "Besides, what's the likelihood his pampered ass will even show up?"

"Not likely," Miller agreed, looking hopeful. "I could use some more volunteers. Do you know of anyone who might like to spend a day digging for centuries old war artifacts while freezing his nuts off with his boyfriend? I bet a guy like that would be rewarded mightily in the bedroom."

"Yeah?" I replied with an enthusiastic nod. "I'm in, Bones." He rewarded me with a toe-curling kiss that held the promise of more to come.

"I have some exciting news to share with you too. Gray stopped by and asked me to represent him and Chase in adopting a baby girl."

"What? When? I can't believe he didn't call me." Miller's excitement for our friends was so cute. He looked a lot like Indy did when I snuck him table scraps. I told him what I knew so far and passed along Gray's parting words about keeping his mouth shut. Miller pretended to lock his lips and throw away the key.

"You better hope you can find that key, Bones. I have plans for that mouth later, and it involves more than eating dinner." I playfully tackled him to the couch as his laughter echoed around me. I forgot about my hunger, my irritation over Baxter creeping back into our lives, and everything else except pleasing Miller.

CHAPTER
Eighteen

Miller

T HE THANKSGIVING HOLIDAY STARTED AS A FUN DAY SPENT WITH my family. Jag fit in so well that it seemed like he'd been a part of our lives forever. As much as I loved including him, there was a small part of me that was afraid someone would open their mouths and ask when we were getting married. I worried that once it happened, it would be the beginning of the end of us. I didn't think my heart could handle hearing Jag say we'd never get married because somewhere along the way my aversion to happily ever after and one ass forever had disappeared. I wanted to be tied to him for the rest of my days. I knew he loved me and wanted to be with me too, but I wanted something permanent.

Luckily, my family happily accepted our relationship without asking us probing questions about a future we might never have. We stuffed ourselves full of scrumptious food and watched some football before we played board games until nearly midnight.

"I thought families like yours only existed in sitcoms," Jag had said from the passenger seat on the way back to his house where our pissed-off animals were waiting for our return. "I love that they've welcomed me into their lives and made me feel like one of them."

"You are one of us." I reached across the console and linked my fingers with Jag's on his lap. "They love you too. You know that, right?" I took my eyes off the road long enough to glance at him.

"Yeah." The smile in his voice made me happy. "I think your mom is worried she's smothering me and that I'll get tired of her, but there's no way that could happen."

"She's just happy I met someone special." Jag scoffed at my remark. "You are special to me, and she knows that. I've never brought a guy home to meet my family, so she knows how important you are to me." We didn't usually have discussions about our feelings; we chose to show our affection with actions instead. Telling him I was in love with him rolled off my tongue easily and he told me just as frequently. I didn't feel like our relationship was lacking anything, but sometimes words were needed too. "You're the most important person in my life, Jag. My family knows that, and I hope you know it too."

He lifted our entwined hands up and kissed the back of mine. "I do know, Bones, but that doesn't mean there aren't moments that I ask myself why you love me the way you do." It wasn't often I saw or heard the broken boy in him anymore, but every now and then, he appeared. "Then I remind myself it doesn't really matter how or why you love me. It only matters that you do. I'm horrible at expressing my emotions, Bones. Please tell me you have some inkling about how much I love you."

"I do, Jag. You show me rather than tell me, and I think it's more meaningful that way."

The Friday after Thanksgiving was just as wonderful. We spent the day vegging on the couch as we watched movies and ate leftovers. Two guys can get into a lot of playful trouble with leftover pumpkin pie and whipped cream. We started out fully clothed sitting beside each other on the couch eating pie. I caught a wicked gleam in Jag's eye, and the next thing I knew, my shirt was off and Jag was smearing pumpkin pie and whipped cream over my nipple, which tightened almost painfully beneath the cold custard. Chills gave way to unadulterated heat as his warm tongue licked the dessert off my chest. Spikes of lust went straight to my groin as he sucked and nibbled on my nipple before he turned and repeated the same sexy torture on the other.

I palmed his hardening length through his jeans and worked him until he was hard as steel. Unwilling to be left out of the fun, I rolled him to his back on the couch and kissed my way down his bare chest until I reached his waistband. I made quick work of his button-fly jeans and pushed them and his underwear down to his thighs so I could have access to the treat I craved the most.

"This is going to be a little cold at first," I warned right before I smeared pumpkin filling on his cock. Jag's breath was a startled hiss, and I couldn't help but smile at his discomfort. I scooped some whipped cream off the top of the pie and smeared it over the head of his dick. "This is my new favorite way to eat pie."

I lowered my mouth to his crown and licked the cream off before I slid the length of him into my mouth, not stopping until I felt his coarse pubic hairs tickle my nose. I sucked hard as I eased up until only the head of his dick remained in my mouth.

"Bones." Jag fisted my hair in both hands and urged me back down on his cock, but I was too busy savoring his salty precum. "I'm dying here."

My chuckle vibrated around his cock as I eased him deep into my mouth once more. He made desperate sounds when I repeatedly changed the tempo from slow and teasing to fast and hard. I didn't let up until he shouted my name and came in my mouth.

Once I'd cleaned up every drop of his release, I climbed up and shared a kiss with him, allowing him to taste the heady mix of the pie and his cream. When I pulled back, he looked at me with a wicked smile.

"You look like you have rabies." He swiped a thumb along my mouth and pulled it back to show me the whipped cream I had smeared around my lips. I grabbed his thumb and sucked it clean. "Your turn, Bones." Jag rolled me over to return the favor, but I felt too edgy for a blow job. I wanted to fuck. Hard.

We made quick work of stripping off the rest of our clothes, then I was stretching him open while catching his sighs and moans with my mouth. "Jag." His name sounded like a prayer as I eased myself into his heat. There were many uncertain things in my future, but the one certainty was that I would never tire of joining my body to his. Each time felt just as wonderful and exciting as our first time, and I refused to take his body, or him, for granted.

I reached above his head and grabbed onto the armrest of the couch once his body had adjusted and opened completely to me. I dug my knees into the couch and took him hard and fast, both of us yelling out the pleasure we found in each other. It didn't take long for Jag to harden again once I found that sweet spot inside him.

"Stroke yourself," I commanded as I pounded into him. I wanted us to come together, and all the signals of a pending orgasm were going off in my body. I looked down and watched Jag stroke his dick, which only turned me on more. I angled my dick for his prostate on every stroke and was rewarded with the tightening of his body beneath mine.

I unclenched my muscles and allowed myself to fill the condom the second his ass squeezed my cock and the first spurt of his cum landed on his stomach.

"You've made a horrible mess of us both, Bones."

"We're a beautiful mess," I said looking down at our joined bodies. "Besides, now we get to shower, and you know the mischief we can make in the shower." I wiggled my eyebrows at him, and he laughed before I eased out of him and held out my hand to help him off the couch.

"I'll never be able to look at pumpkin pie again without seeing you swallowing my cock," Jag said as we made our way upstairs.

"It's time to make our own traditions," I replied, earning a sexy swat on the ass.

"I'll refrain from saying that as one of the things I'm grateful for when we go around the table next year at your folks' house." I laughed at the image his words conjured up, but what made me happiest was the fact that he planned to be at my parents' house with me a year from then.

"Save it for Chase and Gray's on Sunday. Gram will get a kick out of it."

"Bones, we can't upstage Gram. That just wouldn't be right."

Our blissful minivacation was shattered on Saturday when we showed up at the dig site. The day started off beautifully with another shared shower, coffee, and pastries. Things didn't go to hell until after we arrived at the farm and saw Senator Thompson had indeed shown up to assist with the dig. Jag got out of my passenger seat, and the stunned look on Baxter's face was priceless. It was apparent he hadn't known about my relationship with Jag when he'd invited me to dig.

"Uh-oh," Jag muttered quietly so only I could hear. "He looks like someone just took away his ice cream cone."

"Yeah, you did," I told Jag wryly.

Like most politicians, Baxter swiftly replaced his surprise with a camera-ready smile. "It's good to see you again, Dr. Brexler. I wasn't aware you were acquainted with JJ."

"We're *well* acquainted, Bax," Jag said. He might as well have peed on my leg with the tone he used. I had to work hard not to smile at his possessiveness. That kind of macho bullshit should've made me angry, but it didn't.

"I didn't know you were bringing a friend," Dr. Halverston said.

"He's not my friend, sir. He's my boyfriend." I made sure to keep a professional tone as I set the record straight. My sexuality had never been discussed nor was it relevant to my ability to do my job. "Jag, this is Micah Halverston. He's head of the archeology and anthropology departments. Sir, this is Jag Jackson. He's volunteered to help us today since a lot of my students are away for the holiday."

"It's nice to meet you, Jag." Halverston reached out and shook Jag's hand. "You must be the reason behind the frequent smiles I've seen on Miller's face these last several months."

"I'd like to think so, sir." Jag offered him a friendly smile.

"Thank you for helping us out today." Halverston gave Jag a friendly pat on the shoulder before he walked off.

"Jag, huh?" Baxter asked.

"Only he gets to call me that," Jag said. They stared each other down for several minutes before Baxter shrugged and walked away.

Jag leaned into me and gave me a quick kiss, shocking me with his PDA. "Let's get moving. The sooner we get started, the sooner we can get back home. There's still more pie in the refrigerator."

If only it had been that easy. Baxter Thompson was there every time we made a discovery, yucking it up and getting his photo taken with every artifact we pulled out of the ground. Unfortunately, he pulled me into the photos with him and threw his arm around my shoulders each time. I was so caught up in the excitement of discovering an unknown Civil War battleground that I didn't stop to think what it might look like to Jag and the others.

I took one look at Jag's clenched jaw and the firm set of his lips as I approached him at the end of the day and knew he was furious. The brief kiss he had given me eight hours before was the last interaction I'd had with him all day. I'd been surrounded by students, faculty, and the senator every second. The happiness I felt over the discoveries faded when I realized how selfish I'd been. Jag turned and headed to my car without a word.

"Miller." Dr. Halverston hollered my name just as I had started to follow Jag. I stopped and turned to face my boss and saw that he and the senator were walking toward me. "We're having a get together to celebrate at my house tomorrow evening at five. It won't be too late since we're all back to work on Monday, but I couldn't let everyone's hard work go uncelebrated."

"I already have plans, sir, but thank you for the invitation."

"Miller, your plans can't be more important than celebrating today's discovery," Senator Thompson said. I thought about the exciting news

Gray and Chase would be sharing with us the next day and knew in my heart that was where I needed to be. I loved my career, but I loved Jag and my friends more.

"Actually, they are very important, and I won't break them. I sincerely thank you for the invitation to your home, sir, and if I could be there, I would. I don't miss any of our department meetings or celebrations, but tomorrow is a very special day for people I hold dear."

"It's not a problem, Miller," Halverston said. "I'll plan something more official in a few weeks and give everyone plenty of notice." My opinion of my boss had shot up several notches that day—first because of the welcoming way he'd greeted Jag and then the way he'd defended my plans.

I thanked my boss and continued to my car where Jag waited. I knew I had some serious apologizing to do, and I wasted no time. "I am so sorry for the way I acted today," I said as soon as I climbed into the car and shut the door. "I got so caught up in the excitement that I didn't stop to think about your feelings." I turned slightly in my seat so I could look at him. "Please forgive me."

Jag looked at me, and his harsh expression eased a little. "What did they talk to you about back there?" I told him about the dinner invite and watched as his anger returned. "He just expects you to drop everything to hang out with him? Tomorrow is a huge day for Gray and Chase. Please tell me you're not going to blow them off and go to the dinner." I loved the way his eyes turned nearly black when he was either angry or really, really horny. I wanted to get past the anger and onto the horny phase of the night.

"I told them no." I reached over and took his hand. "I got carried away by excitement today, but I do have my priorities straight." I leaned in for a short and sweet kiss but that changed the second his lips touched mine.

Jag pulled back, leaving me panting and aching. "Press is still here. Take us home so we can finish this in private, Bones."

Like the last time Jag had perceived Thompson as a threat, he claimed me with a possessive fervor that I loved. There was no doubt in my mind who I belonged to as he bent me over the end of my couch as soon as we entered the room. It was rough, raw, and real. I didn't have to worry about biting down on my tie to keep quiet. I could make as much noise as I wanted—yell his name as often as I liked—and I did.

Jag and I didn't edge each other very often because we rarely had the discipline to pull it off, but that night was different. Jag felt like he had something to prove, and I loved the lesson. I lost count of how many times he pulled me back from climax right as I was about to tip over the edge. My legs were sore and began to cramp from being bent over the couch for so long, but I loved every second of it. I literally begged for it, and he was only giving me what I wanted.

"Mine," Jag had said several times as he kept pegging my prostate.

"Yours." My voice sounded raw from shouting the word repeatedly. "Love you, Jag."

"Bones." The word sounded like it was ripped from his chest. "Love you too." And we came together. "Was I too rough with you?" he asked once we were in the shower.

"Look at me." I pointed at the blissed-out expression I knew I wore. "Do I look displeased to you?"

"You look pretty satisfied."

"I am thrilled with every aspect of our relationship, Jag." I ran my hand over his heart while I searched for the right words to say. "Do you know how much it means that you've given your heart to me?" He shook his head. "No one, and I mean this, matters as much to me as you do."

"You had me at hello, Bones."

I woke up the next morning eager to take on a new day. I stretched and reveled in the delicious soreness I felt in my backside. I wasn't in any pain, but I'd be feeling Jag's possession all day if not longer. I headed downstairs and poured myself a cup of coffee. I had just sat down at the kitchen table when Jag came into the room with a scowl on his face.

"What's the matter?"

"It's all over Baxter's social media sites." He spat his words angrily.

"The dig?" I couldn't imagine why he'd be so angry, then I remembered all those pictures of the senator standing with his arm around me. "Oh."

"Yeah. You're practically engaged." He handed me his phone that showed hundreds of comments beneath a picture Baxter had posted on his Facebook page. Most of them referred to me as "the new boyfriend."

"Oh, come on." I yelled loud enough to scare Indy under the table. "Where'd they get that?" Then Jag flipped through the rest of the photos posted to the senator's page. They were of the two of us smiling at each other. I could see how someone would misinterpret my joy of discovering artifacts as infatuation with the senator. "Fuck! My name is even listed in the caption."

"Yep. Gay men everywhere are crying over the loss of the hottest bachelor in the United States." I looked at him incredulously, then he showed me the comments that were being plastered all over Twitter, and I saw he was actually quoting them verbatim.

"You've got to be kidding me! I'm sorry, Jag. I'm sure this will all blow over soon. Surely, Thompson will deny the relationship to the media."

"That's where you're wrong, Bones." He ran a hand through his hair in a sign of agitation. "According to a source close to the senator, he said it was too early in the relationship to discuss details." Jag read that line from an online tabloid.

"Relationship? What relationship?"

"You should've known he was up to something when his hands were all over you the way they were." *He was blaming me?*

"So this is my fault? I apologized for the way I acted, and you accepted my apology, or at least I thought you did when you pounded the hell out of my ass last night. Now, you're mad at me because strangers are jumping to conclusions on social media. I understand being frustrated…"

"How would you feel if the situation were reversed? It's humiliating that our friends and your family might see and hear these things."

"So this is about you? What about me? My face and name are smeared all over the internet, and you're worried about what people will think about you?"

"You'd be just as angry, and you damn well know it." Jag's voice was growing louder with anger.

I pointed to the online photos and said, "These images were all taken out of context and can easily be explained."

"You're not getting the point, Miller." He hardly ever called me by my given name. "I would never have disrespected you the way that you did. Yes, you apologized for your behavior, and I accepted your apology. Seeing these images first thing in the morning made me remember the seven or eight hours of misery yesterday. I guess I'm not ready to accept your apology after all. I'm going home to be by myself for a little bit."

"Jag..."

"Please, just give me some space."

He left without kissing me goodbye, and we barely spoke to each other at the Wrights' unless it was to snipe at one another. He didn't come over to my house that night nor did he invite me home with him. My phone calls and text messages were ignored for several days. I was miserable without him in my life. I had hurt his feelings and his pride, but I had no clue how to make it right. I had done all I could, and our fate was in Jag's hands. All I could only do was hope that he missed me as much as I ached for him and that he would reach out to me and let me try to fix what I had inadvertently broken.

CHAPTER
Nineteen

JJ

I WAS FULLY AWARE MY ACTIONS WERE UNREASONABLE AND HURTFUL, yet I felt powerless to stop myself. I replayed all of Miller's voicemail message just so I could hear his voice. I read every pleading text message multiple times each day. Still, I didn't reply. I couldn't. I tried. I honestly did. I would pick up my phone to call or text him, and I'd see another Google alert that Miller and Baxter were being discussed again, and I just couldn't take it. I should never have set up the alerts in the first place because all it did was make me physically ill. I thought the rumors of their romance would fade, but they didn't.

Every insecure thought I ever had about myself taunted me day and night. How could Miller want me over Baxter who could give him the world? I hated how good they looked together in those photos. I licked my wounds in miserable silence for more than a week, aching for Miller every second of the day.

One morning, I woke up and decided enough was enough. The only thing I was accomplishing with my inaction was pushing Miller away. My mind began to spin with ideas and romantic gestures I could use to apologize for my behavior. I thought of singing telegrams, flowers, or something playful like one of the puzzles we made and gave to one another. Then I realized the only thing that made any sense was to talk to him from the heart. I simply needed to drop the pretense and bullshit and tell the man what he meant to me.

I sent Miller a text when I finished talking to Gray. I knew he'd be teaching and wouldn't get my text until later, but I couldn't go another minute without doing something. A text was a piss-poor solution, but it was a start.

I miss you like crazy, Bones. I'm sorry for the way I've acted. I'm going to make this up to you. Can we have dinner tonight and talk? Love, J.

I went to the florist at lunchtime and ordered a huge bouquet of roses. Instead of all red, I asked the florist to put one rose of every color he had on hand. On the note I wrote: *I've been a complete ass. Can you forgive me?* I stopped at the pet store on the way back to my office and bought a few things for Indy and the girls. I missed that little dog almost as much as I missed his human. Mal and Urs had been bored to tears without Indy chasing them all around my house. I picked up a few catnip stuffed mice for them as a special treat for their suffering too.

I had just sat down in my office chair when I received a text from Miller. I held my breath while I opened the text to read his response.

I miss you too. Indy and I will be over at 6.

I breathed a huge sigh of relief and tried to figure out what to do for dinner. Takeout wouldn't impress him, but I could barely boil water. Inspiration struck and I texted Miller's mom for one of her recipes. She was happy to help me plan a surprise and emailed me instructions on how to make stuffed peppers. I finished work early so I could do some grocery shopping and set a romantic atmosphere with candles and soft music. They weren't empty gestures either. Miller meant the world to me, and I would do whatever I could to prove it.

Mal and Urs wound themselves around my legs as I followed the recipe instructions. The stuffed peppers were easier to make than I'd thought, and I felt a sense of pride when I put them into the oven to bake. "Let's just hope I don't give my man food poisoning," I said to the cats.

I lit candles all around the dining room and put on some music—all things I never thought myself capable of—while I waited for Bones and Indy to arrive. Miller meant the world to me, and my stupid pride would need to take a back seat to showing him how I felt. I heard Indy barking on my front porch before I heard Miller's key in the door. My heart beat erratically, and butterflies took flight in my stomach. I tried to look casual as Miller came through the door, but one look at him and I was a goner.

"I've missed you so much, Bones." I wrapped my arms around him and breathed in his scent. "Never again…" I couldn't complete the sentence, but he knew what I meant.

He held me just as tight. "I've missed you too."

My world had returned to its peaceful order with Miller in my arms. Well, until I heard the cats hiss followed by Indy's high-pitched bark before our pets tore through the house. They were the happiest sounds I'd heard in several days until I heard and felt laughter rumbling through Miller's chest.

He pulled back and looked into my eyes. "Thank you for the beautiful flowers, Jag."

"I'm glad you liked them." I leaned in and kissed him softly. "I meant every word I wrote on that card, Bones. I'm very sorry for the immature way I handled the situation. I promise to do better the next time I get jealous."

Miller's baby blues twinkled with happiness. "We'll work on it together because I would've behaved just as badly if the situation was reversed."

"I hate the time we lost because we can't get it back. Hell, it's December already." For so long, I'd hated the month of December. I wanted nothing to do with Christmas decorating, shows, music—none of it. I would still have sad memories of losing Will, but being with Miller made me want to focus on the future and not my past. "It's our first official Christmas as a couple, and I want it to be special. Will you help me pick out a tree and decorate it?"

Miller knew the significance of what I was asking. I could see it in his eyes and the way he touched my face. It was a big step forward for me, and I wanted him to be part of it. I wanted Miller to be a part of everything I went through.

"How about we go this weekend?" he asked.

"Perfect." I leaned in and kissed him again. I planned on kissing him a bunch that night to make up for the lonely days we'd spent apart. I laughed as I realized we were still standing in the foyer. I had snatched him up as soon as he'd shut the front door. "How about we move this reunion a little farther inside the house? I have a surprise for you. I linked my fingers with his and led us into the dining room.

Miller smiled gently when he noticed the romantic touches. "You didn't have to go to so much trouble. Don't you know by now that I would've been just as happy with pizza on the couch?" He tilted his head back and sniffed the air. "Smells like my mom's stuffed peppers in here."

"That's because I got the recipe from her today. I wanted to do something special to show you how much you mean to me. Have a seat, and I'll bring dinner out." I carried the casserole dish into the dining room and set it on the table. I leaned forward and kissed him softly before I sat at the table. "You deserve to be wined and dined. Damn, I forgot the wine." I started to rise from my seat, but Miller placed his hand on my arm to keep me in place.

"I'll get it."

While he was gone, I tried to pull myself together. I was feeling anxious again, but I wasn't sure why. Everything was going smoothly, so I didn't understand where my anxiety was coming from. Miller walked back into the room and placed the bottle on the table. I was lost in my thoughts, and it startled me a bit. I looked at Bones; he looked a little confused. "I'm feeling anxious, and I don't know why."

"I do." He reached out his hand to me and gave me the crooked smile I had missed so much. "I know just what you need." I placed my hand in his and he tugged until I stood up. He dropped my hand and picked up our plates. "Grab those dishes or our pets will be in our food while we're upstairs."

"What about our dinner?" I did as he asked and followed him into the kitchen.

"We've been apart for more than a week, and you're worried about your stomach? I must be losing my touch. The best thing about stuffed peppers is that they reheat nicely." Miller spotted the toy I'd bought for Indy on the counter after we safely stored the food away. "You were going to use my dog to get to me, weren't you?"

"I'm not proud," I said in mock shame. Indy spotted the toy in Miller's hand and began to wag his tail in excitement. I took the toy and gave it to Indy. "Here you go, boy. I missed you too."

"It worked," Miller said with a leering grin.

We practically ran to my bedroom in our haste to get reacquainted with each other's bodies. I wanted to relearn every part of him like it was the first time because that was how it felt. That was the source of my anxiety. Once Miller had his way with me, I could relax and enjoy our dinner.

Our pets were in hot pursuit, thinking we were playing games. Indy was going to town on his new hot dog squeak toy as he gave chase. Miller pulled us inside my room, shut the door, and locked it. I gave him a quizzical look. Did he think the pets could somehow unlock the door? He just shrugged. We sent our clothes flying as we made our way to my large bed.

Miller fit himself between my spread thighs and lowered his head for a kiss so full of passion and promise. He kissed me until my anxiousness disappeared and all I could think about was the pleasure we'd bring one another. Miller reached between my legs and cupped my sac. He gave my balls a firm massage at the same time Indy bit into his squeak toy again. Miller grinned at me from above and gave my balls another squeeze. *Squeak!* He did it a few more times, and each time, Indy simultaneously chomped on his toy. We burst into laughter at the ridiculousness of the moment.

"No wonder you were so anxious," Miller said. "It's been so long since we've had sex that your balls are squeaking."

"Fix me, Bones."

"With pleasure."

We tried to take our time and go slow, but we had been without each other too long. I promised myself that next time I would sip and savor instead of begging to be taken. His every touch and kiss wiped away the sadness and misery I had felt while we were apart. The words we whispered to each other were about love and need as we joined our bodies together.

"All mine," I said as I slid inside Miller. I knew it, could see it in his eyes, but I needed to hear it too.

"Yours." Miller pulled my head down for a searing kiss that branded me as his. Once I came inside him, he rolled me to my back, suited up, and claimed me with just as much passion as I'd shown him. "All mine." He repeated my words as he slid home.

"Yours."

Much later, we ate reheated dinner in my bed while we watched television and our pets slept by our feet. It might've seemed lame to some, but it was what felt right to us. Being with Miller was as natural as breathing for me, and I vowed to never let him go.

CHAPTER
Twenty

Miller

I DID MY BEST TO MAKE OUR FIRST CHRISTMAS THE ABSOLUTE BEST one Jag had ever experienced. I wasn't foolish enough to think I would be able to wipe away all the sadness he felt from missing his mother and brother, but I thought I could at least give him something happy and hopeful to cling to when things got rough for him.

I was planning an outrageous twelve days of Christmas to work some sexy humor into the season. I was calling it the Twelve Days of Sexmas as I made a list of things to buy from the adult toy store. My game didn't include multiple sets of the same item like the song. I mean, what the hell would we do with three sets of handcuffs or five cock rings?

I finished my list and smiled when I read it back: dildo, masturbation toy, handcuffs, scented massage oil, cock ring, butt plug, nipple clamps, flavored lube, riding crop, blindfold, flavored condoms, and vibrating bullet. We were going to have the best Sexmas ever.

The cutest thing about the holiday was that I'd brought Lucas and Lily over to help Jag decorate his tree. We put strands of popcorn and homemade ornaments on the branches along with other ornaments we'd picked out at the store. Jag seemed touched by the ornaments that Lucas and Lily had made for him. Personally, I thought it was the prettiest tree I had ever seen.

After decorating, we ate cookies from the bakery—neither of us could bake worth a damn—and drank hot chocolate. Lily curled up in Jag's lap, and he read Christmas stories to her. Lucas tried to act like he'd outgrown that tradition, but I saw him hanging on every word that came out of Jag's mouth. Lucas wasn't the only one either. I was completely captivated by the deep timbre of his voice as he read. We had a fabulous day together, and we were both sad when Darryl and Destiny arrived to pick up the kids.

Lucas and Lily hugged and kissed us goodbye and grudgingly went home with their parents. Jag and I curled up on the couch in exhaustion. It was hard work being on our best behavior and not using foul language all day. Plus, I had to keep my contact with Jag G-rated. That's not to say I wouldn't kiss him or hug him in front of the kids because it was appropriate for them to see affection between us. I just couldn't sneak in any crotch grabbing or grinding against his groin like I would have if we were alone. The sacrifice was worth it, and the delayed gratification made the sex that night more intense.

We attended the work Christmas parties as a couple and had a great time. The best celebration by far was the ugly sweater party Chase and Gray hosted. Their new house was packed with merry makers wearing the ugliest, gaudiest sweaters ever created. My aunt Susan had made sweaters for Jag and me to wear. They'd started out as red sweatshirts, but once she was done, the original fabric couldn't be seen beneath all the appliqués.

Jag had chosen a *National Lampoon's Christmas Vacation* theme and had Griswold mishaps all over his sweater, including cousin Eddie's RV and the famous sled ride with sparks shooting out from beneath the round medal disk. I was a little bit jealous because I felt Aunt Susan had put more effort into Jag's sweater.

I'd chosen a *Home Alone* theme and was super excited about all the different pieces of the movie until Jag showed me his. My sweater must have been damn good too because people came up to me all night, pointed out different parts of the movie, and laughed. Most everyone was freaked over the tarantula sewn onto the shoulder and acted like it might crawl off and get them at any point. I named him Tyrone and petted him just to creep people out.

Even the babies got in on the action. Ellie's newborn daughter, Sofia, wore a knitted bonnet, sweater, and pants that made her look like a gingerbread cookie. Ava's little boy, Jacob, was dressed in a knitted outfit that had reindeer and snowflakes all over it.

I really thought Jag and I were contenders for the prize, but Gram won the contest and took home the first ever Ugly Christmas Sweater trophy. Her sweater had all the things from "The Twelve Days of Christmas" plastered all over it with enough silver and gold to blind us all when the lights reflected off it.

Jag handed me a cup of spiked punch in a plastic moose glass like the ones they used in the movie his sweater represented. I leaned in and gave him a light kiss on his lips because we were the only ones in the kitchen. I debated pulling him into a bathroom to do a little more than light kissing when we were interrupted.

"Aren't you boys adorable?" Gram said as she stepped into the kitchen to get a cup of punch.

"Careful, Agnes, that might interfere with some of your old lady medications," Jag said. He loved to try to get under her skin, though it rarely worked.

"Drinking water tonight, JJ?" Gram nodded to his unopened bottle. "Afraid you won't be able to get it up later if you have a few drinks? They make a pill for that too, you know?"

Jag threw his head back and laughed so loud people in the living room turned to look. He hooked an arm around her shoulders and pulled her into a hug. Her head barely came up to his armpit. "I love you, you crazy old woman."

Gram jabbed her elbow hard into Jag's ribs, making him groan and rub the afflicted area. "Listen here, boy. You can call me any vile name you want, but don't you call me *old* ever again." She pointed a finger at him. "Do you hear me?"

"Yes, Agnes."

She frowned and tried to jab him again, but he moved quickly enough to avoid her bony elbow. "How many times do I need to tell you to call me Gram?"

"At least one more." Jag gave her his patented shit-eating grin.

She narrowed her eyes at him, then cast her gaze to me. "So, are you idiots done with your 'I don't believe in love' nonsense? You two aren't fooling anyone anymore. You might as well embrace the fact that you two love each other and are as sappy as all the others." She waived her hand around, gesturing at the couples who were dancing to Nat King Cole's "Christmas Song." I hadn't really thought of Christmas music as romantic before, but I was learning a lot of new things once I opened my eyes to the possibilities. "Boys, there's so much more to life than sex, and it's past time you realize it. You can waste time pretending you're not madly in love with each other, or you can get on with living and loving."

"Gram, not everyone wants wedding bells and babies," Jag told her. "It's not a secret that I'm in love with Miller. I may not broadcast it all over for everyone to see and hear, but that's not my style."

"It's not really my style either, Gram, but that doesn't mean I love Jag any less than Gray loves Chase. What we're doing works well for us, and I've never been happier in my life." Jag's dark brown eyes locked on mine, and I saw how affected he was by my words.

"I never said you had to get married and have babies, boys. I simply said you needed to quit pretending you're against love and commitment." She focused her piercing blue eyes on Jag and said, "I've never seen you this happy in as long as I've known you, and I'm including the time you dated Chase. You two weren't meant to be together like that, but you've continued a beautiful friendship over the years. Chase found the man he was meant to be with, and because he did, you've found the person you're meant to be with too." She turned and looked at me next. "Thank you for bringing joy and happiness to JJ's life. I no longer see the shadows of sadness in his eyes, and that's all because of you." She stood on her tiptoes, and I leaned down so she could kiss my cheek. "You boys have a very Merry Christmas." Jag bent over so she could kiss his cheek too before she left as fast as she'd arrived.

"I hope I'm as spunky as she is when I'm her age," I said as I watched her walk over to her fiancé.

"I can make you spunky as soon as we get home. There's no need to wait another forty years." Jag purposely misconstrued what I meant. "I haven't had too much to drink, and I promise you I can get it up."

"Why wait? There has to be an empty bathroom somewhere in this house." I said it loud enough for Chase to overhear as he made his rounds with a tray full of snacks. Chase narrowed his eyes as he tried to fight off a smile.

"Santa is going to bring you a lump of coal, Miller," he replied teasingly. He stuck out his tongue and continued on with his tray of goodies, purposely skipping us.

"I guess he told you." Jag pulled me close and whispered huskily in my ear. "I want to go home and open my next Sexmas gift." Jag was enjoying the gifts even more than I thought he would. I got pleasure from seeing his laughter and being on the receiving end of whatever his gift was that day. I couldn't remember a time I'd loved Christmas more.

We spent Christmas Eve at my parents with my brother and his family. Lucas and Lily were all over Uncle Jag the minute we walked through the door. I'd never forget the look on his face when the kids started referring to him as their uncle. His widened eyes and slack jaw had turned into a broad smile and a joyful expression.

My mom cooked an extraordinary meal for all of us, and we ate so much we practically had to roll ourselves to the Christmas tree to exchange gifts. Jag was surprised by how many gifts he received from my family and that he had a Christmas stocking with his name on it, but like I'd reminded him on the way home, he was one of us. My mom never called to talk to me without asking about Jag. An invitation to dinner at her home always ended with "Bring Jag."

My parents didn't need us to make a formal announcement that we were together or in love. It was accepted and understood that Jag was the part that made me whole. Hell, I didn't even know I was only half a person until I'd met him. Every day we shared seemed to bring us closer and closer. I never questioned how he felt about me or worried he would tire of me and move on someday. On the other hand, I wasn't opposed to making our commitment permanent. I would gladly marry him if it was what we both wanted, but it wasn't make or break for me.

Jag and I exchanged gifts when we got home from my parents' house. We said we wouldn't get too carried away, and we mostly stuck to that agreement. I did buy him an expensive watch, and I got a secret thrill seeing it on his wrist. His extravagant gift for me was season tickets to the Nationals. As much as I loved the baseball tickets, my favorite gift was the glow-in-the-dark dinosaur boxer shorts. He loved the boxers I'd bought for him that said *Jingle These* above a giant set of silver bells that hung over his crotch. Later, we modeled our new undies for each other, but we didn't get to wear them long before we yanked the shorts off each other and tossed them to the floor.

The next morning, Jag surprised me with another gift. "It's from Santa Claus," he said as he laid it on the coffee table.

"Why is it wrapped in the same paper as your other gifts? Are you saying Santa bought his wrapping paper from Target too?"

"Apparently, he did, Miller. Quit being silly and open the gift." He sounded a little nervous.

I stared at the large rectangular box for a few minutes before curiosity got the best of me and I ripped into it like a child. "Huh?" I said when

I lifted the lid and found a miniature sand box filled with white sand. On top was a child's sand shovel and rake. I looked up at him, and he grinned wickedly at me.

"Use those tools to excavate until you find your gift."

"You haven't left this anywhere Maleficent or Ursula could find it, right? That's not the kind of gift I want to dig up."

"No cat poop. Scout's honor." He held up his hand and gave me the *Star Trek* salute, not the Boy Scout one.

"You're no Boy Scout, Jag."

"I'm always prepared." He pulled a condom and a tube of lube out of his robe pocket, both from his Twelve Days of Sexmas gifts.

"Wow, this must be some gift *Santa* brought me. You're all prepared to receive thank-you sex on his behalf." I picked up my shovel and rake and began to comb through the sand. The box was deeper than it appeared. The first thing I dug out was a pair of cheap sunglasses. I looked at him with a raised brow.

"Keep digging, Bones."

"I suppose this is to keep my lips supple for the blow job I'll give you once I figure out my gift," I said, holding up a tube of lip balm I'd unearthed.

"Now that you mention it…" He laughed again at my skeptical expression after digging up the first two items. "Get to digging so I can get my thank-you sex."

I rolled my eyes so hard it hurt, but then I began digging again. I didn't admit it just then, but I thought this was the coolest gift I'd ever received. I dug out a bottle of suntan lotion followed by a plastic suitcase that probably belonged to a Ken doll. I shook the little suitcase and realized it had stuff in it. I pulled out a pair of doll-sized flip flops and a pair of swim trunks. My heart started to speed up as I realized what I was uncovering. At the very bottom was a folder that contained two airline tickets and a pamphlet showing gorgeous pictures of a resort in Turks and Caicos.

"Jag." I was completely shocked by the gift. "Oh my God. I can't believe it."

"You're going to take me with you, right?" He gave me a pouty look and pleading puppy dog eyes like Indy would give me when he wanted a bite of steak.

"I wouldn't dream of taking anyone else." I looked around me on the couch where I'd laid the treasures I'd uncovered. "Where's that lip balm?" Jag laughed happily and pulled out the pair of handcuffs from his pocket before he began peeling out of his robe. "After thank-you sex, you can tell me when we're leaving on our vacation to paradise."

"Anywhere you are is paradise, Bones."

"Oh man, you're going to make me gag." I smiled to let him know I was only teasing. I hoped he saw how happy his words made me.

"I have something you can gag on," he said, stroking the erection beneath his new boxers.

"There's the guy I know and love."

Much, much later I snuggled up next to him on the couch and tucked my head beneath his chin after I nearly thank-you sexed us into a coma. Just as I was about to fall asleep, I heard Jag say, "We leave on January second. We get to start living, loving, and making new memories."

"I'm not going to bottom for you on a sandy beach. Nature's exfoliant has no business anywhere near my junk." Jag's deep chuckle vibrated against my temple, where he had pressed his lips.

"I fucking love you, Bones."

"I fucking love you too." I closed my eyes and mentally ticked off the days until we left and the things I needed to do before then. The trip was a little last minute, but who cared? I was going on a dream vacation with the man I loved. I couldn't wait to make new memories in the new year.

CHAPTER
Twenty-One

JJ

MILLER AND I SENT THE OLD YEAR OUT WITH A BANG. WE WENT
to the New Year's Eve party Jack and Liam hosted at Bottoms Up.
We felt everyone's eyes on us for most of the night and all their spec-
ulation. At first, it had been a fun game keeping them guessing about what
was or wasn't going on between us. I also realized no one was buying our
cavalier attitudes about love and commitment anymore, so I thought we
should give the people what they'd been waiting for once they'd found
out about our relationship.

I gently pressed Miller up against one of the columns that divided the
sections of the bar. I knew I had caught the attention of most of our friends
in the room. I stepped into him until our bodies were almost touching. I

lowered my head until my lips were pressed against Miller's ear. "I think the time for playing games has passed, don't you, Bones?"

I nearly forgot there were other people in the room when I pulled back and saw the answer in his eyes. I started to bring my hand up to touch his face, but I knew the moment called for a more drastic demonstration. Instead, I captured his mouth in a fierce, hot kiss so there was no mistaking the way I felt about him. I poured every emotion I felt for him into that kiss. Catcalls and whistles broke out all around us while Miller and I smiled at one another.

"I think we need to take this a step further." Miller had a wicked gleam in his eyes, and I wasn't exactly sure how far he wanted to push the envelope.

"Um, I'm not much of an exhibitionist, Bones, and I really don't want anyone else to see the look in your eyes or hear the dirty, dirty things you say when I'm deep inside you."

Miller smacked me on the arm, but I could tell his body was reacting to my words. "I was thinking about taking the stage and doing a little karaoke duet, but now you've got me thinking about a totally different kind of entertainment."

The idea of us singing a lame-ass, sappy love song as a duet on stage for our friends to see made me throw back my head and laugh. "Let's do it."

Jack was more than happy to help us pull off the surprise a little bit later in the evening. We looked through the music selection and pointed to the same song at the same time, which caused us to burst into laughter.

"It's perfectly sappy," Miller said. "We're not brothers, but then again neither were they," he said about the artists.

"We're not righteous either." I smirked at Miller, and he replied with a playful wink.

We told Jack which song we wanted to perform, and I thought he was going to bust a nut laughing at us. Once he caught his breath, he took to the stage and announced a surprise performance as the entertainment for the night. I knew Miller and I were the last couple the crowd would expect to take the stage, which was evidenced by the complete silence in the room as they all stared at us, mouths agape.

We had already decided Bones would go first, and he didn't miss a beat once the music for The Righteous Brothers' song "You're My Soul and Inspiration" began to play. It was the sappiest song we could find, and we really amped it up with facial expressions and hand gestures to fit the tone of the song. We swayed along with the music and sang our hearts out, not caring if we were off-key or sounded terrible. I meant every word I sang, even if I played it off as stupid or sappy. Bones was my heart, and he gave me purpose.

We received lots of applause and cheers once the song was over. When we stepped offstage, we received our fair share of teasing too. We gave as good as we got, and the rest of the night was spent celebrating with our friends. Miller gave me a kiss hot enough to curl my toes when the clock struck midnight. It was the first time I'd received a New Year's kiss, and I decided it was my new favorite tradition.

We packed up our pets and their supplies and took them to Chase and Gray's house on the first day of January. They were so excited about our sexy getaway together that they'd offered to babysit our pets and take us to the airport the next morning. Oliver was pissed about the intruders and gave me an evil death glare as he sat on the arm of the couch beside me. I scratched his ears just how he liked, but he was still outraged. His fluffy orange tail never stopped swishing furiously from side to side.

I was so excited the night before our trip I hardly slept. Miller tried his best to fuck it out of me, but not even his talented hands, mouth, and cock could calm me enough to sleep. I finally dozed off a few hours before the alarm went off. I probably would've felt less zombie-like if I had just stayed awake.

I didn't relax until we were in the air and on our way to paradise. We drank mimosas to celebrate the occasion, so it wasn't long before I slipped my hand in Miller's, leaned into him, and fell asleep on his shoulder. I slept through breakfast, but Miller saved me some fruit and pastries. I kissed him to show him my appreciation, then dug into my breakfast.

"Are you guys going on your honeymoon?" our flight attendant asked when she brought me some coffee. I nearly choked on the bite of banana nut muffin I had just taken. I feared a walnut would be permanently lodged in my lung.

"Just a vacation." Miller chuckled while pounding my back to help me stop choking. "Scary thought, huh?" he asked once I was able to breathe without coughing. His eyes only held humor, not disgust that I might get choked up over marrying him or contempt at the idea of marrying me.

"No, I was just surprised by the question," I replied. "I don't know why it surprised me. It's obvious we're a couple from all the handholding and the way I curled into you to sleep. It would be a conclusion a lot of people would make if we were a straight couple. Still, it just caught me off guard."

I hoped that I'd explained my reaction well enough to him because the last thing I wanted to do was ruin the surprise I had planned. Inside my carryon bag was a small box from Tiffany and Co., and it contained something I hoped Miller would accept and wear for the rest of his life. Nerves tried to set in, but I pushed them aside. I wanted to enjoy every second of our vacation together and not spend any of it worrying about what his answer would be when I finally found the right moment to ask him that all-important question.

The flight only lasted about two and a half hours, so it was still bright and beautiful when our plane landed in Providenciales. The bright sunshine and warm temperature reinvigorated me once we stepped outside the airport and hailed a cab.

"This is so beautiful," Miller whispered in the back seat of the cab as we traveled along the ocean to our villa. "I've never seen water so blue in my life."

"It reminds me of your eyes." Miller's head whipped around to look at me. The ornery smile he wore told me he expected me to be joking, but I wasn't. It was the first thought that popped into my mind when I laid eyes on the water. His smile turned sweet when he saw I was sincere, and he leaned in to give me a kiss to match the moment.

"Smooth talker," he whispered against my lips.

The seaside villa was stunningly beautiful. The décor was a clean and crisp mix of stark whites, creamy beiges, and the occasional pop of blue or green. The shower was built for two and something I wanted us to experience. I loved sharing showers with Bones, and I would love it even more if we had a little bit more room, better water pressure, and a few more showerheads at home.

The canopy bed was something out of a fantasy with billowy white fabric draped around the four posts. I instantly envisioned making love to Miller with the French doors open and the wind blowing the sheer fabric around us. *Jesus, what was happening to me?*

"That bed," Miller said. "We're going to be making a lot of memories in that bed." He turned his lustful eyes on me, and I felt like there was no reason to wait until dark to begin making those memories.

I stripped the clothes slowly from his body, and he did the same for me. I captured his mouth in a seductively slow kiss as we tumbled onto the bed. The ocean breeze blowing through the open doors felt like a kiss against my skin as I worshipped every inch of Miller's body. I reveled in the combined scent of soap and man as I left no part of him untouched, loving the way he trembled beneath my lips and fingers.

I wanted so much more than just a new year for us; I wanted a new start to a life that marked him as mine forever. "Mine," I reminded him— as I often did—when I slid inside him. "All mine." I saw the same pleasure in Miller's expressive eyes I always did when I claimed him.

"Only yours, Jag." He wrapped his legs around my hips, holding tight to me. He gripped my ass cheeks with his hands and pulled me deeper inside him, which tore groans from both of us.

I resisted his urging to go faster and harder for a long time, drawing out our pleasure until I was nearly out of my mind with the need to come.

"Mine," I repeated as I pinned his arms above his head and pressed my chest to his. There wasn't a part of us that wasn't touching—hot, sweaty, and masculine skin on skin.

"Yours."

I kissed him feverishly to match the increased tempo of my thrusts. Miller's cock was pinned between our bodies, and I knew the combined friction of our rutting bodies and the angle of my penetration would be enough to send him over the edge. I dug my knees into the mattress and drove into him with everything I had and was rewarded with his shouts of pleasure as he came all over both of us. The slickness of his release and the way his body gripped me inside and out sent me tumbling after him into my climax.

"Welcome to paradise," Bones whispered against my lips.

We did make a lot of memories in that bed, in the gorgeous shower, in the ocean, and on the patio of our villa. We did other things that were non-sexual too like snorkeling, scuba diving, parasailing, and kayaking. Those things just usually got our blood pumping and led to the sexual memo-ry-making part of our vacation.

Before I knew it, I was running out of time to ask Miller the question that made my heart thump every time I thought about it. I was down to my final two nights, and I wanted to plan something spectacular, but I didn't know how when we were together all the time. I woke up before him the next morning and snuck out of our villa like a thief in the night. I made my way to the concierge and asked for a recommendation for the best, most romantic restaurant on the island. She helped me make reservations for six o'clock that evening, and I went back to our room after picking up some baked goods as an explanation for where I'd gone.

"Can we just lie around on the beach and be lazy today?" Miller asked when he woke up a short while later.

"Absolutely."

We alternated between splashing about in the ocean and lazing around on the beach before we climbed back into bed for a long nap. Once again, I woke up before Miller and had a lot of time to panic about the plans I had for that night. I hoped the seaside restaurant, candlelight, wine, and a *yes* would lead to the happiest moment of my life.

I decided to get into the shower to wake myself up, then start getting ready for the evening. I had convinced Bones to pack one nice outfit in case we went to a snazzier restaurant. He rolled his eyes at me, but he'd packed dressy clothes anyway. I thought the clothes might need to be pressed and decided I'd need to seek the assistance of our helpful concierge when I heard the phone in our room ringing.

We had kept our cellphones turned off the entire time we were on vacation. We decided no calls, texts, social media, or news while we were on our trip. Our friends and Miller's family knew to call our room if there was an emergency. The ringing felt like a bad omen, and I went cold all over, even though I stood beneath the hot spray of the shower. I shut the water off and wrapped a towel around my waist without bothering to dry off.

Miller answered the phone just as I exited the bathroom. I heard the hesitation in his voice and saw the worry in his eyes when they met mine. He also knew something was wrong. His face scrunched up as the person on the other end of the line began to speak. I couldn't tell what was being said, but I heard a frantic female voice coming through the phone.

"Mom, slow down. What's wrong?" Miller's voice was firm and urgent. My heart stuttered to a stop and threatened to shatter when I heard his anguished voice say, "No, Mom. No." His body trembled and his baby blues glistened with unshed tears. "That can't be. They made a mistake. It's a mistake." I rushed to his side and wrapped my arms around him, pulling him close to my side. I heard his mother's voice but not her words. Miller laid his head against my shoulder and gave in to the tears that had been threatening since the moment he'd answered the call. "I'll be home as soon as I can. I love you too, Mom."

I heard his mom disconnect the call on her end, but Miller still clung to the phone. I gently took it from his hand and hung it up. "What's wrong,

Bones?" It took him several long minutes before he could stop sobbing long enough to tell me what had happened.

"Darryl and Destiny were involved in a fatal car accident an hour ago." The words sounded like they were ripped out of his chest as he struggled to come to terms with what he'd just learned. "Someone ran a red light and hit them. I can't believe they're gone, Jag. They can't be gone."

"Where are Lucas and Lily?" I asked in a panic.

"Darryl and Destiny had just dropped them off at my mom and dad's so they could go on a dinner date." Miller turned his body and wrapped his arms around me. I held him tight and cried with him because I knew all too well how bad it hurt to lose someone you loved so much. We clung to each other for several minutes before he said, "I need to go home, Jag. Please take me home."

I laid him down on the bed and caressed the face I adored so much. "I'll make the arrangements," I told him. "I'll take care of everything, Bones." I pushed my sadness aside so I could focus on getting us back home to his family where he was needed.

He lay there quietly as I called the airline and moved our flight to the first available one, which happened to be early the next morning. I called Gray to let him know what had happened and asked him to pick us up at the airport when we arrived. I handed the phone to Miller because Gray wanted to talk to him, and I let his best friend offer him comfort while I packed our suitcases.

I climbed onto the bed once I was done and pulled Miller into my arms. We clung to each other and cried out our sorrow. It still didn't seem real, even though I knew it wasn't just a bad dream. I had known this kind of bone-deep devastation before and knew only real life could produce this kind of pain.

"Jag." Miller whispered my name in the dark at some point in the middle of the night. "Darryl and Destiny named me as Lucas and Lily's guardian in their wills." He took a trembling breath before he said, "My life is going to change drastically when we get back. Lucas and Lily have had their whole world turned upside down. I'll need to make them my top priority." My heart squeezed painfully in my chest from fear that he was ending our relationship, but his next words shattered that notion. "Please don't give up on us."

"Never going to happen, Bones." I spent the rest of the night telling him how much I loved him and how I'd never give him up. "I'll be there with you every step of the way." I whispered the words against his temple as the sun rose over the ocean.

CHAPTER
Twenty-Two

Miller

THE DAYS LEADING UP TO DARRYL AND DESTINY'S FUNERAL WERE spent in a grief-stricken fog with only a few moments of clarity, each one involving Jag. I recalled the way he'd guided me through the airport and the flight home. He'd never let go of my hand unless he needed his own to perform a function. He always knew what I needed before I did, whether it was a hug, a hand to hold, or a chest to lay my head on as I tried to come to terms with the fact that I would never see my only brother or his amazing wife ever again. The moment that stood out the most in my mind was the night before the funerals.

I had moved Lucas and Lily into my house because I just couldn't stay in Darryl and Destiny's house right then. My pain was too new and too raw, and I needed to be strong for my niece and nephew who were heartbroken, confused, and scared. I had been holding in every emotion, and it felt like I was going to explode. Just like he had on the previous days, Jag knew exactly what I needed.

"The kids are sound asleep. Urs and Mal are curled up with Lily, and Indy is sleeping with Lucas," Jag said as he got into bed beside me. He wrapped his arm around my shoulders and pulled me to him. "Talk, Bones. Get it all out because it's eating you alive. If you're angry, scream into your pillow. If you want to cry, lay your head against me and let it loose. Scared? I'm here to listen. Please don't pull away from the world like I did because it's not the answer. That's a lonely, horrible existence and not a place you want to go. I'm a big boy, so lay it on me."

I had so many thoughts firing through my brain that it was almost hard to organize them into anything that would make a coherent conversation, but that wasn't what Jag had asked me to do. He didn't want me to give a prepared lecture. He wanted me to unburden my heart and share what I was going through.

"I feel all those things." I leaned in as close to him as I could get. "I'm beyond angry, Jag. I'm so fucking furious, and I worry I am capable of doing horrible things. What email notification on that asshole's phone was so fucking important it couldn't wait?" I hated the man who had run the red light and struck Darryl's car. "Senseless, Jag, completely senseless. He's a forty-year-old man who knows better. I want him to pay, Jag. I'm not sure jail is harsh enough. Then I realize he must live with what he did for the rest of his life. He can never escape his actions. Ever. He killed two people in the prime of their lives and stole parents from two young children. The mature, reasonable adult in me realizes no amount of jail time or financial penalty will ever bring Darryl and Destiny back, and a vengeful mind is a complete waste of energy." Tears of frustration began to leak from my eyes. "I don't want to be mature and reasonable about this, Jag. I want to kick his ass and rage at the unfairness of it all."

"Me too, Bones. Me too." Jag kissed the top of my head and ran his hand up and down my arm. He didn't try to tell me I was wrong. He didn't use any clichéd phrases about time healing all wounds or putting one foot in front of the other. He listened as promised.

"I'm devastated, Jag." My voice broke. It seemed like my heart kept breaking over and over as grief flowed through my veins in a never-ending loop. "Darryl was my champion, my dragon slayer." I swallowed hard to dislodge the emotion choking me. "So many memories of us flash through my mind. The forts we used to build as kids, the tricks we played on each other as teens, and the unconditional way he'd accepted me when I told him I was gay. Darryl was the absolute best big brother I could ever have, and now there's this gaping hole in my life. I want him back. I want this to be a nightmare. I want to wake up." Jag repositioned us so we were lying down instead of sitting up. We rolled so we were facing each other, and his arms folded around me. He had lost a brother too, so he knew exactly how I felt. I accepted Jag's love and comfort and let them wash over me as I tried to come to terms with my new reality.

"I'm really scared. I'm so afraid of doing the wrong thing for Lucas and Lily." I wasn't ashamed to admit my worries to him. There was no judgment in his eyes, only understanding. "What if moving them here was the worst thing I could've done? Maybe they need to be surrounded by their mom and dad's things, Jag. Maybe I'm being too selfish and not putting their needs first. Being their favorite uncle for the day or the weekend is not the same thing as being their parent. I could really mess this up."

"You're amazing with them, Bones." Jag's praise soothed a little of the panic I had been feeling. "Can I make a suggestion, though?" he asked hesitantly.

"Of course." It wasn't like him to ask before he offered an opinion, but we were facing a completely different set of circumstances.

"You might consider contacting a child psychologist who can help you work through things like where the kids should live and give you advice for their different stages of grief." Jag paused to gauge my reaction and continued when he didn't see hesitance in my expression. It was the best suggestion I had heard about handling the kids, and I had received a lot of unsolicited advice on the matter. "We work with several psychologists through our law practice, and I've learned they have a lot of ways to help determine what kids are going through and offer suggestions to ease the turmoil. Kids go through the same stages of grief as adults, but they process each one differently. Sometimes they internalize things more, and other times they act out because they don't know how to deal with their emotions. I've heard so many people tell you what you should be doing these last few days. They mean well, Bones, but unless they've been in this exact situation, it's just a lot of hot air. What Lucas and Lily need right now is love, patience, and comfort, which you've provided in spades."

I expelled a breath as I realized I wasn't alone. Jag had been right there with me as we comforted the confused and heartbroken children. Not only did I have Jag, but I had all our friends too. Chase, Xavier, and Liam had brought us food every night since we'd gotten home. Ava and Gram had packed up the kids' clothes and toys and brought them to my house. Gray, Ben, and Jack took turns playing or coloring with them when I needed to handle funeral arrangements or just needed a moment to take a breath. Then there was Jag, my constant, loving shadow. As heartbroken as I was, I was still aware of the amazing people and awesome love surrounding me. Darryl and Destiny would be pleased to know Lucas and Lily had such a wonderful extended family.

"One of us needs to learn how to cook," I said randomly. "Chase, Xavier, and Liam aren't going to feed us forever. Destiny will haunt my ass if I feed her babies takeout until they leave for college." I pictured the scowl she used to wear when she discussed my eating habits, and I couldn't hold back the laughter. Then I wished she could make fun of me just one more time, and my laughter changed to tears. My laugh had sounded foreign to my ears as if I had expected grief to totally consume every part of my personality. My tears felt like an old comfortable friend by that point, and I allowed them to flow.

"I only know how to make your mom's stuffed green peppers," Jag said. "We can't eat that every night. Liam wants to be a chef. Maybe he can give us some basic lessons so we won't starve or be forced to exist on pizza rolls, chicken patties, and stuffed peppers." Jag's suggestion warmed my heart and helped me focus on doing something positive versus just wallow in sadness. I had accepted I would experience many phases of grief in the days, weeks, and months to come, but it made me feel better if I could find solutions and not just discover more problems. Snippets of conversations I'd overheard from Destiny's parents floated to the forefront of my mind. "I think I'm going to have a whole other set of problems that may require your services."

"Destiny's parents." Of course he knew who I meant. "You're worried they'll sue for custody of the kids." Jag pulled me closer as if he could shield me from the possibility.

"Be honest with me, Jag. Do they stand a chance?" I held my breath while I waited for his answer.

"Based on what?" Jag ran his hand over my face in a tender gesture, but I saw the shrewd, brilliant legal mind shining in his dark eyes. "Darryl and Destiny chose you to be the legal guardian of their children. They were of sound mind when they made the decision. You have the means to provide for them and, more importantly, the desire to do so."

"I think this is coming from a place of grief and guilt more than a true desire to raise Lucas and Lily," I said. It felt so good to be able to admit my feelings out loud. "Destiny was never close to her parents, and they've never really taken an active role in the kids' lives. It seems like Destiny and Darryl chose to celebrate holidays and occasions with our family rather than hers."

"What about the sister?"

"Vanessa and Destiny were very close, even though there was a fifteen-year age gap between them. She's a great person and super smart like her sister. She's in med school at Johns Hopkins and will start residency after she graduates this summer. She supported me as the choice for guardian when Lucas was born six years ago, and I don't see her changing her mind at this point."

"Do you think she'd be supportive enough to defend you in court if needed? I know it's not something we want to think about, but going to court and having a judge decide custody is the worst-case scenario." He dropped a kiss on my lips before saying, "You asked for my legal opinion, and I'm trying to look at the whole picture. I'm not trying to scare you, Bones. I don't think they'll win if this goes before a judge. They'd have to prove you're unfit or that they're better fit to raise Lucas and Lily. You are the best choice for those kids. A judge might grant them visitation rights, so you might want to let that sink in and process." Jag took a deep breath, and I could tell he was pondering whether or not he should share the rest of his thoughts.

"Say what you're thinking, Jag. Don't hold back on me now."

"Are they going to make an issue of your sexuality? Have they ever given any indication or have you had the feeling that they'll make an issue of a gay man raising their grandchildren? I'm just trying to cover all our bases."

"They've never said anything or behaved in a manner that makes me think that, but I've been around them more over the last two days than I have in the fifteen years Darryl and Destiny were married." I blew out a frustrated breath as, once again, my mind became overwhelmed with thoughts and feelings. "I guess we'll just have to be patient and see what happens."

"I'll do anything you want me to, except stay away from you. I'm not going anywhere, Bones. I love you."

I loved hearing his words of commitment, but the look in his eyes was what penetrated through my tumultuous feelings. "I'm sorry we haven't…" Jag pressed his hand over my mouth to prevent me from talking.

"Don't." Jag closed his eyes and shook his head. I saw worry in his eyes once he reopened them. "I'm sorry if I've given you the impression you're nothing more than sex to me." His voice broke, and he cleared his throat before he spoke again. "It was so much more from the very first kiss, and we both know it. You breathed life into me, and I knew I was irrevocably changed." He gave me a sweet smile before he continued. "We made jokes about love, we had fun with our puzzles and games, but the truth is, I meant every sappy word and gesture. The truth is, I've always felt like one of those oddly shaped puzzle pieces that never fits no matter how you turn it or how hard you push. I just didn't fit. Then I met you, and I knew you were the piece I had been missing all along. You're my perfect fit. Don't you dare apologize for not feeling like having sex when your universe has been turned upside down and your heart is broken. Don't think for even a second that I won't wait patiently for you to be ready. Because I will. There is no sexual encounter with a stranger that would ever be worth losing you."

"Jag." I hadn't realized I was crying again until Jag wiped my tears. "At least they're happy ones this time." I gave him a watery smile before I kissed his firm lips. "You're my perfect fit too. I didn't even know I was missing anything until you came into my life." I burrowed my head beneath his chin and closed my eyes as exhaustion from the emotional roller coaster ride I was on set in. I felt a lot better after talking my worries over with Jag.

"We'll get through this together, Bones. I won't let you down." Those were the last words I heard before I drifted off to sleep.

CHAPTER
Twenty-Three

JJ

I LEARNED A LOT ABOUT MYSELF AND MILLER—BOTH INDIVIDUALLY and as a couple—in the days following the tragic loss of Darryl and Destiny. I discovered I was able to put Miller's needs before my own and give him the love and support he needed. I realized Miller was the most beautiful person ever put on this earth, and I was beyond lucky to have him in my life. I recognized there was nothing we couldn't handle, and there were no limits to what I would do for him.

It sounded ridiculous to say someone was beautiful in their grief, but it was true. Miller handled himself with poise and dignity as he arranged both the funerals and moved his niece and nephew into his home. He accepted the help our friends offered with grace instead of falling on foolish pride. He allowed himself to mourn in the privacy of our bedroom where

I held him each night as he released everything he had kept buried during the day. I couldn't bring Darryl and Destiny back, but I could be his safe place to let go and grieve openly.

I was afraid I was smothering him in my attempt to help, but Miller assured me that wasn't the case with a few simple words. "I need you." He'd said the words out loud, but even if he hadn't, I would've recognized the look in his eyes. I tried my best to be everything Miller, Lucas, and Lily needed, even if I wasn't sure what I was doing half the time.

The day of the funeral was frigid and gray to match the somber mood of those gathered to say their final farewell to Darryl and Destiny. Ava stayed with Lucas and Lily at Miller's parents' house because it was decided they were too young to understand what was going on and it could be a very traumatic experience for them. Every decision Miller and I made going forward would put their needs first. Sometimes I was scared as hell I wouldn't be enough and would fail them, but then Lucas or Lily would reach for me for comfort, and I'd forget to be scared.

"I struggled with what to say today," Miller said as he stood at the podium in front of the mourners gathered at the funeral home. He cleared his throat as he gathered himself and continued. I sent him vibes of strength so he could get through the eulogy. His eyes met mine briefly as if he felt them. "I can't seem to find the words to properly express the sorrow I feel over losing my brother and his amazing wife. All of you are feeling their loss just as deeply, so those words aren't needed. Instead, I want to talk about the people they were and the ways they made me a better man." There wasn't a dry eye in the room as Miller spoke eloquently about the love he had for Darryl and Destiny. He added lighthearted stories that also made the crowd laugh. "As painful as it is that we lost them both, I know my brother would not have wanted to live in a world without Destiny, and I'm certain she felt the same way. I'll spend every day remembering the love they shared and the joy they brought into my life, and I will raise Lucas and Lily in a way that will make them proud and honor their memory."

Miller reached for my hand when he returned to the seat beside mine. He held himself together for the rest of the funeral but couldn't hold back his grief during the graveside service. It was the worst day of his life, and I wished I could do something to take away his pain. All I could do was hold on to him and hope he took some comfort in my presence.

Everyone gathered at his parents' house after we left the cemetery. Lucas and Lily rushed to us the minute we walked through the door. They may not have understood what was happening that day, but they felt the somberness of the occasion.

"I missed you, Uncle Jag," Lily said as she tucked her head beneath my chin. She wrapped her little arms around my neck, which matched the viselike grip they both had on my heart.

"I missed you too, buttercup."

I had noticed over the last few days that both Lucas and Lily showed signs of anxiety when Miller and I left them for even short periods. Miller had decided to contact one of the psychologists my firm worked with because he wanted to make sure he was doing his best by them. My eyes met Miller's, and I knew he'd be making the call first thing in the morning.

"I want to go home to Indy," Lucas said to Miller. The kids found a lot of comfort in the pets, and it was amazing to watch how the animals instinctively knew how much they were needed.

"We'll go home soon, big guy. I'm sure Indy misses you too."

The kids stuck close to our sides as the late morning carried into early afternoon. I could tell Lily was dragging, but I also knew Miller felt obligated to spend time with the people who had stopped by to share memories and offer a kind word.

"How about I read you a story, buttercup?"

"Please, Uncle Jag." The girl loved her books more than any toy she owned. "You want to hang out with us, champ?"

"Sure." Lucas wasn't ever as excited about story time as his sister, but he did appreciate a book with an adventurous storyline. He was so much like Miller sometimes that it wasn't funny.

Marilyn kept a basket of books for her grandchildren in her sitting room, which was a quiet nook away from the main flow of the house. I immediately felt better once I walked into the comfortable, quiet space.

They both picked out a book, then tucked themselves against my sides. Lily fell asleep before I was midway through her book, but I continued to read until the end. Lucas handed me the book he'd chosen, and I held it for him while he read it to me. There were only a few words he got stuck on, but I helped him sound them out. When he was finished, he set the book aside and snuggled his head against my chest just like his sister. It wasn't long before he was asleep too.

I heard high heels on the hardwood floor in the hallway outside the sitting room. Destiny's sister, Vanessa, rounded the corner and came to a stop when she saw both kids were sound asleep. I could tell by her expression that she wanted to talk but didn't want to wake them.

"They're sound sleepers," I told her. "Come on in."

"We haven't had much of a chance to talk," she said softly. "It's been so crazy, and I keep telling myself it's just a dream. I'm going to wake up and all this heartache"—she covered her heart with her hand—"will go away. But I'm not dreaming. My sister and Darryl really are gone, and these sweet angels have had their lives turned upside down." She crouched down in front of me and ran her hands over their heads. "My mom and dad are upset because I refuse to challenge Miller for guardianship of Lucas and Lily." She looked into my eyes and offered a sad smile. "Miller was always Darryl and Destiny's choice, and it's the right one. Now they have you too, and they're just where they need to be." She stood and sat in the wingback chair beside the sofa.

"Are your parents going to make things harder than they already are for Miller? I have to be honest with you, Vanessa, they're going to have to go through me first to get these kids away from him. I will use every resource available to me—and they are considerable—to make sure Lucas and Lily stay with Miller because no one will love them more than he does. No one will look out for them the way he will." Outrage started to build, and I took several breaths to calm myself. "This is a terrible and tragic loss, but them deciding they want two small children out of guilt and grief is not the answer."

"I agree," Vanessa said calmly, "which is why I told them I would not support their decision if they pursued custody of the kids. I also told them I'd give a deposition in favor of Miller if they persisted."

"What did they say?"

"They're pissed, of course. I think my mother more than my father. I feel like it's a knee-jerk reaction for my father right now, but once he's had time to think things through, I hope he'll calm down and use his influence over my mother." Vanessa blew out a frustrated breath. "Honestly, my parents weren't that involved in our lives growing up or even as adults. They've engaged very little with Lucas and Lily, so it's really absurd to think that they suddenly want to be guardians of two active, rambunctious kids. I agree with your assessment that their decision right now is being based on grief and guilt."

"Thank you for your honesty and candor, Vanessa. It's a very difficult time for them, and I can understand their grief over losing their daughter and the anxiety of not seeing her children. Miller would never want to keep Lucas and Lily away from them. You have to know he doesn't operate that way."

"I do know that, and once they get to know him better, they will too."

"I must ask you something, and I'm sorry if it makes you uncomfortable. If you really support Miller raising the kids, then I need to be fully aware of all the circumstances of any potential custody hearing." I looked down to make sure my snuggle buddies were still sound asleep before I asked my question. "Are they going to make an issue out of Miller being gay or that he and I are practically living together?"

"They have honestly never said anything negative about Miller's sexuality. They knew he was gay when Darryl and Destiny signed the documents to make him the kids' legal guardian upon their deaths, and they never made any derogatory comments then. However"—she tilted her head to the side—"they probably never thought something like this would happen. Who does? No one really thinks it will, but they plan just in case. Luckily, Darryl and Destiny were prepared, and their wishes should be honored."

"I guess we'll just have to wait and see what happens," I replied. I didn't learn anything new, except that Vanessa was willing to support Miller as Lucas's and Lily's guardian. That part was great news.

Vanessa leaned forward and patted my knee. "I'll give Miller a call once I know what my parents decide to do." She rose to her feet. "I'm going to retrieve them and take them home. It's been nice meeting you, Jag, but I wish it were under happier circumstances."

"Likewise," I said. "I'm sorry for your loss, Vanessa."

"Thank you. Thank God I have these two as little reminders." She leaned in and kissed their heads. "Give them extra hugs from me later, okay?"

"You bet."

I stayed in the sitting room for a long time after Vanessa left. I wanted to seek Miller out and tell him what Vanessa said, but I didn't want to wake up the munchkins to do it. I could tell him later once we got back home. I leaned my head back against the couch to rest my eyes for just a few minutes. The next thing I knew, Miller was waking me with a soft kiss on my forehead. The light in the room had faded, and it was obvious we'd been asleep for quite some time.

"Let's go home," Miller said softly.

CHAPTER
Twenty-Four

Miller

I DECIDED TO TAKE A BRIEF LEAVE OF ABSENCE FROM THE UNIVERSITY so I could handle some estate issues and spend as much time with Lucas and Lily as possible. One of the first things I did after the funeral was meet with Dr. Lauren Tannehill, who was one of the child psychologists Jag had recommended. I needed to be certain I was doing the right things for my niece and nephew.

"All kids react differently to grief," she told me kindly. "Kids are resilient and most cope remarkably well. The most common emotion they feel is fear, but sometimes they show it differently. Some act out, some stop talking or eating as if they're depressed, and some try to mask what they're feeling with humor and a smile. The most important thing for them right now, Miller, is a consistent routine they can rely on."

"That makes a lot of sense," I replied. "My boyfriend and I worry they're showing signs of separation anxiety when we leave. They cling to us when we return as if they were afraid we wouldn't come back. I mean, that's what happened with their mom and dad, so I think they're worried the same will happen with us."

"That is an understandable reaction for children who just lost both parents. The only thing that will assuage their fear is time, patience, and routine." She leaned forward and offered a warm smile. "No one expects you to quit your job and stay home around the clock. That isn't reasonable, and it could be unhealthy. In fact, you can't give in to their fears or enable them to allow their fear to take over."

"I've taken a leave of absence to be with them and make sure they feel settled. I hate to leave them when they get so upset." Tension and worry were evident in my voice.

"Try this, Miller. Leave the house for short periods of time at first, then gradually prolong your absence. You'll have to return to work eventually, so it would be better to work them up to a longer absence than to just one day be gone for your entire workday. When you get home, you should comfort them briefly, then ask about their days. Get their minds off your absence and their worry. It's part of the routine they need to get used to. Did their mom stay home with them?"

"No. They had a nanny who came in each day to look after the kids while they worked. I've been lucky enough to retain her services, which I think will be great for the kids. They know Chloe and love her as much as she loves them."

"That's great news. She's someone they're familiar with, and she'll bring them comfort as they transition into their new routines."

It was late afternoon before I left her office, and I was eager to get home. Jag had taken the day off to hang out with the kids so I could meet with the estate lawyer, life insurance agent, and Lauren. It was an emotionally draining day, and I was looking forward to a big hug from my guy. There was a lot I needed from Jag, but I wasn't sure when we were going to get some alone time so he could give me what I'd been craving from him for days.

Realistically, I knew couples with kids still found time to be intimate, but there's sex, then there's good sex. Sure, Jag and I found time to be together once the kids fell asleep, but we were always careful not to wake them. I needed to make noise. I needed to ride his cock until I forgot all the worries that kept building inside me until it felt like my head might explode. My body started to react to the image of riding Jag like a bronco. It was a very uncomfortable ride home, and in fact, the fantasy caused me to sit out in the driveway for a few extra minutes as I willed my dick to settle down.

I found Jag in the kitchen when I walked into the house. I inhaled, smelling zesty beef. "That smells so good," I said as I wrapped my arms around his waist. "Liam's lessons are working."

"It's just tacos," Jag replied.

"Where're the munchkins?" The smell of food was the first thing I noticed, and the second was the silence.

"Your mom and dad picked them up for dinner and a movie," he said. Just like that, my dick was hard enough to pound nails. We were finally alone and could make as much noise as we wanted. I pushed my erection into his ass. "I see you don't have a problem with that."

"Stop cooking and fuck me." I dropped my hands from around his waist and walked out of the kitchen. A few seconds later, I heard Jag's footsteps behind me. "Don't forget to turn off the stove."

"Fuck." I laughed as he retreated to the kitchen to prevent a ruined dinner and potential fire. That gave me a tiny bit of extra time, so I dashed up the stairs, ripped my clothes off, and laid myself in the middle of our bed. "Damn, Bones, you're so sexy. I can't believe you're mine," he said when he came through our bedroom door.

"I'm all yours." I spread my legs to give Jag incentive as he peeled out of his clothes and climbed onto the bed.

"Roll over so I can give you a massage." Jag's dark, velvety voice was a caress against my ear before he nipped my earlobe sharply.

"You don't have to seduce me, Jag. I'm yours for the taking." I thrust my hips so my cock rubbed against his to demonstrate how ready I was for him.

"It's not about seduction tonight, Bones. It's about demonstrating all the ways I love you, not just lubing you up and plowing into your body. Roll over." The look in his eyes promised that having his hands on my body would be the hottest foreplay we ever had. I rolled over without another word and was grateful I had when his skilled hands began working the knots out of my neck and shoulders. "I promise you'll get to do plenty of screaming soon."

His mouth joined in on the action as he kissed my skin while massaging his way along my spine. My need was so great I couldn't keep my hips from gyrating against the bed beneath me. The dual sensation of my cock rubbing against the duvet and Jag's hands and mouth working my flesh had me closer to the edge than I wanted to be.

Jag left the bed briefly to get a condom and lube from the nightstand. I started to roll over, but a firm swat on my ass stopped me. "I wasn't done massaging you, Bones."

"I got your bone," I replied tartly but complied with his request.

"And I've got yours too." Jag slid his erection along the crease of my ass while his hands kneaded my ass cheeks.

I was never so happy to hear the *snap* of the lube bottle opening as I was right then. So much had been building up inside me, and I needed intimacy with Jag to feel centered again. My ass clenched tightly in anticipation and excitement as he drizzled the lube along my crack. Jag chuckled darkly when I raised my ass in search of friction and penetration.

"Slow down, Bones. We have plenty of time. I don't want to hurt you." I preferred a smaller amount of lube so I felt more friction and a little more bite when he penetrated me. Jag always worried he would hurt me, so he took his time stretching me open beforehand.

"I need to feel you, Jag. Please." I wasn't ashamed of begging for his cock. Given the chance, I'd beg for it daily. "I want it hard, long, and rough."

Jag began to tease my hole before he stretched me with one finger, then two.

The images I'd had earlier of riding him in a frenzy returned, and I took what I needed. I rolled away from him and looked up into his chocolate eyes. I tackled him to the bed and caught his surprised gasp in my mouth as I ravished his lips. I blindly searched for the condom packet while I sucked his tongue into my mouth. I pulled away from his kiss and held up the condom in victory once I found it.

"What are you up to?" Jag asked as I kissed a path down to the cock I couldn't get enough of. "Bones…Oh my…Christ that feels good." I loved when I turned him on so much his words came out jumbled and incoherent, which was usually the case when I sucked his dick as far into my mouth as I could take him. "Fuck, Bones. I won't last." He reached down to pull my head off his cock, but instead, he gripped my hair and thrust his hips upward, rubbing himself against my tongue. His words indicated he wanted me to stop, but his actions were the exact opposite. I tasted his precum on my tongue and could tell he was right on the edge. "Evil bastard," he grouched when I wrapped my hand tightly around the base of his cock to prevent him from coming.

I crawled on top of Jag and kissed him until he came back from the edge and only then did I roll the condom down his hard length. We kept our eyes locked on one another as I positioned myself above him and lined his dick up with my opening. I felt greedy and hungry for him, so I wasted no time taking Jag inside me. I groaned loudly as the bite and slight burn of his penetration sent thrills throughout my body. I welcomed the contradiction of feelings that he always gave me because any brief discomfort was followed by the highest pleasure I had ever known.

That night was no different as I started my ride at a slow, leisurely pace while my body adjusted to his girth and length. Worries and concerns about the future were the furthest thing from my mind when I placed my hands on his shoulders for leverage and raised and lowered myself on his dick at a quicker pace. My head felt so heavy I wanted to close my eyes and let it fall back as pleasure rippled through me, but I didn't want to look away from him.

"Take what you need, Bones. Ride me. Use me." Jag's words were raw as they escaped through gritted teeth.

I pinned his arms above his head, leaned my body over him, and adjusted the angle of his penetration. I took Jag's mouth in a kiss as rough as the wild ride I took us on, only separating long enough to shout in pleasure as I came all over his stomach. I collapsed against Jag's chest, not caring that I was lying in my own cum. Jag grabbed my hips and thrust upward a few more times before he bit my shoulder and filled the condom.

We lay there, holding one another for a while longer, before showering together. Even there, I didn't want to be separated from him for longer than it took to wash off. I was afraid I was becoming too needy and would drive him away. The soft look in Jag's eyes said differently, and I decided to quit worrying about our relationship because it seemed like the one solid thing I could count on.

"You're better for me than any drug or mixed drink," I said as I snuggled closer to him as the shower rained down on us.

"I do what I can," he said with false bravado, which made me laugh.

"Save your bragging until after we've eaten the food you prepared." He slapped my ass hard in retaliation for doubting his kitchen skills. The sound of a wet hand smacking wet taut flesh and my responding yelp echoed through the shower.

It felt so good to have that carefree moment with him, regardless of how short it would be. I had no regrets about accepting guardianship of Lily and Lucas. None. But that didn't mean I wasn't exhausted most of the time nor did it mean I wasn't grateful for the break.

"I'm starving," I admitted. As much as I wanted to continue our bedroom Olympics, I hadn't eaten since breakfast.

"Let's feed you, then." Jag gave me a long kiss before he turned off the water and grabbed our towels off the hooks outside the shower.

Once dressed, I helped him put together the rest of the simple meal. It might not have been five-star quality, but it was delicious. It was better than any tacos I'd ever had, except for the ones I'd eaten at authentic Mexican restaurants.

"This guacamole is delicious," I said as I spooned more onto a third taco. "This is so much better than I expected. I can't wait to see what else Liam teaches you."

"*Us,*" Jag corrected. "You're going to learn some skills too." The look he gave me dared me to argue with him.

"Fine," I said huffily, "but don't get pissed if my food turns out better than yours." There was absolutely no chance of that happening, but I could at least try not to poison us with undercooked meat.

"Not likely." I launched a tortilla chip at him across the table. "Someone wants to get rough, huh?"

I was about to accept the offer I heard in his words and saw in his dark eyes, but my cellphone vibrated with an incoming text from my mom.

This is your ten-minute warning. The prince and princess are ready to come home so we left the movie early. Put your clothes on and be ready. She followed her warning with a smiley face emoji.

My mom has jokes. "Playtime is over," I said to Jag, then relayed the message. "Thank you for a wonderful night."

"It was hot sex and tacos," he said to downplay his role in my peaceful mood. He was never comfortable accepting compliments or praise.

"It was so much more than that, and you know it." I stood from the table and reached for his hand. I led us to the living room and pulled him down to sit beside me on the couch. I angled my body to lean into him and threw my legs over his. Jag wrapped me in his arms and laid his head on top of mine. "This is what I want to do for the next ten minutes."

"You got it, Bones."

One thing always pierced through the heartbreak and sorrow of losing Destiny and Darryl, followed by the riotous emotions of trying to comfort two shattered, innocent hearts—Jag's unwavering love for all of us.

CHAPTER
Twenty-Five

JJ

TWO VERY IMPORTANT THINGS HAPPENED ON THE SAME DAY IN THE middle of January—one was expected but disappointing while the other was beautiful and heartwarming. Miller was notified by certified mail that Destiny's parents, Herbert and Joann Candless, were challenging Miller's guardianship appointment of Lucas and Lily, and Gray and Chase's little girl arrived safely into the world. We chose to focus on the beautiful gift the Wrights had received that day instead of the forthcoming custody battle with Destiny's parents.

"We're going to need a bigger vehicle," Miller stated as we made our way to the hospital to meet the newest member of our ever-expanding family. Chloe came over to spend time with the kids so we could celebrate with our friends. I loved how Miller refused to entertain the notion that

Lucas and Lily would live with anyone except us, making the need for a bigger vehicle a necessity.

"I'm not driving a minivan," I replied, leveling him with a serious look. "I've accepted and embraced every single challenge that has come our way, but I'm drawing the line there. I can see us with a sleek crossover SUV but not a van."

"I don't think you're embracing the beauty a van could bring into our lives," Miller said. He sounded serious, but it was hard to tell with him sometimes. Miller could say the most ridiculous thing in a humorless voice while wearing a deadpan expression, so it was hard to tell if he was being serious or joking. "Some of those vans are very luxurious," he said defensively. "They have comfy leather seats that probably recline back really far and television screens that fold down so you can watch movies."

"Hell no." I shook my head playfully. "I'm rolling up to Lucas's and Lily's games, concerts, art shows, or plays in something badass. I think you should leave family transportation to me. I'll make sure the kids aren't mortified. I'm thinking a Range Rover."

"White?"

"Shows too much dirt," I rebutted. "Dark gray or black," I countered.

Miller pursed his lips and tipped his head slightly while he pondered my suggestion. "I could see us driving a Range Rover." He nodded as the idea took root. "Tell you what, let's take the kids to look at them this weekend so they can help us pick."

"Deal." Like Miller, I refused to play it safe. There were no guarantees a judge would side with us, but I loved our chances. My gut told me everything was going to be okay while my heart continued to expand with more love than I'd ever thought possible.

The waiting room was packed with familiar faces as we waited to meet little Miss Wright. Abigail had gone into labor in the middle of the night. They didn't call any of us because they were focused on Abigail, who was scared out of her mind. I'll never forget the happy tears in Gray's voice when he called to tell us their daughter had arrived.

"It won't be much longer," Gram said excitedly when she greeted us.

"I can't wait to meet her. I wish those brats would have at least told me her name."

"You don't know either?"

"They wanted it to be a surprise." Gram rolled her eyes in exasperation. "I get that she's their little princess, but they're not William and Kate who need to make some royal announcement."

"Okay, guys, they're ready for us." Chase's voice pulled us away from our conversations, and we all turned to look at him. His eyes were red and swollen from crying, but the smile on his face told us they were happy tears. "They gave us a private room so we could stay with her tonight since she can't come home until tomorrow." We all converged on Chase at once. He made sure to hug each one of us to thank us for coming as if we'd miss out on the happiest day of their lives.

Gray was sitting in a recliner rocking his little angel when we entered the room. There were so many of us that we could hardly fit, and I half expected the nursing staff to tell us we'd have to visit in shifts.

"Me first," Gram said as she threw elbows to get to her great-granddaughter. "What's my girl's name?"

Gray rose from his chair with the sleeping infant. He placed his daughter in Gram's waiting arms. "Everyone, meet Grace Abigail Wright." Gram started to cry as she kissed Grace's little forehead. Chase wrapped his arm around Gram's shoulders and kissed the top of her head.

"We named her Grace after my mom and Abigail to honor her birth mother, who is a remarkable young lady," Chase told us.

"It's a beautiful name," Gram told him. She sat in the vacated recliner and gently pulled off Grace's knitted hat. "Look at all that hair," she cooed. The kid was sporting a head full of curly, black hair. "I can't wait to see what color eyes she has." Gram ran her finger softly against Grace's cheek and kissed her forehead several times.

"You're going to share her, right, Agnes?" Ava asked.

Grace spent her very first day getting passed from one joyful person to the next. That little gal had no idea how much she was already loved, but it was a beautiful thing to witness. If I had learned anything the last several months, it was that families came in many different forms. There's the family that you were born into, the family you chose, and the family that chose you. Each was beautifully unique in their own way. For those of us who hadn't had a great start in life, the families we chose and those that chose us were the ones that meant the most.

Not only had I redefined the way I thought of families, I'd learned to forgive my mother. Xavier helped me to see past the addiction to the person she was beneath. By doing so, I allowed myself to remember the happy times and all the ways she tried to make up for my early childhood once she got sober. I forgave her for the crappy choices she made and no longer blamed her or myself for Will's death.

The sad reality was that tragic events touched us all at some point. We could give up and quit living, or we could live for those we'd lost. We could put up a Christmas stocking to remember them or eat a piece of cake in honor of their birthday. We could donate to a charity they believed in and make them proud of the person we had become. We could choose to focus on living and loving, or we could choose to focus on the loss.

As much as Miller was missing his brother and Destiny, he put one foot in front of the other and focused on living. He made Lucas, Lily, and me his primary focus and his source of comfort on tough days. Grace's birthday was a great day. I probably wouldn't admit to anyone just how precious I thought Miller looked holding a tiny little girl in his arms or the sudden urge I felt to see him hold a child of our own someday. I loved the way he cooed to her and how comfortable he was holding a newborn, where I was terrified I'd break her.

I was quiet on the way home because so many thoughts were cycling through my brain. I kept wondering when I should ask Miller to marry me and how. It clearly wasn't the right time when we were heading into a custody battle, but as soon as it was over, I wanted to show him how committed I was to our future and our family.

Lucas and Lily had their typical reaction when we got home, but we did as Lauren had instructed. We greeted them exuberantly, then quickly changed the focus to take their minds off their worry. It seemed to be working so far, and I had hope that in a few weeks they wouldn't panic when we left the house.

The kids went back to coloring the pictures they'd been working on when we came in, and I pulled Miller into the kitchen. We could keep an eye on them, but we had a bit of privacy so I could talk to him about the custody issue.

"I think it would be best if I let Paul represent you at the hearing," I told Miller. I could tell he was going to object, and I quickly continued so I could finish what I needed to say. "I'm too personally involved in your case. I worry I can't be objective when it comes to you and the kids. Paul is brilliant, and he's agreed to meet with you in the morning."

"I don't want Paul, Jag. I want you." I loved hearing how much he wanted and needed me in all aspects of his life, but he needed someone who would maintain their professionalism. "I don't want someone who is cold and detached. I want someone who passionately defends my right to these kids." He tilted his head toward Lucas and Lily. "You're the one who's helping me take care of them and sees firsthand how much I love them and how devoted to them I am." Miller moved closer and wrapped his arms loosely around my waist.

"I don't want someone who's going to recite family law by rote," he added. "I want someone who will go to the mat for me and the kids. You're that someone, not Paul. I'm sure he's a good guy, but he's not you." Miller shook his head vigorously. "He doesn't love me, and he doesn't love Lucas and Lily, but you do. I need this to be personal because it's the most personal thing to ever happen to me. These are *our* kids now, Jag. They trust us, and they need us. I trust you to protect them better than anyone else."

I knew he was right, but that didn't erase the fear I had of letting him and the kids down. If the unthinkable happened and the Candlesses were awarded custody, I selfishly wanted someone else to blame. Miller had seen right through my objection to the fear I didn't want to admit.

"You won't lose, and you won't let us down. I know it in my heart. You need to do this to prove it to yourself more than you need to demonstrate it to me or them."

I pulled Miller tighter against me and kissed his forehead. "Okay." I felt his relieved breath against my neck. "Thank you for having faith in me."

"Perfect fit," he said, repeating the words I had said to him the night before the funerals. I dropped a sweet kiss on his lips to show him how much his words meant to me. They tasted so sweet I couldn't resist another little taste, then another. Miller didn't hesitate to show appropriate affection in front of the kids. Their parents had kissed and hugged all the time, and he felt it would seem unnatural to them if we didn't do the same. I heard Lucas's and Lily's childish giggles and turned to see what had made them so happy. They were both looking at us and smiling with so much innocence that their laughter became contagious. "It seems our puzzle turned out to be bigger and to have more pieces than what we'd first thought."

"Uncle Miller and Uncle Jag, sitting in a tree. K-i-s-s-i-n-g." Lucas sang the same song we'd heard him sing to his parents on several occasions. Miller was right. The kids accepted our love just as they'd accepted their parents' love. They had no concept of bigotry or hate, and I wanted to shield them from it as long as we could.

"I'm thinking it's a pizza and a movie kind of night," Miller said. "It's Lily's turn to pick the movie." Lucas groaned because he knew what she was going to choose. It was the same movie each time.

She jumped out of her chair and did a little ballerina twirl followed by a graceless leap. "*Frozen!*" I could've recited every word by then. "I'll need my Elsa dress," she said before she scampered off to her room to put it on.

"Not again," Lucas said, laying his head on the table. "We've seen that movie at least four billion times." Lucas often sounded like a junior adult, and it always made me smile.

"We have to take turns, champ," I reminded him. "I'm sure Lily isn't thrilled about *Indiana Jones and the Temple of Doom* either."

Miller gasped and clutched his chest as if he couldn't comprehend why anyone didn't like the *Indiana Jones* movies. I didn't care how many times we watched them because I always reaped the benefits once the kids went to bed. Occasionally, Miller asked me to put on my Indiana Jones costume.

"I guess," Lucas said, giving in. "At least you guys don't make me dress like Olaf."

Thirty minutes later, the four of us sat on the couch with Miller and me acting as bookends. We had paper plates of pizza in our laps, glasses of milk on the table, and begging pets at our feet. I looked at the little munchkins beside me as they went to town on their pizza and then over at Miller who was smiling at the scene playing in the movie. Never in my wildest dreams had I pictured this as a typical Friday night. I never could have conjured up this level of love because it was something I hadn't known existed until I'd met Miller.

Miller's eyes met mine in the semidarkness of the room. I knew he was worried about the custody hearing and still deeply sad over losing Darryl and Destiny, so it did my heart good to see genuine happiness in his eyes. He was pushing all the things he had no control of aside to live in the moment and focus on the positives in his life, which included greasy pizza and kid-friendly movies with the people he loved the most in the world. I hoped the smile I gave him showed him how proud I was of him and how happy I was to be with him in that moment. If not, I would tell him later. Life was a fragile gift. and I wasn't willing to leave anything to chance.

CHAPTER
Twenty-Six

Miller

NEITHER MY HEART NOR MY MIND WAS READY TO RETURN TO WORK, but everyone told me it was best for all of us to get back to our normal routines—well, our new normal routines. I was worried about being away from Lucas and Lily all day. I was worried about the future custody battle with the Candlesses. I was worried everything would end up being too much for Jag to handle, even though he'd said he wanted to be there, and his actions backed up his words. Still…I worried about everything.

My colleagues were very welcoming when I returned, which made it easier. Gavin was there to greet me with a friendly hug and then I noticed the huge bouquet of flowers sitting in the middle of my desk. I didn't need to read the card to know who they were from, but I did anyway.

Bones,
I'll be there at noon with lunch so send the kid on a very long errand.
Love,
J

I smiled as I put the card in my drawer where I kept all the others he had sent me. I loved how Jag still considered Gavin competition and referred to him as "the kid." There was absolutely no challenge for my heart where Jag was concerned. I'd handed it over to him a while ago, and I didn't want it back. In fact, our lives had become so entwined I could hardly recall what mine had been like before he'd come into it. I couldn't imagine a future that didn't include Jag, and just the thought was enough to cause a stabbing pain in my heart.

I pulled my cellphone out of my briefcase and sent him a quick text. **Thank you for the flowers. I can't wait to see you at lunch.**

I was just about to set my phone down on my desk when it started ringing. I saw it was Vanessa calling, and my heart rate accelerated, which caused my anxiety over losing the kids to kick up several notches.

"Hi, Vanessa." My voice sounded hesitant and wary.

"Hello, Miller." Vanessa's voice was soft and reassuring, the same one she'd use on a patient someday. "Do you have a few minutes to talk, or should I call you back later?"

I really needed to focus on the lectures I would give that day, which wouldn't happen unless I found out why she was calling. My mind would turn over every possible situation again and again until I made myself sick. I had never been like this before, but then again, I had never faced so much grief and turmoil at once.

"I have time for you, Nessy," I said, using the nickname Destiny had used for her sister. I heard my office door shut quietly, and I looked up to find Gavin had left to give me some privacy.

"Never stop calling me that, okay?" Grief slipped through Vanessa's composure, and I heard her sniffle a few times before she spoke again. "I've tried and tried to talk sense into my mom and dad, but nothing I've said has sunk in. I'll give a deposition or testify on your behalf. Whatever it takes, Miller."

"I don't want to cause a bigger rift in your family. I'll try my best to find another way, but if it comes down to it..."

"I won't hesitate. I appreciate your concern for my relationship with my folks, but our family isn't like yours. We don't have Hallmark moments in our home. My niece and nephew need to grow up with the Brexlers. Destiny loved you all so much"—her voice broke—"and I just can't fathom a judge not honoring her final wishes."

I heard Jag's reassuring words in my mind and repeated them to Vanessa. "They don't have grounds to overrule their wills. They'd have to show I'm unfit, and there's no way they can prove it. This will all turn out okay." *It had to, or I didn't know what I would do.*

"I know you're right, Miller. I just want it to all be over with for you. I know it must be stressful to take all this on while trying to get back to work and help Lucas and Lily cope with their grief. How are my beautiful niece and nephew doing?"

"We're doing good, Nessy. They're adjusting to their new life with just a few hiccups here and there. Lily doesn't want to part with her Susie doll. Ever. It was hard convincing her to go to preschool this morning without it. Lucas is very cautious at times like he keeps waiting for something bad to happen. Jag and I got a few books to read, and I've met with a child psychologist on how to handle these types of situations. It's not easy when we're trying to get out the door on time, but I've realized nothing is more important than their feelings. It's a juggling act. It's trying to be patient and understanding without encouraging their fears. It's harder than one might think, but Jag and I have handled it well."

"You've just confirmed what I knew all along. The kids belong with you."

"And Jag," I amended.

"And Jag." I heard the smile in her voice. "I like him, Miller. He's fierce and protective but also loving and nurturing. That's a beautiful combination in a man. If you find a straight guy with those qualities, can you send him my way?"

"Absolutely." We shared a brief laugh before it was time to wrap up the call. "Nessy, do you want to help me decide what to do with Darryl and Destiny's possessions? I've decided to put their house on the market, and the money left over after the mortgage is paid off can go into college funds for the kids. I'm just not sure what to do with the clothes and furniture. There might be things of Destiny's you or your parents want to keep."

"I'm free this weekend if you want me to make the trip. I'd love to help you out and spend time with the kids. Maybe give you and Jag a night off for a date night."

"That sounds awesome. Call me later this week and let me know what time works best for you. Jag and I need to go car shopping, and we wanted to take the kids so they could help us pick one out."

"I'll call you in a few days. Give the kiddos a kiss from me."

"Will do."

I felt lighter after receiving the flowers from Jag and talking to Vanessa. I wasn't alone, and I needed to stop feeling as if I was. I had a huge support system of family and friends who would step up and help me no matter the time of day. I just needed to have some faith—in myself and others. I took a few more minutes to pull myself together, then I headed off to my first class.

Jag showed up promptly at noon with a sack full of delicious Italian takeout from my favorite restaurant. I took the food from him and set it on my desk before I kissed him like I hadn't seen him in a month. Jag pushed me against the edge of my desk, placed his hands on both sides of my head, and kissed me back with just as much fervor. I knew I would never tire of feeling his lips against mine or tasting him on my tongue.

"That is some kind of welcome," Jag said breathlessly after our kiss ended.

"I just wanted to show my appreciation for your thoughtfulness."

"Do I get extra credit points if I brought cheesecake for dessert, Professor Brexler?" The pouty pleading look he sent my way had me laughing.

"Did you bring cheesecake?"

"No, but I will next time for the proper incentive."

I leaned in closer and pressed my lips to his ear. "You don't need to entice me to get on my knees for you, Jag." I felt his body stiffen against mine. "I love the feel of your cock in my mouth and the way you taste when you're really turned on."

"Bones." His hands gripped my shirt where they had been resting above my ass. "I didn't know it was possible to need anyone the way I need you. I'm not talking about sex either."

"I need you too, Jag." I pressed small kisses to his full lips. "My need gets stronger every day." Funny how I would've made fun of someone for saying those types of things just a short time ago. Telling and showing someone how they made you feel didn't make you weak or less manly; it made you smart. Jag and I still joked about turning into sappy suckers, but we both appreciated the romantic gestures we gave to one another. Jag's smiling eyes didn't lie.

We stayed in our embrace for several long moments before we broke apart to eat the food he'd brought. I told him about the discussion I had with Vanessa and passed along the compliments she'd paid him. He blushed a little and tried to play it off like what he did was no big deal. He was complete shit at accepting praise or compliments because he hadn't received many in his life. I couldn't go back and change his terrible past, but I had his present and future, and I would work on making him see what others saw in him.

"Were you serious about coming with me to help pick out a new ride this weekend?" He nodded because he had a mouth full of pasta. I found it amazing how seamlessly we'd melded our lives together. There was no hesitation about including him in decisions regarding my future because I couldn't see a future without him. We needed to have a conversation at some point because he was paying for a home he didn't use, and my house wasn't quite big enough for all of us to be comfortable. The more I thought about it, the more I didn't want to put the conversation off.

"Jag, I think it's time we started looking for a larger place too." I didn't pause to let him respond. "Lucas and Lily will need their own rooms, you and I could use a home office, and I'd love a big backyard so they could have one of those giant wooden swing sets with a fort and a slide." He sat blinking at me, so I continued. "It makes no sense for us to have two mortgages. I love the safety of your gated community, so I thought we might look for bigger houses for sale in your neighborhood." Jag still hadn't said anything or moved anything but his eyelids. I thought for a second that I had pushed too hard or expected too much, but his slow smile assured me that I hadn't.

"Funny you should mention that," Jag said, pulling his phone from his pocket. "I think I found the perfect place." He clicked a few things on his phone, then handed it to me. "It's not in my neighborhood, but it's still a gated community." I flipped through the photos of the house on his phone and felt an immediate connection. "There's a third-floor bonus space that would make an awesome media room so we can have movie and popcorn nights with the kids. There's more than enough bedrooms to have a guest room, an office, or even space for someone else someday."

His voice broke slightly during the last few words, and I jerked my head up to look at him. Jag licked his lips nervously as his eyes met mine. I thought I couldn't possibly love him any more than in that moment. He helped paint a bright and hopeful picture of a future we could have together, and I wanted to grab it with both hands and not let go.

"It's perfect. Let's make an appointment to view it." Jag's nervousness faded at my words. I looked through the photos again. "There are plenty of extra bedrooms for future someones."

"Yep."

People would think we were nuts for thinking along those lines soon after Lily and Lucas had come into our lives. I said screw them because only we knew what fit for us.

CHAPTER
Twenty-Seven

JJ

THE NEXT SATURDAY FOUND THE FOUR OF US AT A RANGE ROVER dealership. Miller showed no hesitation over trading in his sleek BMW for a family-sized SUV. We made a big deal out of it by taking the kids to a pancake breakfast before we went to pick out the car. I couldn't help but smile when Miller pulled baby wipes out of the glove compartment in his car. I raised my eyebrow at him in question, wondering just how long they had been in there and what uses he had for them. Of course, he read my mind.

"I just bought them yesterday for this exact reason. We don't need sticky kid fingers fondling shiny new cars. It's frowned upon."

I leaned forward and pressed my lips against his ear so only he would hear my words. "I love when your sticky fingers fondle me." I pressed a quick kiss to his cheek as innocent giggling came from the backseat. Then the little heart snatchers made kissy noises at us. I turned so I could look at them. They both wore mischievous smiles, and it melted me right on the spot because it had been the roughest week yet.

Lily had had a few nightmares, and Lucas had acted out at school. Miller and I used every tool we had learned from Lauren and the books we had read about helping children cope with grief. We were patient yet firm in both situations. We both comforted Lily and let her cry her little heart out over missing her mom and dad, but we insisted that she stay in her own bed. Sleeping with us was not a habit Miller nor I wanted to start, and Lauren cautioned it was an easy habit to slip into when it was the middle of the night and you were dealing with a distraught child. She cautioned that everyone needed boundaries, even in grief. With Lucas, we talked to him together about the behavior that was expected of him at school. We took away his tablet for a day as a punishment and urged him to talk to us instead of holding things inside.

Lucas resisted our efforts and was sullen for a few days. It broke our hearts, even though we knew we had done the right thing. I told Miller I thought maybe Lucas needed some physical activity to help him work through his frustrations. He told me Lucas had played t-ball the previous year, and he loved to swim. I signed us up for a family pass to the YMCA the next day during lunch. That night, we took the kids to the pool at the Y before dinner. The physical activity was just what Lucas needed. Later, when we tucked him in, he broke down and cried. He clung to Miller like a life raft as he poured his little heart out.

"I miss Mom and Dad so much. I miss Mommy's singing and Daddy's laugh."

"I do too, Lucas." Miller laid his head on top of Lucas's. His eyes met mine, and I could see how much it hurt him to see his nephew suffering so much. I wished I could do something to make them all better, to take their pain away, but I knew it wasn't possible. I had been down that road myself, and it would take a long time before sorrow didn't overshadow everything.

Hearing them giggle in the back seat, looking happy, was worth the teasing they gave us. "Someday you'll fall in love too, wise guy, and you'll want to do things like smooch and hug that person."

"Uncle Jag and I will make kissy noises at you when you do," Miller added. An eye roll was Lucas's response, but the smile never left his face. "Remember what I said about your behavior today. No running. No touching everything in sight. You will be polite and respectful."

"Yes, Uncle Miller," they echoed from the back seat.

Miller pointed his finger at me. "That goes double for you."

"Yes, Miller," I said, imitating the kids and making them giggle again.

We all ended up liking the same overpriced but sexy-as-sin SUV. It was charcoal gray with black leather interior and totally badass like something Batman might drive if he ever became Batdad. Miller let me take the kids to the Y in it while he met with Vanessa to decide what to do about Darryl and Destiny's belongings. They were still at Darryl and Destiny's house when we got done, so I took Lucas and Lily to meet baby Grace.

I didn't know a person could appear exhausted and exuberant at the same time, but that was the only way I could describe how Chase and Gray looked when they let us into their house. They had bags under their bright, sparkly eyes and tired but happy smiles.

"Nice wheels," Gray said, then bumped my fist. "Plenty of room in there for more passengers." He gave me an impish smile as if the thought would scare me. Ha!

"So you'll understand if I consider my visit to my littlest client as billable hours to help pay for the shiny new toy?"

"Very funny," Gray said before he turned to Lucas and Lily. "What else have you guys been up to today?"

"Uncle Jag took us to the Y so we could swim for a bit," Lucas told him.

"I bet you could use a snack," Gray offered. "We have fresh chocolate chip cookies from Gram."

"Yay!" The kids skipped into the kitchen with Gray, and I took a seat next to Chase, who was feeding his daughter, on the couch.

"Hey there, Gracie Lou." I kept my voice soft because it looked like she was just about to drift off.

"Dang it," Chase said without venom. "I owe Gray twenty bucks. He swore up and down you'd be the first one to call her that."

"We don't have to tell him," I suggested.

"Too late," Gray said as he entered the room with a tray full of drinks and a large plate of cookies. He set the tray down and looked at me. "I already heard what you called our baby girl." He turned to Chase and said, "I'm willing to let you pay me in trade instead of cash."

"Yeah?" Chase sounded hopeful.

"Mmm hmmm," Gray replied suggestively. "You let me nap for an hour, and we'll call it even." Gray smiled wickedly while Chase groused under his breath.

"I can't believe I'm about to offer this, but why don't both of you take a nap, and the munchkins and I will take care of baby Grace. She's asleep"—I nodded to the bundle in Chase's arms—"so you should be sleeping too. I'll turn on Nickelodeon, and Lucas and Lily will be asleep in a few minutes too after all their exercise today."

"Seriously?" Gray sounded shocked I'd offer.

"It's been a while since I changed a diaper, but I'm sure the technique is still the same—wipe off any poop or pee, powder their butts, and close up the new diaper."

"You don't have to tell me twice," Chase said as he gently leaned over and placed their daughter in her bassinet. "She sleeps pretty soundly for about an hour to ninety minutes."

"Get some sleep, take a hot shower, and I bet you'll feel brand new. Miller texted me and said they'd be a few more hours, and I don't have any place I need to be. I want to help." I directed my words at Gray.

"Thank you," he said sincerely before they went upstairs.

I turned on the TV to the kids' favorite channel, kicked my shoes off, and got comfy as I ate a cookie on the couch and watched cartoons until Lucas and Lily fell asleep. Little Grace slept through it all and didn't wake for nearly two hours. By that time, the guys had napped, showered, and looked like they'd fooled around a little too. They'd either had sex or smoked a joint because they were looking pretty damn mellow as they made their way down the stairs. I knew neither did drugs so that left only one thing.

"Shut up," Chase said when he caught sight of my smirk.

"I didn't say anything," I said defensively. I gave him my most innocent expression, which only made him laugh.

"Thank you for staying and letting us rest," Chase said once I started to put my shoes on.

"It was my pleasure. I need to wake up my little sleeping angels, or they won't go to bed tonight." I saw the smile on Gray's face and realized I'd referred to Lucas and Lily as mine. It seemed natural and right to me, and I didn't second guess my words. "Vanessa is staying with us tonight so Miller and I can go on a date."

"I hope you guys have a great time," Chase said as he walked us to the door. "I'm so happy for you, JJ. I'm proud of you too. I'm glad everyone else is getting to see the guy I've known all these years." This time his hug was not accompanied by a snarling growl from his husband. All that was behind us as we both built our new lives with our families.

"Thanks for never giving up on me, Chase. Your friendship was a lifesaver, and I mean that."

We still beat Miller and Vanessa back to our house but not by much. The kids were so excited to see her that they talked over one another to try to speak to her. I used the distraction to lead Miller upstairs so he could talk to me. I felt tension rolling off him in waves. He shivered beside me as we entered the bedroom, so I guided him to the bathroom where we could take a hot shower together.

Once under the spray, I began rubbing the tight muscles in his shoulders, back, and arms. I knew he was struggling to keep it together, but I didn't think holding it in was the answer. I turned Miller around and wrapped myself around him. All the pain he had felt being in Darryl and Destiny's house released in a torrent of tears.

"We don't have to go out tonight, Bones. We can stay in and take it easy." I rubbed my hands up and down his back while he rested against me.

"Darryl wouldn't want me hiding from life and giving in to my sadness that he's gone. He'd want me to enjoy every damn second I have on this great big rock. We're going out tonight, Jag. You gave me exactly what I needed just like you always do. I want to go out to dinner with you and maybe catch a movie or make out in our new ride."

"I, um, kind of planned something for seven o'clock, but it probably won't take long. We can eat dinner before my surprise, then catch a movie afterward if you want. I shouldn't have made these plans tonight. I should've known today would be difficult for you. I'll reschedule the surprise." My sudden case of nerves had me prattling on and on until Miller's laughter penetrated my mind.

"Whoa, you're really wound up about this surprise." Miller shook his head slightly. "Don't you know by now that I'll love anything you give me? Whatever you have planned will be exactly what I need."

Our evening started at Gruff's, our favorite steak and seafood restaurant. We agreed that date nights meant we talked about things besides the kids. As much as our world now revolved around them, it didn't mean they had to occupy our thoughts and discussions twenty-four seven. Our conversation never lulled because we had so many common interests. I knew nothing about archeology and anthropology, but I loved to hear his passion for his job. He listened just as raptly to me talk about my job and my hope for much needed changes to assure all people were equal in the eyes of the law.

We skipped dessert to make our surprise on time. Miller looked at me oddly when I pulled into a coffee shop. I turned the car off and removed my seat belt. "There's your surprise," I said, pointing to the tall blonde standing next to her SUV.

"She's really pretty, Jag, but she's not my type." He looked into my eyes and smiled wickedly. "I like them tall, dark, handsome, and with a cock." He reached over and slid his hands between my thighs. "You're my type."

"You don't recognize her, Bones?"

"Of course I do. She's that real estate agent with the billboards all over the place. She looks pretty and nice, but I bet she's a real tiger. We better watch our wallets," he said as he slipped off his seat belt. "It's freezing out here, and she's standing there like it's no big deal. Ice in her veins, Jag. Don't fall for her telling you there are multiple offers on the place just so we offer more money. Don't look her in the eyes, or you'll be buying a house before you know what hit you."

"That's the plan." I leaned over and kissed him softly. "Come on, Bones. I'll protect you from the scary realtor."

Cynthia greeted us with a kind smile and ushered us into her warm SUV so she could take us over to look at the house Miller and I both felt was perfect for our family. She kept the conversation light and friendly while she drove us over to the house. Contrary to what Miller said, I didn't get the impression Cynthia was a high-pressure salesperson. Her reputation was that of an agent who listened to what you wanted and worked very hard to find the perfect home for her clients. That was why I'd chosen her, even though she was not the listing agent for the property. Cynthia greeted the attendant at the gate by name, and it was obvious she spent a lot of time there.

"Wow," I said as we pulled up to the house. "It's even better in person."

"I know, right?" Cynthia sounded as happy as I did. "Wait until you see the interior. If you're serious about the house, you'll want to make an offer quick because it won't stay on the market for long."

Miller elbowed me lightly in the ribs and widened his eyes as if to say he told me so. "Don't sound so overeager," he warned between gritted teeth, drawing a laugh from both Cynthia and me.

"You guys are too damn cute," she said. "I'm going to unlock the door and let you look around on your own. It's vacant right now, so you can take your time and check it out to make sure this is your forever home." She looked back at Miller before she got out of the car. "I don't have the place wired for sound, so it's okay if you show your excitement inside the house. It will be your secret," she said, gesturing back and forth between Miller and me. "I'll also let you in on a little secret. I think you could offer the sellers thirty-five thousand dollars less, and they'd accept your offer. As wonderful as this home is, it's overpriced, and their listing agent knows it."

Miller turned a little pink over being called out, but I laughed my ass off. I'd definitely be buying a house from Cynthia, even if it wasn't this one. I nudged him and nodded my head in the direction of the front door. "Let's go check it out, Bones."

True to her word, Cynthia unlocked the door and let us in, then returned to her SUV. We took our time looking at every room. We didn't say much because we were overwhelmed with the rightness of the space. There wasn't a single space I couldn't see us in, and if that didn't mean this was our place, I didn't know what did.

Our private tour ended in the third-floor bonus area I'd referred to as the media room. I could easily see the four of us sitting on the couch, watching our favorite movies while eating popcorn. Miller and I turned and faced each other at the same time. The emotion I saw in his eyes matched the feelings inside me that had my heart thumping wildly in my chest.

"Let's go tell Cynthia we've found our forever home," Miller said to me before he pressed his lips to mine to seal the deal.

CHAPTER
Twenty-Eight

Miller

THE MONTH OF FEBRUARY ROLLED OVER OUR LIVES LIKE A HURRI-
cane, and the result was a scattered mess, but unlike with a hurricane,
it was a beautiful mess. Jag and I were approved for our loan to buy the
house together. We listed our individual homes and both received offers
within days of Cynthia putting them on the market. We had two houses
to box up and figure out what we were keeping and what we were donat-
ing to Habitat for Humanity with very little time to do it.

Lucas and Lily had already picked out their rooms in the new house
and were so excited about moving. I let them decide if they wanted to
get new furniture for their bedrooms or keep the stuff they had from the
house they'd lived in with Darryl and Destiny. I didn't want to guess their

feelings or make the wrong decision. They chose to keep the furniture their parents had chosen for them, and I found that comforting.

Throughout all the chaos, and with Chloe's help, we found a schedule that worked for our family. I only had a late lecture once a week, and Jag made sure he was home by five thirty on those nights. We enrolled both kids in classes at the YMCA so they could learn new things. Lily had chosen gymnastics, and Lucas wanted to swim. Sometimes we took them separately, but mostly we all went as a family. Lucas and Lily seemed to enjoy cheering each other on, and I felt like it brought us all closer.

I caught the ladies and a few of the dads sizing up Jag like he was some hot mountain they wanted to climb on several occasions. I would just sit there smugly because only I got to climb Mount Jag, and I did so at every opportunity. I too had started some stress-relieving activities like running, weightlifting, and even coloring with the kids. I discovered some amazing coloring books for adults at the bookstore when we'd taken the kids shopping. As much as those activities helped, nothing could ever make me feel as good as Jag. His hands, his mouth, and his magic cock melted my stress away like nothing else.

"After today, we can put all this behind us, Bones." Jag reached over and placed his hand over mine where it rested on my thigh. "Judge Burrows will come through for you. I'm sure of it."

"How can you be certain?"

"She's an amazing advocate for children and families. I've seen her in action enough times to know she cuts through bullshit and gets right to the heart of the matter, which is the best interests of the children. There is no one better suited to raise Lucas and Lily than you, and she'll see that. Hell, Vanessa's deposition alone should be enough to sway her, but add in Lauren's testimony and the caseworker from DCS's notes and it should be a slam-dunk decision." The confidence in his tone made me feel better, but I was still afraid.

Lucas and Lily had no idea any of this was going on. We'd kept it away from them because the last thing they needed was to think they might be taken away from us. Lauren advised us, as she did the court, that removing

Lucas and Lily from my home could be very detrimental to them coping with the loss of their parents. It had been a little over a month since the accident, and the kids could regress if they were faced with the upheaval of being relocated again.

"Have faith, Bones." He squeezed my hand once more before he replaced it on the steering wheel. As riotous as my thoughts and emotions were, I still noticed what he said and realized how far he had come too. This was a man who used to not have faith in anyone, not even himself, and there he was lifting me up and giving me hope.

"I'm a lucky man." My observation was random and out of the blue but totally called for in the moment.

"*I'm* the lucky one," Jag countered. He gave me a firm look that dared me to contradict him as he pulled into a parking spot near the courthouse.

"We're both lucky." I leaned toward him, and he met me halfway for a kiss. His touch soothed me like it always did, and I took my first calm breath since leaving the house. I ran my thumb over his full bottom lip and couldn't wait until we could be alone so I could explore it more. "Let's go make this official." I was referring to the kids but hidden in my message was a desire to tie myself to him through more than just a joint mortgage. I wanted it all with Jag, and I wanted it forever.

"It won't take her long to rule in your favor." One last kiss and we got out of Jag's car and briskly walked inside so we could get out of the brutal cold.

My mom and dad were waiting for me inside the courthouse. I had told them they didn't need to be there, but they'd insisted. Looking at my mom broke my heart because she tried her damnedest to smile through her pain, but it usually came out as a grimace. The only exception was when she was around Lucas and Lily. I missed my brother every single day, and the loss hadn't gotten any easier a month later. I had assumed the ache would lessen over time, but it had remained the same. The despair I felt must have been magnified a thousand times for my parents. Losing a child had to be the most horrible thing a person could experience.

The Candlesses were probably hurting just as badly, which was why

I couldn't be mad at them. They hadn't made heinous allegations about me during any of the custody proceedings. The worst thing they'd said about me was that I was a bachelor, and the kids would be better suited in a home with two parents. My rebuttal was that I was in a committed and loving relationship and provided the lifestyle Lucas and Lily were accustomed to when their parents were alive. Regardless, I didn't think their complaint had merit. There were plenty of single moms and dads out there raising remarkable children. That argument might have worked in the sixties, but I believed it wouldn't in my case.

"Thanks for coming, Mom." I pulled her into a hug and held her a little tighter and a little longer. "I know I told you it wasn't necessary, but having you here really helps."

"I wouldn't be anywhere else when you need me." She pulled back and pecked my cheek with a kiss. "I am so proud of you, Miller. I'm confident everything will go your way today. I just can't see an alternative ending."

My father hugged me next, and I noticed he lingered a little longer than usual too. "You're an amazing young man, and I'm proud to call you my son."

"Thanks, Dad."

Herbert and Joann Candless arrived with their attorney, Brady Barnes, and tension filled the hallway. I had wanted to try to talk to them before things got to this point, but both Vanessa and Jag had advised me against it. Even though I had good intentions, Jag told me it could look like I was trying to pressure or harass them. Vanessa told me that it wouldn't do a bit of good and told me the best thing to do was to let the court decide once and for all who would be the best guardians for Lucas and Lily.

What Jag and everyone else had told me had finally sunken in. I was going to win that day, and it was obvious the Candlesses knew it. Their attorney had surely informed them their case was weak, and they hadn't proved I was unfit to raise the children. The hostility they had felt toward me had faded, and now I saw resignation instead. In my mind, the only unknown was whether Judge Burrows was going to grant them visitation rights or if that would be left up to me.

A bailiff opened up the door to the courtroom and looked at us. "Candless versus Brexler?" she asked.

"Yes," I said.

She stepped aside so we could all enter the small courtroom. It wasn't as grand as the ones on TV, but then again, our case didn't require a jury box or a lot of seating that larger trials needed. It would be a judge, a bailiff to keep order, and a court recorder. Once we were seated, the judge entered the room from a side door. We all rose to our feet and stood until we were instructed to sit.

Judge Burrows went through the process of introducing herself to both parties and named the case for the record. I put all my focus on not bouncing my knees or giving away the sudden nervousness that washed over me. The confidence I'd felt in the hallway had completely fled. I felt Jag's hand brush the side of my leg beneath the table in an effort to reassure me.

"I've had the time to review all the depositions and evidence provided to the court." Judge Burrows looked at me, then at the Candlesses. "None of the documentation I've read indicates that Darryl and Destiny were not of sound mind when they named Miller Brexler as the legal guardian of their children in their wills. Furthermore, evidence has not been provided that Mr. Brexler isn't fit to be their guardian or that Mr. and Mrs. Candless would be the better candidates for guardianship of Lucas Brexler, age six and Lily Brexler, age five. I am ruling today in favor of Miller Brexler, and permanent guardianship will be granted to the prior temporary guardianship order. In addition, I do not see any reason to award visitation rights to Mr. and Mrs. Candless, as Mr. Brexler has stated they can have free access to their grandchildren." She leveled a firm look in my direction. "However, if he fails to deliver on his promise, I will reconsider setting visitation." The judge dropped the gavel and exited the room.

"Congratulations," Jag said warmly in my ear. He put an arm around me and pulled me into him. "It's finally over, Bones."

I turned to look at him. He was smiling happily at me, and had we not been surrounded by people, I would've melted into him. "Thank you, Jag. I can't imagine going through this without you."

"I'll always have your back."

"Miller." Joann's voice pulled me away from Jag. I rose to my feet and turned to face her.

"Mrs. Candless." I wasn't exactly sure what to say to her. Sorry wasn't right because I wasn't remorseful they'd lost their case. I could tell she wasn't going to apologize either, but I also saw fear that I would make this harder on them. What mattered was not how Joann or I felt; what mattered was what was best for Lucas and Lily. Having a relationship with Destiny's parents was good for them. I didn't want the kids to lose that connection to their mother. "When would you like Lucas and Lily to visit?" I extended the olive branch because it was the *only* way to proceed. I knew it was the right thing to do once I saw the tension fade from her face.

"How about this weekend? I would like to pick them up for dinner on Friday and bring them home on Sunday afternoon." She fidgeted slightly as she waited for my response.

"Sounds great. How about you pick the kids up at five at my house, and I'll pick them up at your house at three on Sunday? We'll be moving into our new home, so I'll be back and forth between the houses, and it might be easier for me to pick them up."

"That sounds great. Thank you, Miller." She offered me a small smile.

"You're welcome, Mrs. Candless."

Joann nodded and returned to her husband's side. My parents were waiting to give me congratulatory hugs once I finished the conversation. They offered to take us to lunch, but I needed to get back to the university to give my afternoon lecture. I promised to have a big celebration as soon as we moved into our new home.

"Feel better?" Jag asked once we were alone in his car.

"Much," I admitted. "I knew you were right all along, but I was afraid to get my hopes up too high. I kept picturing our life together with the kids, and I wanted to believe so badly that it would happen. Have you ever wanted something so bad but were afraid you'd never have it?"

"You." Jag's voice was deep with sincere emotion. "You were the one I was afraid would always remain out of my reach. I still feel that way sometimes." His confession shocked me, and it must have shown on my face. "It took me a long time to believe you really wanted me. I was afraid to let you get too close because it would only be a matter of time before you got tired of me. I took you seriously when you said you would never want forever with anyone. It was always in the back of my mind even when you told me how you really felt about me."

"That's because I hadn't met you. I crashed hard into love with you, Jag. Pride and fear of you not returning those feelings had me playing it all off as fun." I reached over and placed my hand on his face. "We were truly meant for each other. The guy who didn't believe in love and the guy who was afraid he didn't deserve to be loved. Somehow, we were just what the other needed."

"Perfect fit."

"Perfect fit," I agreed. "You know what holiday is coming up, don't you?"

A serious scowl marred his handsome face as he thought about it. "It's not a holiday, Bones. It's a sappy-ass occasion created by greeting card companies to make money. I refuse to participate."

"We celebrated it last year, and it was one of the most memorable nights in our relationship. I loved it." I waggled my eyebrows at him.

"My gift to you was a bright red cock ring. That's hardly romantic."

"It was fucking hot." I noticed the temperature inside the car was rising too as we both recalled the way he'd tortured me until I begged him to let me come. My voice had been raw from pleading, and my body had been covered in sweat. The delayed orgasm had ripped through me and left me in a boneless heap in the middle of his bed. "Best Valentine's Day gift ever."

"You're so easy to please, Bones." He leaned forward and kissed my lips. "We probably should buy something for our little Valentines, though. They'll be coming home from the Candlesses that night, so we should do something special. Any suggestions?"

"Just a little gift and their favorite dinner. Those are the kinds of memories I want to make with them. I don't want to turn it into something material and meaningless." I cocked my head and smiled wickedly at him. "We'll have some time to ourselves to have a private celebration, and I know where I hid my gift from last year."

His eager smile matched my own. "Break in the new house properly? Sounds like a perfect night to me."

Jag drove me back to the university where I'd left my car. My lips lingered against his for a few extra minutes during our goodbye kiss. It was my late night, and I wouldn't see him again until it was almost time to put the kids to bed. Our kiss ended, and we sat there with our foreheads pressed together. Something huge and momentous had happened to us that day, and it deserved a few extra moments of appreciation.

It was the first official day of moving forward as a family—Jag, Lucas, Lily, and me.

CHAPTER
Twenty-Nine

JJ

I WAS EXHAUSTED ON THE MORNING OF MOVING DAY FOR ALL THE right reasons—marathon sex with Miller the previous night. The kids had genuinely seemed excited to spend the weekend with the Candlesses, and we took advantage of our first night and morning alone in over a month. I wanted to stay in bed with him all day, but we had moving trucks showing up at both houses, and we had to get up and get going.

I was happy and relieved to see all our friends show up at our new house to help us unload the furniture and boxes. I thought maybe it wouldn't take as long with all the guys pitching in to help, and I would have more alone time with Miller so I could give him his gift from me. Actually, it was more like a gift to myself.

We had taken the time to label the boxes so it would be easier to sort through all our stuff, but even so, it took us until lunchtime to get all the boxes and furniture unloaded then moved into the designated areas.

Miller and I wanted to focus most of our energy into having Lucas's and Lily's rooms perfect for when they came home for the first time. It was the home they'd share with us until they went to college and maybe longer. They would have sleepovers here and birthday parties. We'd celebrate all the holidays as a family in the home Miller and I had bought together. I ordered pizza and soda to feed the guys, then we set about putting the beds together. I wasn't worried about our bed because we could work on our room once the guys left. Hell, I'd sleep on a concrete floor as long as Miller was beside me.

"Pizza's here," Liam hollered up the stairs. A chorus of "Thank God" echoed from all corners of the house.

"Be right down, Ace." Jack's reply made me smile. He had changed so much since he'd allowed himself to love Liam. I was certain people were saying similar things about me. Jack looked up from the screwdriver he was using to secure the headboard of Lily's bed to a side rail and caught me smiling at him. "What?" he groused.

"Nothing." I shrugged and laughed, which earned me a dangerous scowl from the big guy. "There's the look I'm used to seeing on your face."

"That's because you were always looking my guy up and down like he was your next meal," Jack replied with a smirk.

"He wasn't *your* guy then," I corrected. "And I was just admiring the scenery. I never hit on him."

"He was always *my* guy, even when I didn't want to admit it to myself. You never hit on him because of the look I gave you." Jack tilted his head and dared me to argue his point, but I couldn't. "That's what I thought," he said smugly before giving the bed a hard shake to make sure it held firm. "Let's eat."

Chase and Gray were stepping out of the first-floor half bath when I came downstairs. I could tell what they'd been up to by the looks on their faces. "You boys work up an appetite in there?" There was no way I was letting them off the hook. They were still giving Miller and me crap every time we went over to their house. "I hope you cleaned up after yourselves and washed your hands." Jack laughed as he walked past us on his way to the kitchen.

"That's a well-crafted vanity cabinet you have in there," Chase said, then followed Jack.

"It was his idea." Gray pointed at his husband's retreating back, earning a middle finger in return. "I just did that, baby, but we can go again if you want."

"Let's get you some lunch first, Clark. Wait. You have secret superpowers, so you don't need time to recharge like the rest of us mere mortals."

"I'd hate to knock you on your ass in your very own house, Bruce, but I'll do it if I must." Gray brought his fists up, bounced on his feet, and playfully jabbed at me for a few seconds.

"Grayson, get in here and eat," Chase called from the kitchen.

"Uh-oh, someone's in trouble." I covered my mouth with my hand and widened my eyes in pretend fright.

"That goes for you too, Jagger," Chase said. Gray pointed his finger at me and laughed because I was in trouble too. Scary that the two of us were responsible for young lives, but I felt strongly that our playfulness would come in handy many times while raising kids.

Liam was receiving affectionate kisses from Jack when I walked into the kitchen. It wasn't overt PDA, but it was more than he'd showed at the beginning of their relationship. I was happy for both of them.

Miller handed me a paper plate with a few slices of pizza on it. "Cute, aren't they?"

"Did you guys pick a wedding date yet?" Chase asked them.

Liam looked at Chase and smiled. "What if we already got married?"

Chase stood up straight and looked at his younger brother with so much hurt in his expression. "Did you?"

"No, and that look on your face is the reason why. We almost went to Vegas last month, but we decided to wait until we could plan something so all our friends and family could share the day with us." Liam smiled at Jack.

"My mom would've killed us," Jack said. "We're thinking May, but we still need to pick the date so we can let everyone know."

Xavier and Ben came downstairs after they finished assembling Lucas's bed. "What about you guys?" Liam accosted them as soon as they walked into the room where we gathered around the large kitchen island. I couldn't wait until Lucas and Lily would sit there on stools, coloring or working on homework, while Miller and I stumbled through making dinner.

"What about us?" Xavier asked.

"I'm guessing they want to know when we're getting married," Ben answered. "Gram probably has him wired for sound." This was said in a mock whisper, but it was loud enough for all of us to hear. Ben leaned closer to Liam as if he was speaking into a hidden mic and said, "We're thinking about a June wedding like the majority of engaged couples, but we still haven't decided."

"You should all have one giant ceremony. Make it a triple wedding with Gram," Brandon said, earning a round of groans. "What? Too many divas in one ceremony isn't a good thing?" He pointed to Liam and Xavier. Everyone laughed at his joke except the two men he'd pointed out.

"We should've made him stay at Chase and Gray's house with the kids and let Ava help us move," Xavier replied.

"Can you imagine?" Chase asked. "They'd have to film a reality show for that wedding fiasco."

"We'd have two groomzillas and one bridezilla," I added.

"Just who are you two laughing at?" Liam asked, gesturing to Miller and me. "Aren't you Mr. I Don't Do Love and Romance and Mr. I Can't Suck the Same Cock for the Rest of My Life? Seems to me you just bought a beautiful home and are raising two kids together."

Jack laughed and pulled Liam against him. "I love the sass." He growled playfully against Liam's neck.

"Who in the world would've imagined it?" Gray asked with a laugh. "Ewwww, commitment cooties." I knew the joke was aimed at me, so I flipped him off.

"You're only going to have sex with *him* for the rest of your life?" Chase said, mocking Miller's comments from his bachelor party.

Miller and I just looked at each other and smiled. We knew it was bound to happen. We'd been giving these guys so much shit for nearly two years. I hooked my arm around his neck and pulled him closer before I planted a kiss on his temple. The teasing was well deserved, and I'd gladly take my punishment. I was willing to tolerate anything to have Miller and the kids in my life. We stood there wrapped in each other, eating our pizza, while the jokes continued. I was waiting for them to put on a skit or something.

"Nothing to say for yourselves?" Gray finally asked.

"We didn't want to interrupt our free entertainment," I replied.

"Besides, we had it coming," Miller said sheepishly. "We're mature enough to take our punishment."

"I'm not sure about mature," Chase quipped.

"Yeah, since when?" Jack asked.

"Yesterday," Miller and I answered at the same time. We looked at each other and laughed.

"Awwwww," Xavier cooed. "Aren't they cute?"

"No, we're downright sexy bastards," I corrected them.

"Oh, okay," Gray said with a roll of his eyes.

"I hope they get stuck like that," Miller told him.

The teasing and wedding talk wound down as hunger became the prevailing need. Once finished, the guys all busted their asses to make sure all the heavy furniture was arranged or built so all we needed to do was unpack boxes. We couldn't have gotten half of that accomplished on our own, and not for the first time, I realized just how lucky I was to have this special group of guys in my life. I wasn't one to do a lot of hugging, but that day, it was warranted. I wanted them to know how much I appreciated their friendship and their help.

Gray was the last in line for a hug, and he didn't make it awkward. Instead, he slapped my back and quietly said, "You're a good man, JJ, and you deserve this happiness. Accept it. Embrace it. Enjoy every minute of it."

"I will. Thank you." I shut the door behind him and turned to face Miller. "Where do you want to start?"

"I have no idea." He looked around the huge space filled with boxes and let out a deep sigh. "Let's start upstairs in our bedroom. Let's get our bed made and our bathroom stuff set out so we can at least take a shower soon."

Naked Miller. Wet Miller. No kids. I was starting to get my second wind and was eager to do as he suggested. Besides, I had his special gift, and I was eager to give it to him. "Let's get to it." He wasn't blind. He saw the gleam in my eyes that told him what I'd been thinking about.

We had our bedroom situated and our clothes put away quickly thanks to the premove organization he'd insisted on. I would remember to never balk when he wanted to be that organized again. Instead of going through every box looking for shower gel and toothpaste, it was all in one box labeled "Master Bath." Thank goodness I didn't have to search for lube and condoms either because I wasn't willing to wait another minute to start making this space our own.

"Come here, Bones," I said, pulling him into me by the belt loops on his jeans. "I've waited forever for this."

"You just had me this morning," Miller said, but his smile told me just how much he loved hearing that I needed him.

"That was forever ago," I told him as I kissed his neck and slid my hands beneath his T-shirt. My fingers traced the muscles in his abdomen before moving up to tease his nipples. "I'm never going to stop needing you and the connection we have. You make everything right in my universe."

"That's what you do for me, Jag." He pulled back slightly and cupped my face. "I'm not sure I would have gotten through these last six weeks without you. Your love kept me strong and gave me focus when all I wanted to do was fall apart. I knew you loved me, but I couldn't comprehend just how much until my world was blown apart and you helped me piece it back together."

"Perfect fit." It was our phrase, and it summed us up accurately. We were made for each other, and no other person would understand or connect with us the way we fit together. I reached inside our new fancy-as-fuck shower and turned the water on.

We removed our clothes and stepped inside the glass stall. I squirted body wash into my hands and began to lather up his body slowly and completely while the moans Miller made told me how much he enjoyed my touch. Once he was rinsed off, he returned the favor, and my echoes of pleasure mirrored the ones I'd elicited from him.

Nothing said welcome home better than sliding into Miller while I watched his reflection in the mirror through the glass shower wall. It didn't take long for steam to gather in the room and fog up the glass, but I clearly saw the look of ecstasy on his face when I sank balls deep inside him. That quick glimpse was enough to ignite a fire in me and would be a memory I would hold on to forever.

I wanted to go slow and take my time, but Miller wanted no part of slow and sensual. He thrust his ass back on my dick, reached around with one hand, and grabbed my thigh in a bruising grip. I felt the hungry need from him to be claimed and gave him what he wanted. I held tightly to his hips while I rode his tight ass. I always wanted Miller to tell me what he needed so I could give it to him. I knew I could be just as open with him, and it was a beautiful thing.

It didn't take long for our jubilant cries to echo through the bathroom as Miller's orgasm caused his ass to clamp around my cock and milk everything out of me. I should've been used to the way my body reacted to him after over a year, but I wasn't. Miller electrified me more and more each time we were together.

"Welcome home, Bones."

"You're my home, Jag. Wherever you are is where my home will be. I love this house because it's ours." Hearing those sweet words touched me in ways I couldn't verbally express at the moment because there was a ball of emotion stuck in my throat. I cleared my throat to dislodge it but was unsuccessful. I would need to let my kiss and my surprise for Miller do the speaking for me.

I poured everything I felt for him into my kiss. Every shared breath, captured sigh, and touch felt like it was our first time all over again. In a way, we were starting over—a new home with kids that were legally Miller's, and I hoped someday they'd be mine as well.

Once we were showered and dressed, I took Miller back into the kitchen. We were both famished from the day's physical exertion but didn't want to ruin the family dinner we had planned with the kids. We decided to eat a few slices of pizza to hold us over. I went outside to get my surprise while he reheated the food. I set out candles on the dining room table and hurriedly lit them. I placed a large gift box on the table and took my seat to wait for him.

"What's all this?" Miller asked when he walked into the room with two plates in his hand.

"It's our Valentine's Day dinner."

"You don't do Valentine's Day. I remember you saying something about greeting card companies and swindling." He tilted his head slightly as if he was searching for a memory.

"None of your gifts were purchased from a greeting card company. This gift is unique," I said with a sniff of superiority.

"Good. I got you something too, but I was afraid you didn't get me anything and would feel bad." Miller set the plates down on the table and ran out of the room. He returned with a box he must've hidden somewhere in the house. He placed it on the table with exaggerated fanfare, and I was immediately curious about his gift. "Eat first," he demanded.

Our first romantic dinner in our new house was lukewarm pizza on paper plates by candlelight. It was perfect. We wore ridiculous grins while we consumed our pizza and drank ice-cold beer. I had to admit, beer had never tasted so good.

"You first," Miller insisted once we were done eating. He slid my gift to me.

I removed the wrapping paper and opened the box. Inside was a framed picture of the four of us at the Brexlers' Christmas party the previous year. Lily was sitting in my lap while Lucas stood on the couch behind Miller with his arms wrapped around Miller's neck in one of his favorite wrestling moves. The look of sheer happiness on all our faces made my eyes tear up. The photo had been taken just a few weeks before Lucas and Lily had lost their parents, and I could only hope to see that unbridled happiness on their faces again someday.

The coolest thing about the picture was that it had been printed and cut like a jigsaw puzzle, which was our thing. It was Miller's way of reminding me that we still fit, even though the picture had changed and the puzzle was now bigger, but it was no less beautiful to me.

"I love this, Bones. It's the best gift I've ever received." I leaned over and kissed him, but he pulled back before I could deepen the kiss too much.

"My turn!" Miller pulled the heavy box toward him and grinned because he knew it was going to be another excavating activity. I had put a lot of thought and effort into it, and I wanted him to take his time unearthing all the clues. "I love these gifts," he said.

"Go easy," I told him. There were some pieces that were slightly delicate, and I didn't want him to break them.

Miller looked up at me and gave me a gleeful smile as he slowly started to dig through some type of sugar that looked like sand. I had edible things inside, and I didn't want them to get ruined by real sand. Chrissy from Adam and Steve's Bakery had come through for me big time. She seemed genuinely happy to help me plan this surprise. I'd sworn her to secrecy because Miller frequently went by the bakery on Saturday mornings for donuts and pastries.

Chrissy had baked and iced cookies to look like candy hearts. Then she cut them into jagged halves so they could be pulled apart and put back together again to look like a puzzle. Miller pulled one out and of course only saw half the message. He raised it to his mouth like he was going to eat it until he saw my glare.

"Not until you've found all the pieces."

"Spoilsport." Next, Miller dug out one of the plastic groom cake toppers. This one was blond and resembled the man I loved more than life itself. His eyes jerked up, and he swallowed hard. "Jag." His voice sounded breathless.

"Keep excavating, Bones."

He dug up several more cookie pieces and set them aside as he carefully searched through the sand. He pulled out a bottle of champagne and two plastic flutes. His eyes connected with mine after every item he pulled out. I could only describe the look in his gaze as hopeful. There were only two remaining items left for him to find, and I didn't want him to discover the last one until he formed his puzzles, so I stopped him from digging after he pulled out the plastic groom that resembled me.

"Put your puzzle together, Bones." It wouldn't take him long because each cookie was iced in a different color. All he had to do was match up the halves in the same color. I held my breath as he put the pieces together until he had four hearts that read:

His sweet, happy laugh was music to my ears. I saw the answer in his eyes, but before he could speak, I pointed back to the sandbox. "You're not done yet. There's one more thing for you to find."

Miller didn't move for several seconds, then he slowly began to scrape away the sugary sand until he saw the blue Tiffany's box waiting for him at the bottom. "Oh my," Miller whispered. He gently removed the ring box, held it in front of him, and looked at me with such love in his eyes. I nodded, and he opened the box.

It was a moment I never thought I'd share with another person until I met Miller. Then I discovered what it meant to love someone more than food, water, or air. That was when I found the piece of me I hadn't known was missing.

"What do you say, Bones? Will you marry me?" I bit my bottom lip to keep it from trembling.

"I will." I took the ring out of the box and slipped it onto his finger. "This is even better than the red cock ring," Miller said as he looked at the platinum band on his hand. Bless Miller for making highly charged emotional moments easier for me. "Where's yours?"

"Hidden among my underwear," I answered him. "I'd kept them locked in my desk once we returned from vacation." His eyes widened, and I realized what I'd let slip out.

"You were going to ask me on vacation?" I nodded. "Why did you wait?"

"I was waiting for the right time and had planned a special night, but then we found out about Darryl and Destiny. It wasn't the right time to ask you to make such a commitment. Then I thought it was probably better to wait so you'd know I want all of you to be mine forever. I needed you to know I would commit myself to loving Lucas and Lily as if they were my own too. That was something you needed to see."

Tears leaked out of Miller's eyes and rolled down his face. He grabbed me by the hand and pulled me up the stairs to our bedroom. "Get it out. I want to see it."

"Well," I said, deliberately misunderstanding what he said. I began to unzip my pants. "I like the way you celebrate, Bones."

"Yeah, yeah. Later." He waved away my attempt at being sexy. "I want to put the ring on your finger too."

"Engaged for less than five minutes and sex is already being put on the backburner." I sighed dramatically and dug out the matching ring to his from the bottom of my underwear drawer. I held out my hand and he slid the ring onto my finger while looking into my eyes.

I placed my hand on his neck and pulled him in slowly for a kiss. I loved all the ones we shared, but that kiss felt different as did the love we made to seal our engagement.

"I love you, Bones."

"I love you too, Jag."

It wasn't until much later that I remembered to tell him about the inscription on the inside of our rings. I'd had the words *Perfect Fit* engraved on the inside of both bands to represent our unconventional love.

CHAPTER
Thirty

Miller

JAG AND I WORKED HARD TO GET THE MEDIA ROOM SET UP BECAUSE we wanted to celebrate our new home with an early movie marathon with the kids. We wouldn't keep them up too late on a work and school night, but we wanted to have an early surprise for them with the space we'd created for all of us to enjoy.

Jag had purchased an actual popcorn maker similar to those they used at movie theaters but on a smaller scale, and we'd installed a mini refrigerator so we didn't have to walk down two flights of steps every time we wanted to get a drink. My favorite part was the large electric fireplace built into a wooden entertainment center. We placed a flat screen TV on the mantel and the cable box and DVD player in the compartments. We'd put the couch and loveseat from my house in the media room and Jag's in the living room since his furniture was newer.

We planned their favorite dinner—chicken nuggets, macaroni and cheese, and apple sauce for our family Valentine's Day dinner. We bought them small gifts, and Jag had ordered them each a little cake from Adam and Steve's. We didn't want to go overboard, but we wanted to make it a happy day. Destiny had done those types of things for them, and I wanted so badly to keep up her traditions.

"I can't believe how much I missed the munchkins," Jag said, interrupting my thoughts. "I was looking forward to a break, but I was ready for them to come back Saturday morning. I feel really guilty for saying this, but I was hoping Joann would call and tell us the kids were upset and wanted to come home. What kind of selfish asshole does that make me?"

I chuckled at the perplexed frown on his face. "If you're a selfish asshole, then so am I, but as hard as it is to be away from them, it's good for all of us to have a little break now and then. I was so happy Joann and Herbert didn't make things awkward on Friday when they picked them up." I tilted my head in consideration. "I mean, they weren't smiling all over themselves and hugging us, but they greeted us warmly. That's progress, right?"

"It sure is, Bones. I'm sure in time any remaining tension will dissipate. They're just missing their daughter and are afraid of losing their last ties to her. Once they see that you genuinely want them to be involved in Lucas's and Lily's life, they'll relax." He glanced over and smiled at me when he pulled up at a red light. I noticed he liked driving the new SUV when we went places together. "I was thinking about inviting Herbert and Joann to the open house at the YMCA so they can see the kids swim and tumble. I wanted to make sure you were comfortable with the idea first."

"It's a great idea." He leaned forward and gave me a soft kiss.

I raised my hand to touch his face, and the sunlight reflected off the band he'd placed on my finger the night before. Like every time I saw it, my heart rate increased as I remembered the way I'd felt when I dug up each piece of his puzzle and the symbols of a wedding. I kept looking into

Jag's eyes to see if it was a joke, but his love for me smoldered in his eyes. My insides quaked when I assembled the cookie pieces to form his proposal. My God, when I saw that Tiffany's box at the bottom of the sandbox, my tears started to fall.

"Let's go get our kids," I told him when the light turned green.

Joann and Herbert smiled warmly when they opened the door. They were overjoyed when I extended the open house invitation to them, and Joann went to the kitchen and wrote the event on her calendar. "We'll be there," she said when she returned.

Lucas and Lily squealed and ran to us when they heard our voices. They leapt into our arms and held on to our necks. They were so excited to tell us about their weekend that they talked over one another. It was obvious spending time with their maternal grandparents had been wonderful for them.

"One at a time," Herbert said, laughing.

The constant chatter kept up through their goodbyes to their grandparents and the entire ride home. Jag and I just smiled at one another and reminded them to talk one at a time, but they were too excited about their visits to the children's museum and aquarium.

"We have a surprise for you," Jag said, finally getting their attention.

"Ohhhhh," Lily said, clapping her hands. "What is it, Uncle Jag?" She always poured on the charm for her uncle Jag, and she had him wrapped around her little finger. If I wasn't careful, Lily would be ruling the household, and we'd end up her loyal servants.

"You'll have to wait until we get home, princess."

"That's just mean, Uncle Jag," Lucas said, crossing his arms and trying to look angry.

"When we get home, Uncle Miller and I are cooking a Valentine's Day dinner for our special Valentines while you guys get your rooms set up the way you want."

"I'm only four," Lily said. We laughed at her irate declaration.

"Your beds are all set up, but your clothes and toys need to be put away," Jag told her.

"I guess." She struck a pose to match her brother's, and I had to bite my lip to keep from laughing. I looked over at Jag, and he was doing the same thing.

Once we got home, the kids were suddenly eager to get upstairs and get their rooms set up. Jag and I set about making chicken nuggets from scratch using Liam's recipe for crispy air-fried nuggets rather than frozen ones. Jag cut the chicken breasts into bite-sized chunks while I put the breading together.

Once the nuggets were frying, we turned our attention to the macaroni and cheese recipe. Liam basically cooked the noodles, drained them, and added milk, butter, and fresh American cheese, stirring until the cheese melted.

"This is a really easy dinner," I remarked. "If you can read, you can cook," I said mimicking Liam. "You want to take over here, and I'll start the laundry?"

"Gladly." Jag hated doing laundry more than any chore, but he always pitched in. Often, he did the folding and putting away. He liked cooking more than I did, so I thought it was a fair trade off because I would do the dishes afterward. We had found a balance and rhythm that worked for us.

After a tasty dinner, we gave them their presents. Lily loved her Elsa doll and Lucas was ready to whip out his age-appropriate chemistry set and start working on experiments.

"That's not all," I told them.

"There's more?" Lily's surprised look made me smile.

"What? Where?" Lucas had always acted much older than he was, but when he was excited over something, he showed his real age.

"Follow us," Jag said as he scooted his chair back. Lily took his hand and skipped beside him while Lucas and I followed at a more leisurely pace. He had resorted back to his much calmer and older demeanor. "Are you ready?" Jag asked as he stood by the closed door of the media room.

"Yeah!" Lily bounced up and down.

"It's okay to be excited and act like a six-year-old," I said quietly for Lucas's ears only. He looked up at me with big blue eyes and smiled widely.

"Yeah!" Lucas said, echoing Lily.

"Me too." I clapped my hands and jumped around. Jag threw open the door and we rushed inside.

"Wow!" Lucas said.

"I love it!" Lily squealed and did a happy dance like I had just performed.

"This is our media room where we can come and watch movies and eat popcorn together as a family," I told them. "Someday you'll have friends come over to stay the night and you can come up here and have fun. Do you love your surprise?"

They showed us how much they loved us with hugs and kisses. Jag pulled a coin out of his pocket so he could flip it to see who got to pick the first movie. Luckily, Lucas won so we were able to put off *Frozen* for at least ninety minutes. Once we settled in to watch *Monster's Inc.*, I felt Jag's eyes on me, and I looked over at him. I saw the comical look on his face, and I thought I knew what he was thinking.

How did the kings of no commitment, who hated Valentine's Day, end up celebrating the holiday with happy, sappy hearts in their eyes? How did we end up wearing matching engagement rings with dreams of our happily ever after? It was fate. Chase and Gray had met and fallen in love through some wicked twist of fate, and because of them, we had too. It wasn't love at first sight, it wasn't even love at third sight, but our bond had developed over time into a love just as solid as what the rest of our friends had. We might not be as vocal or as demonstrative, but it didn't make our love any less real or significant.

We were no longer two oddly shaped pieces of a giant puzzle that never fit. We connected and realized that together we were perfect. The puzzle had expanded to include two more beautiful pieces that made an even more amazing picture. I couldn't help but wonder if our puzzle would expand someday down the road to include more perfect pieces. I guessed only time would tell.

Epilogue

JJ

THE CHURCH HAD THE AIR CONDITIONING CRANKED UP TO COMBAT the July heat, but it did nothing to cool me down. Wasn't there a saying about being as nervous as a whore in church? Was that my problem? I didn't feel allergic to weddings anymore after all the ones we'd attended the past few months.

Gram had kicked off the weddings in April in the botanical garden at her retirement community. Jack and Liam were next in May followed by Ben and Xavier in June at the same church Gray and Chase had gotten married. The same church where I was standing and sweating like I had just walked through hell. The same church where I adjusted my bow tie for the tenth time. I couldn't swear out loud, not only because I was in a church but because I had little ears around me almost always. I didn't want to be struck down by lightning before Miller could legally become mine. I didn't want to swear in front of the kids because I wanted to set a good example for them.

I was going to legally adopt Lucas and Lily once we returned from our honeymoon so our family of four would be official in the eyes of the law. I was just as excited about that as I was about the wedding. *Married!* I, Jagger Jackson, former resident Bachelorville, was about to take the plunge, and I couldn't have been happier.

There was a knock on the door followed by girlish giggles. "Are you ready to marry us, Uncle Jag?"

I strolled over to the door and pulled it open. "Yes!" I did the happy Lily dance to demonstrate my happiness. "Are you ready to be the prettiest flower girl in the whole world?" I asked. Lily's answer was a ballerina twirl, which I took as a yes. I looked up and saw Miller and Lucas heading our way. Miller took my breath away every time I looked at him, and seeing him in a tuxedo was a beautiful sight. He stopped in front of me and gave me a quick kiss.

"You're not supposed to kiss me until *after* we're married," I teased.

"I've never been one to follow the rules."

"I love you, Bones. I can't wait to make you mine."

"Wait! *I'm* going to make *you* mine," he countered.

I reached into my pocket and pulled out a quarter. "Want to flip for it?"

The End!

Other Books by
AIMEE NICOLE WALKER

Curl Up and Dye Mysteries
Dyeing to be Loved
Something to Dye For
Dyed and Gone to Heaven
I Do, or Dye Trying
A Dye Hard Holiday
Ride or Dye

Curl Up and Dye Box Set

Road to Blissville Series
Unscripted Love
Someone to Call My Own
Nobody's Prince Charming
This Time Around
Smoke in the Mirror
Inside Out
Prescription for Love

Welcome to Blissville Collection (Both M/M Blissville series)
Volume One
Volume Two

The Lady is Mine Series
The Lady is a Thief
The Lady Stole My Heart

Queen City Rogue Series
Broken Halos
Wicked Games
Beautiful Trauma

Zero Hour Series
Ground Zero
Devil's Hour
Zero Divergence

Zero Hour Trilogy Box Set

Matrimony and Mayhem (Continuation of Zero Hour)
The Magnolia Murders
Marriage is Murder
Killer Honeymoon

Sinister in Savannah Series
Ride the Lightning
Mr. Perfect
Pretty Poison

Sinister in Savannah Box Set

Savannah Standalone Books
Invisible Strings
Bad at Love

Fated Hearts Series (Second Edition)
Chasing Mr. Wright
Rhythm of Us
Surrender Your Heart

Standalone Novels
Second Wind

Coauthored with Nicholas Bella
Undisputed
Circle of Darkness (Genesis Circle, Book 1)
Circle of Trust (Genesis Circle, Book 2)

Acknowledgments

I must give a huge shoutout to my editing team, Susie Selva and Lori Parks, for tackling this rehab project with so much gusto and passion. If not for their guidance and cheerleading, the Fated Hearts series probably would've stayed in the vault. Thank you so very much, ladies.

I've been so fortunate to work with Stacey Blake of Champagne Book Designs since virtually the dawn of my career. In fact, Chasing Mr. Wright was the first book she formatted for me, so it only seemed right that I tapped her to work on the covers for the second editions. Stacey is a brilliant artist, and I'm always so thrilled to show off her pretties.

And I'm sending so much love to the fans who've waited for the Fated Hearts gang to return.

xoxoxo

About
AIMEE NICOLE WALKER

Ever since she was a little girl, Aimee Nicole Walker entertained herself with stories that popped into her head. Now she gets paid to tell those stories to other people. She wears many titles—wife, mom, and animal lover are just a few of them. Her absolute favorite title is champion of the happily ever after. Love inspires everything she does, music keeps her sane, and coffee is the magic elixir that fuels her day.

She'd love to hear from you.

Want to connect? All her links are in one nifty location. Go here:
linktr.ee/AimeeNicoleWalker

www.ingramcontent.com/pod-product-compliance
Lightning Source LLC
Chambersburg PA
CBHW051240250626
47155CB00009B/3109